A Cowboy STAYS

COWBOYS
of Crested Butte

BOOK FOUR

USA TODAY BESTSELLING AUTHOR

HEATHER SLADE

MORE FROM AUTHOR HEATHER SLADE

BUTLER RANCH
Kade's Worth
Brodie's Promise
Maddox's Truce
Naughton's Secret
Mercer's Vow
Kade's Return
Butler Ranch Christmas

WICKED WINEMAKERS
FIRST LABEL
Brix's Bid
Ridge's Release
Press' Passion
Zin's Sins
Tryst's Temptation

WICKED WINEMAKERS
SECOND LABEL
Beau's Beloved
Coming Soon:
Cru's Crush
Bones' Bliss
Snapper's Seduction
Kick's Kiss

ROARING FORK RANCH
Coming Soon:
Roaring Fork Wrangler
Roaring Fork Roughstock
Roaring Fork Rockstar
Roaring Fork Rooker
Roaring Fork Bridger

THE ROYAL AGENTS
OF MI6
Make Me Shiver
Drive Me Wilder
Feel My Pinch
Chase My Shadow
Find My Angel

K19 SECURITY
SOLUTIONS TEAM ONE
Razor's Edge
Gunner's Redemption
Mistletoe's Magic
Mantis' Desire
Dutch's Salvation

K19 SECURITY
SOLUTIONS TEAM TWO
Striker's Choice
Monk's Fire
Halo's Oath
Tackle's Honor
Onyx's Awakening

K19 SHADOW OPERATIONS
TEAM ONE
Code Name: Ranger
Code Name: Diesel
Code Name: Wasp
Code Name: Cowboy
Code Name: Mayhem

K19 ALLIED INTELLIGENCE
TEAM ONE
Code Name: Ares
Code Name: Cayman
Code Name: Poseidon
Code Name: Zeppelin
Code Name: Magnet

K19 ALLIED INTELLIGENCE
TEAM TWO
Coming Soon:
Code Name: Puck
Code Name: Michelangelo
Code Name: Typhon
Code Name: Hornet
Code Name: Reaper

PROTECTORS
UNDERCOVER
Undercover Agent
Undercover Emissary
Coming Soon:
Undercover Savior
Undercover Infidel
Undercover Assassin

THE INVINCIBLES
TEAM ONE
Decked
Edged
Grinded
Riled
Smoked

THE INVINCIBLES
TEAM TWO
Bucked
Irished
Sainted
Hammered
Ripped

THE UNSTOPPABLES
TEAM ONE
Furied
Merried

COWBOYS OF
CRESTED BUTTE
A Cowboy Falls
A Cowboy's Dance
A Cowboy's Kiss
A Cowboy Stays
A Cowboy Wins

TABLE OF CONTENTS

Chapter 1 1
Chapter 2 16
Chapter 3 30
Chapter 4 48
Chapter 5 66
Chapter 6 86
Chapter 7 102
Chapter 8 124
Chapter 9 143
Chapter 10 161
Chapter 11 171
Chapter 12 198
Chapter 13 215
Chapter 14 229
Chapter 15 246
Chapter 16 263
Chapter 17 284
Chapter 18 300
Chapter 19 317
Chapter 20 338
Chapter 21 354
Epilogue 371
About the Author 375

1

It was another bad night, full of dreams about explosions, and fire, and pain. The nightmares were commonplace. She'd had the same dream so many times, yet it still rocked Bree to her core with the same intensity as it had the first time.

In it, Zack was reaching out to touch her face, tears in his eyes. She could handle the horrific images far more easily than seeing her husband's tears. It only made the longing worse when she spent the rest of the night tossing and turning, unable to sleep.

She hoped a change of scenery would make a difference, but she knew better. No matter where she traveled, each place would have one thing in common with the previous one—Zack wouldn't be there. He wouldn't be anywhere. He was gone.

Jace Rice was gone, too. Not in the same way, but still…gone. Every day, Bree told herself she shouldn't think about him. It wasn't Jace she missed, it was Zack. Jace was a distraction, someone she allowed herself to think about when her subconscious refused to let her mourn her dead husband. On an intellectual level, she understood that the way she felt about Jace wasn't real;

it was simply a manifestation of her real grief over Zack's death.

Zack Fox had been the light of her life. The word "soulmate" was thrown around too often, but in this case, there was no better way to describe him. Zack made her laugh. He made her feel safe, secure, confident, smart, and beautiful—all of those things. With Zack by her side, Bree could do anything she set her mind to. It had never occurred to her that, one day, she'd be forced to find out what she could accomplish without him.

Bree had just graduated with her master's degree, something she'd started when Zack was still alive. He hadn't pushed her into it, but he had encouraged her. He told her it was the right time to do it, before they started their family. He convinced her she'd be happy she'd done this for herself later, when there wouldn't be time for it. Now she had all the time in the world.

Maybe she'd consider getting her doctorate. It wasn't as though having a family was still in her future.

Bree had offered to babysit her nephew, Cochran, while her sister Blythe and Tucker, her sister's husband, attended the opening of his show at a local art gallery.

Tucker was an artist who worked in many different mediums. He'd done sculpture, relief carvings, and block prints. Watercolor was his current passion.

Earlier this year, he'd painted landscapes in Black Forest, outside of Monument, Colorado, before a massive fire destroyed much of it. After the fire, he continued to paint the same landscapes. Blythe told her that the paintings in the show were both compelling and heartbreaking. Many of the vistas he'd painted days before became charred remains of what they'd once been.

She hadn't seen Tucker's recent work, only heard about it. She was afraid seeing it would make the nightmares worse. Instead of seeing the Black Forest landscape, Bree would see Afghanistan. Her imagination would replace the images of the burned-out forest with those of a charred convoy destroyed by an IED, like the one Zack had been a part of.

"Where's that sweet baby?" she asked Blythe as soon as she walked in the back door of her sister's house.

"Still sleeping, which means you won't get a break tonight. He'll be wide awake for his Auntie Bree."

"I won't be complaining."

"I know, which is why I let him sleep. If we were going to be home tonight, I would've gotten him up an hour ago. Unlike you, I would want him to go back to sleep before midnight. And before you ask, we'll be home long before then."

There wasn't much nightlife in Monument, Colorado. They'd probably be home by ten at the latest.

Between May and September, the historic town hosted an art walk once a month. Tucker was showing his work in the gallery of the winery that had recently opened downtown. While the other businesses would close up shop early, most folks would end up at the winery, which would stay open later.

"Stay out as long as you want," Bree told her. "Take advantage of your last night with a regular sitter."

"Don't remind me. I can't believe you're going to be gone a whole month."

"I need to do this, Blythe."

Bree was leaving the next day for Stanley, Idaho. The trip was a self-imposed sabbatical, intended to give her time to grieve her husband's death. In the fall, she'd be taking over a junior teaching position at the Air Force Academy while the tenured professor was on maternity leave.

They heard Cochran stirring through the baby monitor that was sitting on the kitchen counter. Even with as big as the house was, everyone always seemed to congregate in the kitchen. The back door led straight into it, and with windows on two sides, the views of the dense forest on one, coupled with that of Pikes Peak on the other, were jaw-dropping. Today was a perfect bluebird day, with billowing clouds resting just below the peak of the fourteener, only one of the fifty-three such peaks in the state of Colorado.

"Do you mind if I get him?" Bree asked.

"Of course I don't," answered Blythe, tears filling her eyes.

"Oh, honey, please don't cry. I'll be back before you know it."

Blythe waved her hand in front of her face. "I know, but I'm going to miss you so much."

"Sweetie, I need this."

"I know you do. I'm being selfish. Now go get your nephew before he climbs out of the crib on his own."

"Is he doing that? At seven months?" Bree gasped.

"Not yet, but I expect he will any minute. That boy is his father's son, and Carol told me Tucker and Jace started walking the day they turned ten months old. She said the twins skipped crawling entirely."

Bree's shoulders tensed, as they did whenever anyone mentioned Jace. She walked across the distressed wood floor that covered the surface of the great room, over to the carpeted curved staircase that led downstairs, to the bedrooms.

She stopped for just a moment, closing her eyes and letting the water that bubbled softly out of the twin sculptures Tucker had built into the stairwell soothe her. The two separate, yet identical pieces were made of bronze and copper, and sat on a base of river rock.

Bree continued down the stairs, willing the tension in her shoulders to release before she opened the door to Cochran's bedroom.

She loved that Blythe and Tucker chose Bree and Blythe's maiden name for their baby's first name. With no boys in their generation, it was the only way their family's legacy would carry on.

"How is Jace? Have you heard?" Bree asked when she came back with Cochran in her arms.

"Only that he's settling into the life of a rough-stocker. I'm glad Carol and Hank are up there with him…"

Bree had heard the twins' parents had partnered with Jace on a rough stock and cattle operation in Montana. The twelve-thousand-acre ranch had been part of the Beiman family holdings for years, but after the death of their father, the two sons decided to sell the Montana property to focus on their larger operation in Alberta, Canada.

"Lyric said she heard there was more to the story, though. Something about them having to sell," said Blythe.

Lyric Simmons was the host of RodeoChat, and often heard industry news before anyone else. Blythe had been working for Lyric for close to a year, although she'd become more than a boss to Blythe; she had become part of their family.

"What did she hear?"

"She said the Beiman brothers got into trouble, smuggling Canadian bulls from Alberta into the States. Consequently, they made a deal to sell their US holdings, which included the Montana property. She heard Jace and his parents got a sweet deal because of it."

Bree hoped so. Jace deserved to have something good happen in his life. It hadn't been an easy year for him. The estrangement between Tucker and him was the worst of it.

Last year, the brothers had a falling out. No one expected Tucker to stay angry as long as he had, but now it seemed as though he might never forgive his twin.

"Does Tucker ever talk about him?" Bree asked.

"Not really, but I know he thinks about him. I mean, he and Jace have always been so close. I can't imagine not having you in my life, Bree. The truth is, as hard as it's always been to get along with Brooke, it wouldn't matter what she did. I couldn't stay mad at her as long as Tucker has been mad at Jace."

Bree understood. Brooke, their older sister, had never been easy to get along with, but she felt the same way. She was still their sister.

It was so much more than Tucker being mad at his brother, though. Jace had betrayed him by sleeping with his brother's girlfriend. And after that woman's death, Jace had kept the secret of their affair from Tucker for years. Bree understood that Tucker's forgiveness might be a long time coming.

"He needs time."

"Have you talked to him?" Blythe whispered, even though Tucker wasn't anywhere near.

"Jace? No. I texted him a few times, but he never answered."

"Oh. I'm sorry."

"There isn't anything to be sorry for. I thought someone should send Jace a picture of this sweet baby." Bree kissed Cochran's forehead while he sat on her lap, quietly playing with her beaded bracelet. "You're such a sweet boy, aren't you?"

"He really is. I've been blessed with a very happy baby," Blythe smiled.

"I'm sure Grandma Carol shows Uncle Jace plenty of pictures of his nephew. I should have thought of that."

"I'm sure he appreciated the photos, Bree. I don't know why he never answered you."

Bree would never know. If she did see him again, which at this point appeared doubtful, she wouldn't dream of asking why he hadn't.

"I love seeing you so happy, Blythe."

Bree never would've predicted her little sister would fall into motherhood as easily as she had. Tucker was a good match for her.

When they were growing up, Blythe was a brat if she didn't get her own way. She was the baby of the family, and she played it well—until she met Tucker. He loved her just the way she was, and she blossomed because of it. He calmed her, settled her, centered her. He was her soulmate. Just as Zack had been Bree's.

"I wish you could get him to talk to Jace."

"I do too. He will, in his own time, Bree. In the meantime, Cochran is growing up so fast." Blythe leaned over and kissed his cheek. "Aren't you, big boy?"

It was a beautiful day for a ride. The blue Montana sky stretched on forever. When he rode the ranch, Jace was content. He felt at peace—even though it was solitary.

The ranch had two main houses. When the Beiman family had owned it, the old man lived in one and his oldest son lived in the other. When the deal went through, Jace's parents insisted he move into the house that had belonged to the old man. It was closer to the center of the ranch, and it was the bigger of the two.

His mom said she felt more comfortable in the smaller house. After all, she told him, they were finished raising their family. She hoped, one day, Jace would fill the bigger house with a family of his own.

He didn't see that happening soon, if ever, since he only fell in love with women who were in love with someone else.

There was one, but she wasn't as interested in him as he was in her. Not that it would make a difference if she was. Her sister was married to his brother, and his brother never wanted to see him again.

Jace and Tucker had shared a tragedy when they were younger, after which, Tucker would often disappear for months at a time. Tucker's part in the accident was public. He'd been as much of a victim as the girl who died. Jace's role wasn't only private, he'd intentionally kept it a secret. When that secret came to light, it was Jace's turn to disappear.

He traveled the rodeo circuit for a while, but his heart wasn't in it. After a few months, he knew he needed somewhere to settle, at least for a while. Even he didn't know what that meant; he only knew he was tired of running.

The truth was, he'd been on the run since that horrible night all those years ago. He ran from himself, afraid of what he might see if he let himself take a good, long look in the mirror.

Owning up to what he'd done had been the first step. If he was ever going to be the man he knew he wanted to be, he had to take that long look and figure out what was inside of him that made him betray his brother in the first place.

Montana was where he settled. He heard the Beiman family was looking for help with the rough stock end of their ranching business, but in the end, it was more than help they were looking for. They wanted to sell. In under two weeks, he'd gone from having virtually nothing, except money in the bank, to having a lot less money and a lot of land.

Jace and his father learned the lay of the land and worked to get a handle on the rough stock business that had been part of the deal to purchase the ranch.

They had fifteen bulls and were looking to add more. It was common for their numbers to be down in the winter, when there were fewer events, but they were behind the curve for the spring and summer.

Jace offered to go out on the road, but when Hank insisted he be the one to go, Jace admitted he'd be glad to stay put. He knew it wouldn't be long before he'd be forced back out on the road. If they were going to make a go of this business, both he and his father would have to be out there, delivering bucking bulls to the rodeos that contracted them.

For now, he spent as much time as he could, riding the twelve thousand acres of the land that was now his, and caring for six hundred head of cattle.

As he rode up to his parents' place, he saw his mother waving at him from the front porch.

"Join me for breakfast?" she called out to him.

"Would love to," he answered, leading his horse into the corral. "Whatcha' cookin'?"

"Huevos Rancheros. Go get cleaned up, and I'll make you a plate."

"You got any coffee brewin', Mama?"

She laughed and shook her head. Yeah, that was a stupid question. Carol Rice almost always had a fresh pot of coffee going. His father was addicted to the stuff.

"It's good to have you in my kitchen," she said when Jace sat down at the table.

"Good to have your kitchen so close."

Carol put her hand on her son's shoulder and kissed the back of his head. "I love you, sweet boy."

"You might be the only one who does these days. You and Daddy."

She swatted his head, the place she'd just kissed. "Oh, Jace. That's a load of nonsense and you know it."

"I don't know 'bout that, Mama," he muttered.

"You got some amends to make, boy. Once you have, your life will come back together the way it's supposed to."

It wasn't only his estrangement from his twin brother that troubled him. Jace was beginning to think he'd never find the kind of love his parents had. For a long time, Tucker believed he wasn't worthy of love. Maybe it was Jace who wasn't, and that was the reason he kept falling in love with the wrong women.

"Would you like to see some pictures of the sweetest grandbaby in the whole world?"

"You know I would." Jace took the phone from his mother's hand and scrolled through the latest photos from Blythe. His nephew was getting so big. As he swiped his finger across the screen, one photo made him stop. Blythe's sister Bree held the baby on her lap. Her head rested against his, and her eyes were closed. Her arms were wrapped around him, and he leaned into her, as though it was the most comfortable place in the world for him to be.

Jace's arms ached. He longed to hold the baby, but it was more. He longed to hold Bree, too.

It had been important that he be the one to tell her what happened with the accident. And, when he had, she accused him of wanting her to smooth things over between Tucker and him. That wasn't it at all, but he hadn't bothered to try to convince her otherwise. If she'd felt any of what he was feeling, she would've known that wasn't why he told her.

When he closed his eyes, he could see those arms, the ones she had wrapped around baby Cochran, folded in front of her. She'd closed herself off to him that day. That was the reason he left the way he had. And never looked back.

Even when she had texted him pictures of the day Cochran was born, he didn't respond. He couldn't. If he did, he might be tempted to…to what? Ask her if she could forgive him? She'd think he'd lost his mind if he had.

Instead, he ignored her. He needed to get Bree Fox out of his head. He closed his eyes and started to hand the phone back to his mother, but he stopped and took one more look. He couldn't help himself.

"I hear Bree is leaving Monument."

"What's that, Mama?"

"I talked to Blythe yesterday. She's torn up about Bree leaving town."

"What do you mean? Where's she going?"

"I'm not sure. Maybe you should give her a call yourself and ask her."

He shook his head. Was she kidding?

Carol sat down at the table, across from her son. "I'm serious, Jace. Why don't you call her? I'm sure she'd love to hear from you."

He waited until his mother went into the other room, pulled his phone out of his pocket, and scrolled through the contacts until he found Bree's number.

2

"Thanks for driving me to the airport," Bree said to her mother.

Paige Cochran was her rock. Blythe was daddy's girl, but Bree belonged to her mama. She could count on her mother to understand how she was feeling, often without her having to say a word. It was true when she was growing up, and it was true now.

She gazed out the window at the pond just off County Line Road, a visible landmark from the interstate. "Whenever I drive by this spot, I feel like I'm leaving home. It's this same place that welcomes me back."

"I know what you mean," answered her mom. "Nothing ever changes on this stretch of land."

There were several thousand acres north of the road that separated Monument, in El Paso County, from Douglas County. The original homesteaders gave the land to the State of Colorado, with the stipulation that it be open space for two hundred years. The only buildings visible were part of the original ranch. Family members kept the operation going, so there were still cattle and horses on the land.

They were almost at the turnoff for the Denver airport before either of them spoke again.

"Are you renting a car in Hailey, or is someone from the ranch picking you up?"

"I decided to rent a car. It'll be easier that way."

"Don't spend all your time off on your own, baby."

Her parents sat her down, the day before, and told her they were worried she'd isolate herself.

Bree had spent most of the past couple of months with Blythe, Tucker, and the baby. The camaraderie of being with her sister had been good for her in some ways, and not good in others.

"She'll spend all her time out on that river," she overheard her father say.

"She needs to, Mark," her mother answered. "She knows what she's doing."

Her mother told him Bree needed this time to mourn the loss of her husband. Zack hadn't been gone very long when Blythe was in a terrible car accident, one in which she'd almost lost her life. Shortly after, Blythe realized she was pregnant.

Instead of grieving her husband's death, Bree took care of her sister. She let herself get caught up in the drama that swirled around Tucker and Jace Rice. Consequently, she hadn't spent any time dealing with her own.

"Thanks for understanding, Mom," Bree said as she hugged her mother on the curb at the airport drop-off.

"I do, baby. Otherwise, I'd be going with you."

It wasn't until the plane was in the air that Bree felt truly alone. It was a feeling she'd been craving. No one on this plane knew her. She doubted anyone at Idaho Rocky Mountain Ranch, where she was headed, would remember her, and that was the way she wanted it.

Instead of staying in the main lodge, Bree booked one half of a two-sided cabin for the month of June. July and August were busier months, although the ranch manager had assured Bree she could stay longer if she decided she wanted to.

Bree's parents needn't have worried about her being off on her own too much, since her only option for meals at Idaho Rocky Mountain Ranch was to join the other guests and ranch hands in the main dining hall.

"Mind if I join you?"

Bree looked up into the greenest eyes she'd seen since the last time she saw Jace Rice. "Of course," she answered, moving her tray out of his way.

"Red Dugan's the name."

"I'm Bree, uh...Fox."

"You sure 'bout that?" he chuckled.

"Yes, sorry." Bree extended her hand. "Nice to meet you, Mr. Dugan."

"It's Red, young lady. I heard a rumor somewhere that you're heading out to do some fishing later this morning."

"Not much later. In fact, I planned to leave in a few minutes."

"If you can wait until I finish my oatmeal, Miss Fox, I'll take you to one of my secret spots."

"Please, call me Bree, and sure, that would be... nice."

"You're saying you can keep a secret, then, right?"

Bree rolled her eyes. "I think I'll be able to."

Red reminded her of someone's sweet grandpa, and as much as she'd prefer to be on her own, tomorrow would be a good enough day to start her sabbatical.

Bree climbed in Red's truck after he put her rod and other gear in the back.

"You sure I can trust ya, girl? Could always blindfold you on the drive over if you're afraid you'll tell."

"I promise," she crossed her heart, "that I will never divulge your super-secret fishing spots."

"Good thing, since the only thing I could've blindfolded you with is this old bandanna that's been in this truck since the day I bought it. We're talkin' twenty years or so."

"*Ew,*" Bree cringed and looked out the passenger-side window.

Red didn't speak again until he pulled off the main highway onto an unmarked dirt road.

"There's been some talk about naming this old road Dugan's Way, but I put the kibosh on that brilliant idea."

"Sounds like your secret's out already."

"This way," he said, pointing toward the woods.

A ten-minute walk later, Red stopped at the edge of a tributary of the Salmon River.

"It's beautiful," she murmured.

The water was high, and a deep shade of blue. The grasses along its edge were green, but not as dark in color as the pine trees that rose above them on either side of the water. The same breeze Bree felt on her face, moved the clouds quickly across the blue Idaho sky. She closed her eyes and breathed deeply, remembering the last time she fished in an area not far from here.

"How long you been fishin'?" Red asked.

"Since before college. About ten years. It was something my husband and I used to do together."

"But not anymore?"

"My husband was…" Bree's eyes filled with tears.

Red held up his hand. "You don't need to say another word, young lady."

Bree shook her head. "It's okay. I'm not used to talking about it. My husband was in the Air Force. He was killed in Afghanistan last year."

Red closed his eyes briefly and shook his head. "I lost my brother in Vietnam. Never got over it."

"I'm sorry."

"I am too. War is hell. There's nothing that describes it better. I miss him every day, even after all these years."

"I understand," she said softly, thankful to talk about his grief rather than her own. Bree closed her eyes and focused again on the breeze on her face.

"There isn't a minute that I don't miss him," she whispered after a while. The tears were back, but she didn't try to fight them. She was here to mourn Zack, and she couldn't keep burying her feelings. She'd never be able to move on if she didn't allow herself to acknowledge her pain. That was what she wanted, wasn't it? To move on?

"Tell me about him."

"What's that?" she asked.

"Your young man, tell me about him."

Bree took a deep breath. She hadn't planned to talk about Zack to anyone. But if she was going to grieve, she needed to talk about him.

"I met him when I was fifteen," she began. "At church."

Jace pulled his phone out of his pocket for the umpteenth time, but he couldn't bring himself to hit the send button and place the call to Bree. He put it back in his pocket and pulled out a pair of pliers instead. He'd been working on one particular section of fencing all morning, but instead of focusing on what he was doing, his mind was on Bree.

He was just about finished when he saw his father's truck pull in through the ranch gates. He'd been in Texas, picking up a year-old bull, which had been sired by Little Yellow Jacket, and his dam was Cowgirl Trash. That lineage made the bull worth every penny of the $15,000 they paid for him.

Jace left the fence unfinished and went to meet his father at the barns. With the bull being so young, Jace was more worried about the older bulls picking on him than him being the troublemaker, but you never knew.

He'd keep a steady eye on him for the next few hours, and pen him off to himself for tonight, at least.

"Long drive, Daddy?" Jace rested his hand on his father's shoulder.

"Not too bad. I stopped in Monument, but you already know that, don't ya?"

"Yeah, I know you did." Jace walked toward the trailer.

"Hold up, there, a minute," said Hank. "I want to talk to you."

"Has anything changed with Tuck?"

Hank hung his head and shook it. "No, Jace. It hasn't."

"Ain't me refusin' to talk to him. You're barkin' up the wrong twin."

Jace's mom came flying out the front door and ran into his father's waiting arms. He spun her around and gave her a kiss that made Jace blush. That was what he wanted, but doubted he'd ever have—a love so strong that after thirty years, their kisses were still as passionate as when they met.

His father distracted, Jace slipped away from the conversation he didn't want to have anyway and opened the back of the trailer to unload the bull.

"Gotta come up with a name for ya. Somethin' fierce is what I'm thinkin'."

"You talkin' to bulls, now, instead of your daddy?" Hank was following Jace into the barn. "And don't you go sayin' the bull's got more sense, or I'll clip you one."

Jace laughed. "No, I wasn't gonna say anything like that. But, can we table the Tucker talk? I got nothin' to say on the subject, and I doubt he did either."

"Your mama and I aren't giving up, Jace. You and your brother need to resolve this thing between the two of you. You're both hurting. In the meantime, you're missing out on seeing your nephew grow up."

That was the hardest part for Jace. His brother's baby was eight months old, and he still hadn't met him.

"How is Cochran? Growin' like a weed?"

"He looks just like you."

Jace laughed again. "Tuck and I are twins, in case you forgot. I'm guessin' he looks more like his daddy than me."

Hank raised his eyebrow. "I could tell the difference between you boys from the minute you were born. And I'm tellin' you; he looks like you, Jace."

"What do you think of Cowgirl Stinger as a name for this one?" Jace pointed at the bull.

"I like it," his father smiled. "Seems fitting."

"Yeah, I like it too. Who knows, maybe it'll be a female bull rider who'll be the first to cover him."

His father put his hand on Jace's arm. "I'm not letting it go, Jace. We're gonna talk about Tucker, and we're gonna do it right now."

Jace sat down on a bale of hay and settled in for the lecture he knew his daddy was going to give him. Once Hank Rice got something stuck in his craw, there was no dissuading him until he got whatever he had to say off his chest.

The dinner bell rang, a half hour later, otherwise his daddy might've talked all night. Both he and Jace knew better than to keep his mama waiting when dinner was on the table.

"What news from Monument?" asked his mother not five minutes into their supper.

"Well, Carol," his father answered. "There's a fella in Larkspur I want to go see, and, Jace, you should meet him too. Ty Rinaldo is his name."

"Heard of him. He's got a good operation goin' down there. But, Daddy—"

She rested her hand on his arm. "Jace Porter Rice."

Jace knew, when his mama used his full name, he'd best keep quiet. Why was it he'd thought living so close to his parents would be a good idea?

"As I was sayin'," Hank continued. "TZ Bucking Bulls has been a family operation for three generations, and Ty's gotten in good with the National Western Stock Show. That's something I'd like us to be a part of. Next year, if we can make it happen."

Jace wondered if he could come up with an excuse good enough to get out of going to Monument. He doubted it.

Sometime in the middle of the night, Jace heard a raucous coming from the barn. He pulled on his Wranglers and stuck his feet in the boots that were always near his bed. When he got outside, he saw his father headed toward the barn from the other direction. The bulls had broken through the pipe fencing, and there was a fight going on.

In his rush to get to the pen, Jace tripped when his jeans caught on a piece of the broken pipe. When his leg twisted around, he felt a pain he'd hoped never to experience again. The pain was ingrained in his memory, and he had no doubt that an MRI would simply confirm what he already knew. He'd just torn his ACL. Four years ago, he'd torn it skiing. At the time, he doubted he'd ever ski, or ride a bull or a bronc, again in his life. It had been a long road of rehab, most of it self-prescribed, but he'd done it.

Given his injury, Jace and his dad postponed the trip to Larkspur indefinitely. Hank wouldn't be able to leave the ranch until Jace recovered, and that might take weeks.

Jace got up and put the brace on his knee. The news hadn't been as bad as he initially thought it would be. The ligament wasn't torn completely, only partially. It wasn't any less painful, but the recovery would be much easier. And quicker.

He'd dodged a couple of bullets. One, with the injury itself, since it wouldn't require surgery. And two, by getting out of a trip to Monument.

He heard his mother downstairs, puttering around in his kitchen. She came by every morning to make him a pot of coffee and a hot breakfast. She also left lunch and dinner for him to heat up later.

Getting downstairs was painful, but Jace was determined to sleep in his own bed on the second story of the ranch house. If he stayed downstairs, he'd be forced to sleep on the couch, and if he did that, his back would hurt as much as his leg.

"Mornin', Mama." He leaned over and kissed her cheek.

"How's the leg?"

"Sore. But better than it was yesterday."

"You take anything for the pain?"

"Not yet. Gonna try to get by with over-the-counter stuff today. I don't like the way the prescription medicine makes me feel."

She set a plate of bacon and eggs on the table in front of him.

"You don't have to come over and make me breakfast, you know."

"I know, but I like to do it." She sat down in the chair across from him. "I'm worried about you."

"I'll be okay, Mama. It'll take time to heal, that's all."

"It isn't your leg I'm worried about, Jace. It's your heart."

Jace wanted to tell her he was fine and that she shouldn't worry about him, but he couldn't. "Me, too," he said instead.

Bree leaned over and picked up a rock near the side of the stream. She and Red had been fishing at different places on the Salmon River for a couple of days. Bree wouldn't have minded going off on her own, but Red was easy going, and she got used to being with him.

"What's the hatch?" he asked when she set the rock back down.

"Caddis." The most common, and meant there'd be plenty of hungry fish. "I'll go downstream," she offered.

He smiled. "Lots of fish right here, Bree."

Other than Zack, there wasn't anyone else she'd liked to fish with, until she met Red. It took her a few minutes to settle in, but soon, she got into the rhythm of casting, and let herself get lost in it.

"Gettin' hungry?" Red asked.

Hungry? Now that he mentioned it, she was starving. She pulled her cell phone out and saw it was just past noon. They'd been fishing for three hours and neither had said a word.

"You won't be gettin' a signal on that thing out here, better to forget you have it with you."

"No, uh, I was just checking the time."

"That's right, you youngins don't wear watches, do ya?"

"You're right. It's been a long time since I relied on a watch to tell me the time." She waved her phone in the air. "Much easier to rely on this thing." She put the phone back in her pocket.

"Whaddaya say we head up to Stanley for a bite to eat?"

3

When Red suggested they go to Stanley, Bree felt the air leave her lungs.

"Stanley Bakery okay with you?" he asked.

She nodded, and they made the rest of the ten mile drive north in silence.

"It'll be crowded," Red said when they pulled into town. "Me and the boys got a table in the back, though. There'll be two seats open."

She nodded but wasn't really listening. The last time she'd been in Stanley was with Zack, five years ago.

* * *

Bree and Zack drove from Colorado, up through Wyoming, and into Montana before they went to Idaho.

The night before they got to Stanley, they'd been in Butte, Montana. Which, in its heyday, between the late nineteenth century and about 1920, was one of the largest and most notorious copper boomtowns in the American West, home to hundreds of saloons and a famous red-light district.

Driving in, the desolation of the city shocked her. The earth had been ravaged by mining. The disparity between it and the extraordinary beauty of the rest of Montana and Wyoming, was heartbreaking.

They spent that night at a bed and breakfast called the Copper King Mansion. It was originally built by William A. Clark between 1884 and 1888. The thirty-four-room, Tiffany-decorated, multi-million dollar home incorporated the most modern inventions available at the time, including a shower which the innkeeper referred to as a plumber's nightmare. It looked more like an instrument of torture, with water shooting from all sides.

Without a wide range of options for dinner in such an economically-depressed place, she and Zack ended up at Mahoney's Bar, where they spent the rest of the night talking to the authentically-Irish bartender.

Their drive to Stanley, the next morning, had been miserable because they were both so hungover. It was pouring rain, and they barely had enough energy to stop for lunch before they stumbled into another bed and breakfast.

That night they were lulled to sleep by the sound of the rain hitting the old tin roof of the one-time boarding house. The bed was small and the box springs, creaky.

* * *

"Everything okay?" Red asked when he came around to open her door.

"Zack and I spent time in Stanley," she answered, hoping he wouldn't ask anything else. If she closed her eyes, she could remember the feeling of the two of them being as close as two people could be.

As he'd predicted, there was a line out the door at the bakery. He took Bree's hand in his big one and pulled her past the crowd to a room in the back, where the locals had their permanently-reserved table.

"Boys," Red began, "I'd like you to meet the woman I spent the last few mornings fly fishing with. Who, I humbly admit, typically out-fishes me two to one."

The men stood, and Red introduced her to them one by one. "Zeke, Emmet, Virgil, Branson…"

Bree lost track of the names, which sounded as though they could be a list of characters in an old Western. Each one shook her hand before sitting back down.

"Where did Red take ya this mornin'? I'm bettin' mile marker 189," said the one she thought was Zeke.

She looked over at Red, who was grinning.

"To his secret spot you mean?"

Her answer was met with laughter. "I take, it isn't a very well-kept secret," she continued.

"You got it, girl," said the one named Virgil.

Red chuckled and ran his hand over his whisker-covered chin. "I'm curious about somethin'."

Oh, no. Would he bring up her husband here, in front of all these strangers? "What's that?" she stammered, hoping he wouldn't.

"Every fish you catch, right before you release it, you hold it up real close to your face, so close I could swear you're kissin' the damn thing. What's that all about?"

Bree's cheeks flushed. "It's a little ritual. I tell them I'm sorry for hurting them before I send them back."

She supposed every man at the table figured she was bat-shit crazy after that story, especially given the way they were still staring at her and not saying a word.

"Well, ain't that cute?" Zeke laughed.

She couldn't tell whether he was confirming her insanity, or if he truly did think it was cute.

She looked at Red who was shaking his head, but still grinning. If nothing else, she'd just given them a story they could repeat for the next twenty years.

"What's good?" Bree asked.

"The sticky buns are world famous," answered one of the cowboys.

That sounded too sweet for Bree's taste. When Red ordered corned beef hash, she did too.

"I know it's well past breakfast," he said, "but it's about the best I've ever had."

She nodded and finished every last morsel on her plate.

Jace's days settled into a routine of physical therapy followed by a ride around the ranch. There wasn't much he was up to doing, but it gave him the chance to make a list of the things that needed to be done when he recovered enough to start tackling them. As he learned the land, he tried not to let his mind wander.

He had no idea what to do about Tucker. His brother had every right to be angry, every right to hate him. Which was why Jace was hesitant to pursue a reconciliation. What he'd done was unforgivable. How could he ask it of Tucker when he couldn't forgive himself?

He spent as much time thinking about Bree Fox as he did his brother. The harder he tried not to think about her, the more he did.

Other than at the funeral, there had only been two times Jace witnessed her break down over the death of her husband. Both times, he'd been the one who gave her comfort. He wondered who gave her comfort now. He hoped someone was.

He wanted to call her, but the last time they'd spoken, she accused him of using her to intervene with Tucker on his behalf.

"You can't blame me for wondering about your motives," she'd said the day he told her about the accident. How could he explain that his motives were about her? As much as he wished Tucker could forgive him, he needed Bree's forgiveness too.

"How about a break for lunch?" his mother asked, riding up next to him.

"Mama, if you keep this up, I'm gonna weigh three hundred pounds before my leg heals."

"Nonsense. You're still as active as you were before you got hurt. If anything, you're losing weight."

She was right, and that was why she insisted on bringing him meals. He didn't have much of an appetite, so if she didn't, he wouldn't eat.

"Your daddy doesn't want to ask," she began as she laid out a picnic lunch for them.

"Ask what?"

"There's a bull he's interested in, in Idaho. The folks at a place called Idaho Rocky Mountain Ranch contacted him about a bucker they were given." She told him they'd sent his father a video, and based on what Hank had seen, he thought the bull would be worth taking a look at. The ranch wasn't interested in getting into the rough stock business, so they were looking to sell him.

"He has to stay here and oversee the stuff you aren't able to yet, but he wants to get a look at this bull before someone else makes a bid on him."

It was a six-hour drive from their place outside Helena, Montana, to Stanley, Idaho, where the ranch was. If he stopped every hour and stretched his leg, he could probably handle it. It was the least he could do, since his father had been picking up so much of his slack.

"Sure, I can do it. I'll talk it over with him when we get back to the house."

"Good. He'll appreciate the offer."

Each time he tried to ask his dad about the bull, Hank changed the subject. When Jace asked to see the video, he grumbled. "You don't make a decision about a bull by watching a video," he muttered, and glared at Carol across the dinner table.

Jace couldn't figure it out. Maybe his father was irritated at his mom for asking him to go. When he offered to let him go instead, his dad waved him off.

"You go," he said.

Jace set out the next morning, just after dawn. He'd be in Stanley by mid-afternoon. When he asked his dad whom he should ask for when he got there, he told him to ask his mother. As if the whole thing could get any stranger.

"Ask for Red," she told him before he got in the truck and drove away.

"I have no idea what you're talking about," said the ranch manager when Jace asked him about the bull. "But that doesn't mean much. Red doesn't tell us everything he's got a hand in."

"Could you ask him?" Jace ran his hand through his hair. His leg ached, and more than anything, he wanted to get this over with so he could get back home and rest it.

"He won't be back today. He's in Salmon, at a fishin' tournament. I think he said he'd be back sometime tomorrow."

Jace didn't know what to do. According to this guy, there wasn't any way to get in touch with Red. But if his daddy really wanted this bull, Jace knew it only made sense to wait until tomorrow when he got back.

"Can you recommend a place to stay?"

"Sure. See that cabin over there? It's what we call a two-fer. Got two sides to it. One is occupied by the lady Red's off fishin' with. We try not to book the other half, so she can have her privacy, but seein' how she's gone anyway, you can bunk there for the night."

The man shook his head. "It's damn sad."

"What's that?"

"She showed up here a couple of weeks ago, on some sort of sabbatical. That's why we don't book the other half of the cabin. You can hear her cryin' somethin' fierce sometimes, mostly at night. Lost her husband a while back, in the war. I doubt she thinks anyone hears her, but we do. Red took her under his wing right away. They spend a lot of time fishin'."

"Who is this Red guy anyway?"

The man waved his hand in a sweeping circle. "Red owns every bit of land as far as your eye can see. He owns this place, too." He laughed then. "Folks would pay good money to have Red as their fly-fishing guide for even a couple of hours, but he refuses to do it. For her, he does it for free."

"Why?"

"Can't say, but he seems to be enjoyin' himself, so who are we to tell the boss to stop." The man kicked at the dirt. "Red lost his wife about a year and a half ago. We been worried 'bout him since. He's a generous boss and all-around good guy. If he feels like fishin', he can fish. Name's Wyatt, by the way."

"Jace Rice, nice to meet ya."

"Trail ride later on, with a damn good chuck wagon dinner if you'd like to join us."

"Appreciate it."

"Meet me at the main barn at six, and I'll get you seated on a horse."

"I spent a few summers working a dude ranch," Jace told Wyatt as they saddled the horses.

"Oh yeah, where at?"

"In Colorado. A place called Black Mountain Ranch. Ever heard of it?"

"No, can't say I have. Nice place?"

It was nice, but nothing like this place. Idaho Rocky Mountain Ranch was situated in the Sawtooth Valley, with a spectacular view of the mountains by the same name. The front porch of the main lodge offered a view of Heyburn and Horstman Peaks as the backdrop to Pettit Lake, where their sunset ride would take them.

Jace gorged himself on applewood-smoked baby back ribs and soy-glazed local salmon, which were served at the fanciest chuck wagon dinner he'd ever seen.

"Damn, this is good," he said to Wyatt.

"Red likes the best."

Jace looked forward to meeting Red more than seeing the bull he had for sale.

"Can I ask you a question?"

"Ask away, Bree. Ol' Red Dugan only keeps his fishin' spots a secret, everything else is fair game."

"You aren't very good at keeping those a secret either." Bree smiled. "You've spent almost every day of the last week playing my fishing guide. It isn't that I don't appreciate it, but are there things at the ranch you're supposed to be doing? I mean, other than babysitting me?"

"First of all, what makes you think you aren't babysitting me?"

Bree raised an eyebrow.

"And second, they're pretty good about lettin' me do whatever I want over at the ranch. Ain't like I'm much of a hand anymore at my age."

"You could probably run laps around any of the other cowboys over there, and you know it."

Red laughed and threw his arm around Bree's shoulders. "You're good for this ol' guy's ego, but I know better." He stopped and opened the door for her. Bree put her hand on his shoulder and climbed up into the truck.

"My daughter used to do that," he murmured.

Red closed Bree's door and walked around the front of the truck. He got in but didn't start it up right away.

"Tell me about her."

"She was a lot like you. Tiny, but feisty. Smart as a whip. Could out-fish me any day of the week. Could out-ride and out-rope me too. Whatever she set her mind to, that girl could do." Red looked away and took a deep breath. "The only thing she couldn't do was beat the damn cancer."

Bree recognized the quiver in Red's voice. She heard it in her own so often. She also knew that he'd continue his story when he wanted to, and that might mean never.

They were almost to the fishing lodge in Salmon when Red pulled off the side of the road.

"See that there?" he pointed.

Dusk was easing quickly into nightfall, and Bree couldn't see whatever Red was talking about. "What is it?"

"Looks like a grizzly." He pulled out a pair of binoculars from under the seat of the truck, and looked in the direction of the hillside.

Suddenly there was movement and Bree realized a herd of pronghorn antelope was scattered on the hillside.

He handed the binoculars over to her. "Look that way," he pointed again. "She's stalking them."

Bree moved the binoculars back and forth until she caught sight of the grizzly. "How do you know it's a female?"

"Look there," he said.

Bree lowered the binoculars and looked where he pointed. When she raised them, she could see a bear cub staying just off to the side.

"She's goin' in," he said.

And sure enough, the grizzly bounded forward and caught one of the smaller antelope. Bree lowered the binoculars, not wanting to see the rest.

"Circle of life, young lady," he said, putting the binoculars back under the seat and starting the truck.

"I know," she answered with a sigh.

"My daughter would've done the same thing. Watched to a point, then set the binocs down."

"How long has it been, Red?"

"Goin' on thirty years now."

"She must've been very young when she died."

"Twenty-seven. 'Bout your age, if I'm right."

"You are."

When Red asked Bree to enter the tournament with him, she knew she'd be fishing the same places she and Zack once fished. She tried to convince herself it would be good for her.

What it ended up being was gut-wrenchingly painful. And it started as soon as they drove up to the main office of Salmon Creek Outfitters. She'd taken her first fly-tying class right here. She wondered if the owners, Annie and Dave, would recognize her.

Before Red could introduce her, Annie pulled her into a bear hug. "Bree Fox, is it ever good to see you! Where is that devilishly handsome husband of yours? Parking the car?"

Bree took a deep breath. She looked at Red, whose soft eyes told her he was right there with her.

"Annie," she began, hoping her voice wouldn't quiver. "He was deployed to Afghanistan two years ago. His convoy hit an IED. Zack didn't make it."

Annie gasped and threw her hand over her mouth. "Oh, Bree," she said, pulling her back into the hug. "I'm so sorry, sweetheart. I don't know what to say."

There, thought Bree, she'd done it. She said it out loud and she hadn't fallen apart. Red rested his hand on her shoulder and squeezed tight.

"Let me go get Dave, honey. He'll want to see you. Wait, how do you know Red?"

"Kind of a long story. I'll wait until you get Dave, and fill you both in," Red answered for her.

"How ya doin', Bree?" Red asked when they walked back to the truck.

"If I said I was fine, would you believe me?"

"Nah. But I wouldn't question ya 'bout it either."

The next morning they got out on the water early. Bree walked farther downstream than she normally would've when she was with Red, but today she needed time alone. She and Zack had fished this very stream. She hadn't told Red, though. It might have made him feel bad about bringing her here.

"This is what I'm here for," she told herself. She looked up at the sky. "I'm gonna do this, Zack."

She closed her eyes and cast, imagining he was standing close enough to put his hands on her waist, to gently guide her as her body twisted just slightly and slowly came back around. She could feel his breath on her neck, whispering how well she did.

Right away, she felt a tug. It was almost too much. Through her tears she brought the fish in.

"Back to mama," she said before releasing it back into the stream.

She dropped down on the rock behind her, put her head in her hands, and cried. What had she been thinking, coming here? Why had she thought it was necessary to immerse herself in her grief? Why hadn't she just let it happen naturally?

She felt a hand resting gently on her shoulder. She knew it was Red. She didn't need to look.

"I can't do this."

"Come on, then. Let's go."

"It's okay, you can fish. I'll just walk back to the truck."

"Let's go, Bree. We're done for today."

Bree let Red guide her, without an argument. He didn't drive back into town, he went south toward the ranch instead.

"I'm sorry about the tournament, Red."

"Now, now, none of that," he answered. "We can fish anywhere we want. Doesn't have to be up in Salmon."

Red turned the truck off the road in the direction of the lake, opposite of where Bree expected him to go. She didn't care where he was headed, though, she was just happy they weren't in Salmon any longer.

Knowing she'd be back on the ranch felt safer. There were nights she cried herself to sleep, but she could do that in the dark by herself, with no one to witness her sadness. Out on the stream, today, felt too raw, too public, although she doubted anyone saw her, other than Red. She appreciated his comfort, even though she couldn't bring herself to tell him so.

There was only one other person whose comfort she'd appreciated more. In the weeks after Zack's death, it had been Jace who held her when she cried. Jace, who, at the time, she couldn't stand.

She couldn't understand why she'd let him. Maybe it was because he was so damn pushy he wouldn't take no for an answer. She could still remember how it felt to have his arms wrapped around her the day she admitted for the first time that she and Zack had fought before he was deployed to Afghanistan, and that he'd left without saying goodbye.

She'd cried for what seemed like hours, that day, and Jace held her through it all. It hadn't mattered how hard she pushed him away; he refused to let go.

What she'd give to have him here now.

Something had been eating at Jace all day. It had started the night before, when he got into bed. It was something Wyatt said about the woman who was staying on the other side of this cabin. He said she lost her husband in the war. He also said that they could hear her crying at night, when she thought no one could.

Every word he said made him think of Bree. Where was she? Was she feeling the same way? He wished, now, he'd asked his mother more about her plans. He hoped she wasn't alone, like this woman was.

Several times last night and even today, he thought about texting her. He started to type a message to her three or four times, but never hit the send button. No matter what he wrote, it didn't sound right.

How could he ask her anything without explaining why he'd never responded to the messages she sent him? None of it belonged in a text, but it would've been harder to call. So he didn't do anything, except spend the whole day thinking about her.

He walked to the barn, in the middle of the afternoon, and asked Wyatt if he would mind if he rode one of the horses out on the trail. Rather than exploring anything new, Jace took the same trail they'd been on the night before, over to Pettit Lake.

Last night he'd seen what he thought was a pathway that wound its way all around the lake. He was three-quarters of the way there when he saw a truck pull up and stop near the dirt road that led back to the ranch.

When it didn't look as though the people in it were getting out, he stopped paying attention and continued making his way around the lake.

4

Bree rolled down the window and looked out over the lake. It was beautiful and she said so. It was hard to tell which was real—the mountains and trees, or their reflection in the lake. Both were so clear.

"I grew up on this lake," Red told her as he opened her door and helped her out. He pointed toward the north bank. "See that cabin? I spent every summer there for most of my life."

"It's idyllic," she said wistfully. "Almost surreal in its perfection. Who owns it now?"

"I do."

"Oh. Is this where you live? Convenient that it's right across the road from the ranch."

He didn't answer, but it didn't matter. Bree didn't feel like talking any more than it seemed he did. The breeze from the lake was colder than it had been on the stream, and when she shivered, Red went back to the truck to get her jacket, just like Jace would've.

Bree closed her eyes and let her thoughts drift back to him. She knew she shouldn't be thinking about Jace. She should be thinking about Zack. Why did she have to remind herself of that over and over again?

When she opened her eyes, she saw movement across the lake. Off in the distance and through the trees, Bree could see a man on horseback. From where she stood with Red, she could swear it was Jace. She blinked her eyes and looked again.

Jace saw the passenger door open and a woman climb out of the truck that had parked near the lake's shore. She wore a baseball cap, and she was a sprite of a thing, just like Bree. Her t-shirt hugged her small body the same way too. Rather than taking the turn to go back to the ranch, he turned the horse in her direction.

The woman walked slowly toward him, so Jace stopped and climbed off the horse. He lifted his hat, removed his sunglasses, and wiped the sweat from his brow. By then she was much closer to him.

"Jace?" he heard her say.

Was this real or was he dreaming? It wouldn't be unusual; he dreamed about her all the time. He'd know soon enough, because in a matter of seconds, she'd be close enough to touch.

"Bree?"

"Jace, what are you doing here?"

He had no idea what to say. He couldn't remember why he was there. Why had he come to Idaho in the first place?

Bree was a couple of feet away from him when he came out of his stupor. "A bull."

"What?"

"Uh, I'm here about a bull."

He dropped the horse's reins and reached out to her. He was so afraid she would hesitate, or back away, but she didn't. She walked the rest of the distance between them, and let herself fall into his arms. He could feel every inch of her as she pressed herself into him.

"I missed you," he thought he heard her say.

"I missed you, too," he answered.

"I can't believe you're here." She pulled away and looked up at him. "Tell me again why you are."

"I'm supposed to see a man named Red about a bull. He's been off fishing with a woman…"

Bree waited for him to finish his sentence, and when he didn't, she pointed in the direction of the truck. "Red's right over there," she told him. When she turned back, Jace's look of confusion turned into a smile.

His ash blond hair was longer, closer to the way his brother, Tucker, kept it. He looked as fit as the last time she saw him, maybe more so. She knew he'd been competing as a saddle bronc rider and working the ranch in Montana. His skin looked weathered, with a few more wrinkles surrounding his deep green eyes.

"Bree," he whispered. "You've been on my mind, girl, and now, here you are, in Idaho. It's almost too crazy to be a coincidence."

"Let's go ask Red about this bull."

Jace put his hand on her shoulder as they walked toward the truck. Just moments ago, she was thinking she'd give anything to have him here, and now, he was. She slowed her pace, and when she did, Jace put his arm around her and pulled her close to him.

"You must be Red," she heard him say. She struggled with explaining who Jace was, but she had nothing.

"I am. Red Dugan. Nice to meet you."

Jace moved forward to shake Red's hand, but his other arm remained around Bree's shoulders.

"Jace Rice. Nice to meet you, sir."

"What brings you to Idaho, young man? I take it you know Bree."

"I do know her. And as far as what brings me to Idaho, I'm guessing it has more to do with Bree than I was initially led to believe."

Red laughed. "I think I'm gonna like this story." He motioned for them to take a seat at a wooden picnic table on the lake's shore.

"I was sent here to see you about a bull. You know anything about that?"

"A bull?" Red laughed again. "Don't know nothin' about any bulls, young man. Who'd you say sent you?"

"That's the thing. My mama said my daddy wanted me to check out a bucking bull at your ranch. When I asked my daddy about it, he clammed up in a way that should have told me somethin' was fishy."

Bree noticed Jace rubbing his left knee; it wasn't the first time he'd done it since they sat down.

"There isn't a bull for sale at the ranch, is there?"

"Not that I know of." Red shook his head and chuckled. "I'm guessing you're right. This lady is why you're really here."

Bree blushed when she realized they were both looking at her. "I don't know anything about this." She looked back and forth between the two of them.

"I doubt you do," said Jace, leaning closer into her. "But your sister knows you're here."

"Of course she does. My whole family knows I'm here."

"My mama. Your sister."

"Really? Do you think this was planned?"

Jace nodded his head. "As much as this sorta thing can be."

"But...why?"

Bree saw a look pass between Red and Jace. Maybe this was something they should wait and discuss when they were alone.

"Jace, is there something wrong with your knee?" The last time he rubbed it, she saw him grimace.

"It's no big deal. I pulled a ligament in an accident up at the ranch. Which is why it was easy for my mama to get me to make the drive down here. Haven't been much help to anyone up there."

Red turned and faced the other direction, out toward the lake, and laughed harder. "This is quite a set up. Your mama played you pretty good, son." He turned back around to face them. "But by the looks of things, you aren't too disappointed about missing out on a bucking bull."

Red winked at Bree and looked over at the horse. "Tell you what," he tossed his keys over to Jace. "You drive my truck across the road, and I'll ride ol' Spike back myself."

"It's okay, I can—"

Red raised his hand. "I insist. And if my ranch manager hasn't already extended the offer, I'd like to invite you to join us for dinner tonight."

"Thank you, sir. As a matter of fact, I spent last night at your place. Had one of the best meals I've ever had right here at this lake."

"Well, I hope you're able to stay another night with us. Again, I'd like to think that offer has already been made to you."

It hadn't been, because the woman in the two-fer cabin was due back tonight. They'd apologized that the other cabins were booked and there weren't any open rooms in the main lodge. They'd given him the name of a place in town where he could stay, but he hadn't gotten around to calling to see if they had any vacancies.

"I'd love to stay for dinner, appreciate the invite," he answered. He'd deal with where he was going to stay later. He guessed that things might be different now that he knew Bree was the woman on the other side of the adjoining door.

Dinner was served in the main lodge, and the food was as good as it had been the night before, but Jace wasn't paying any attention to what he was eating.

Bree's cheeks were pink. Was it from the time she'd been spending outdoors or the wine she drank with dinner? Whatever it was, it looked good on her. Damn good. Somehow, her eyes were even bluer than he remembered. She kept her dark hair cut short, but it had grown some since he last saw her. It was just long enough that it curled around the edges of her face. He longed to wind his fingers through those curls and pull her close enough to brush his lips over hers.

He heard what sounded like live music coming from outside the dining room and saw other guests making their way in that direction.

"You wanna go see what's goin' on?" he asked her.

"I'm okay sitting here a while longer, unless you want to."

"I'm good," he answered. He leaned forward so he was only a couple of inches from her, rested his arm on the table, and looked into her eyes.

"How've you been, Bree?"

"I've been good," she paused. "No, that isn't true. I haven't been good at all. I've been terrible, in fact." She shook her head and laughed.

Jace laughed too, although he sensed the conversation was about to turn more serious. When she rested her hand on the table, he ran his fingers over her knuckles. "Tell me," he whispered.

"I decided I couldn't hide from it any longer. I had to face it."

"Zack?"

She nodded. "He and I spent a week at this ranch. It was part of our honeymoon. I thought, if I came back here and let myself remember, maybe I could also let myself grieve." Soft tears rolled down her cheeks.

"I'm sorry, sweetheart."

"I have to do this, Jace. I can't keep denying he's gone."

He could tell her he understood, but he didn't. He missed his brother so much there were times he felt as though he'd die from the ache of it. But Tucker was still alive. If he wanted to see him, he could. He might not be welcome, but he *could* see him. Bree couldn't see Zack.

"I'm sorry I never answered your texts."

"Yeah, about that," she laughed through her tears. "What the hell, Jace?"

"I just didn't—"

"You don't have to explain. I understand, and I'm not just saying that."

"You were awful mad at me the last time I saw you."

"I handled that badly, didn't I?"

He leaned closer, so close he could almost kiss her. "You handled it honestly. Somethin' I'm tryin' to do more often."

"Jace...I'm sorry about you and Tucker."

"Nothin' for you to be sorry about, darlin'. Did that all on my own. Can't say as I blame Tuck for not wantin' to see me. I wouldn't want to see him if the situation were reversed."

Jace looked up just as Red turned to leave the room. "Red? Can I help you?"

"Didn't want to interrupt."

Jace recognized the look on Red's face as he gazed at Bree. He looked at her that way too. Red wanted to comfort her, help her through the pain, ease it if he could.

"You aren't interrupting," Bree told him. "What's up?"

"Thought you might give an old fella a dance."

Bree stood, put her arm through Red's, and let him lead her into the other room. She turned back to make sure Jace was following. She didn't want to leave him sitting in the dining room all alone.

He stood and stretched his leg. Just when she was about to turn around and go back to him, he looked up and waved her off.

"Go dance," he said. "I'll be right along, soon as I loosen my leg up."

Red was a good dancer, just like her dad was. It felt good to have his strong arms lead her around the room.

"Seems like a nice young man." He pulled back to look in her eyes.

"Yes, he is. He's very nice," she laughed. "Although I didn't always think so."

"No?"

"I can't remember why not. Except that he was kind of pushy with my sister. She's, uh, married to his brother now. His twin brother."

"Why do I think there's more to the story?"

"There is, but it isn't very interesting." She rested her head against Red's shoulder. "The truth is, he comforted me. He helped me a lot right after Zack's death. He didn't have to, but he did. Even when I pushed him away."

"Must care about you."

"It's a family thing. I love my sister; he loves his brother. We were thrown together, whether we wanted to be or not."

"Uh huh."

Was it that obvious? She supposed it was. Jace Rice made her heart beat faster, and she loved that he was here. She still didn't understand why he was, but they'd get to the bottom of it eventually. In the meantime, she'd take whatever time with him she could get.

"Pretty moon tonight. Maybe you and your young man would like to sit out on the porch, take in the sky. Nothin' like a clear night in Idaho for stargazing."

When the song ended, Bree walked over to where Jace stood, waiting for her. "Red recommends the porch for stargazing."

"I know just the spot he's talkin' about." Jace took her hand in his.

No one else was out there, so they sat on the porch swing. Jace put his arm around her and pulled her close.

"Bree?"

"Yeah?"

"I know I said it before, but it bears repeating. I've missed you."

She rested her head on his shoulder. "I've missed you, too."

Should she tell him that she'd missed him as much as she missed Zack? He would think she was crazy if she did. Or he'd think the same thing she was. Missing Zack and missing Jace got jumbled up together. She couldn't tell the difference between the two sometimes. And that wasn't healthy. It also wasn't real. What she'd had with Zack had been real. She hardly knew Jace.

"I'm here because I need to let myself mourn the death of my husband."

"I know, and I won't do anything to interfere with that. In fact, you say the word, and I'll be in the truck back to Montana come sunrise."

Pain bit her stomach. "No, Jace, that isn't what I'm saying. Please, don't misunderstand."

"I'm glad to be here with you, Bree, but I know there's a road you have to go down. I get it. I'm a detour. You're gonna have to go down that road eventually."

He'd articulated her thoughts perfectly. Jace was a distraction. *A detour.*

"Maybe you could stay another day?"

He smiled. "That could be arranged."

The mountains, with their peaks illuminated by the full moon, took her breath away. Or was it Jace? Probably both. "Oh…uh, where are you staying?"

"I stayed in that cabin right over there last night." He pointed to her cabin. "I think they might let me stay there again tonight if I promise not to disturb the 'little lady' stayin' on the other side."

Bree closed her eyes and felt heat flush her cheeks. They hadn't booked anyone else on the other side of the cabin, and she'd wondered about that. It must have been intentional. "They've been so good to me here."

"They're very protective of you."

"They are?"

"Yep. The only reason they let me stay, last night, was because you weren't here."

"You're kidding?"

"Nope. Think you can put in a good word for me tonight?"

"I'll do that," she said softly.

He wanted to tell her he'd be there for her, on the other side of the cabin. If she wanted him to, he'd hold her when she cried. He'd comfort her, like he had one other night, when she'd begged him not to go.

The door opened, and Red came out on the porch with a key in his hand. "You're welcome to bunk in the same place you did last night," he said and went back inside.

Jace tucked the key in his pocket. "You ready to call it a night?"

"Not yet." She sighed and put her head back on his shoulder.

"No hurry, sweet girl."

"Is your leg okay?"

"What leg?"

He'd been tossing and turning for what seemed like hours when he heard the tap on the adjoining door. At first he thought he might have imagined it, but then he heard Bree say his name. He jumped out of bed, forgetting about his knee. It almost gave out on him, but he managed to hobble over to the door and open his side of it.

"Were you asleep?" she asked.

"No. Not even close."

"Do you mind if I come in?"

"Not at all." He stepped back to let her through the door. "Uh, can I get you anything? Something to drink?" He didn't know why he made the offer. He wasn't sure he had anything to give her if she said she did.

"No. I'd really just like, you know, I mean would you mind, uh…"

"No, I wouldn't mind," he answered, and led her over to the bed.

He held her until he was sure she'd fallen asleep, before he allowed himself to drift off.

When he woke the next morning, she was gone. He looked over at the adjoining door, now closed, and wondered if he'd dreamed the whole thing. There was only one way to find out.

"Bree?" He tapped on the double door. It took a minute, but he could hear her approaching footfalls.

"Good morning," she said as she opened her side of the door.

He took her hand and pulled her toward him. "Good morning, Bree." He put his arms around her and held her close. "When I woke up and you were gone, I was afraid last night had been a dream."

"I'm sorry, I—"

"Shh. Don't apologize. It's okay."

"I don't know why I left."

"It's one thing for me to comfort you in the night. It's another thing entirely for us to acknowledge that closeness by light of day."

"It is?"

He nodded. "It is."

"I'm sorry."

"Stop apologizing," he whispered as he drew her farther into his side of the cabin. "Come here with me, baby."

"Jace, I can't."

"You can. It isn't any different than last night."

When he pulled her over to the bed, she didn't resist. He pulled back the covers so she could crawl in, and got in next to her.

She rested her head on his shoulder, just where he wanted her.

"I want to do this when it's daylight, so I can see you," he murmured. "And know I'm not dreaming."

"Do you dream about me?"

"All the time."

"I dream about you, too."

"Nice to hear."

"Jace, I can't—"

He put two fingers over her lips. "I know. I want to hold you close. That's all."

"Okay," she said and snuggled back into him.

Jace had no idea what time it was. He must've drifted back to sleep. Bree was still snuggled against him, so he kissed the top of her head. He wanted to keep going, to kiss her lips and not stop until he had kissed every inch of her, but he didn't.

Last night she told him she *couldn't*. He understood. As much as he wanted to make love to her, it was too soon. She moved against him, and he cringed.

"Does your leg hurt?" she asked.

He hadn't realized she was awake.

"No, my leg is okay."

"You look like you're in pain, Jace."

He pulled her closer. "I am, darlin', but it isn't my leg that's hurtin'."

"Oh. I, uh...um..."

"Shh, now. It's all good." He closed his eyes, willing his body to stop reacting the way it was.

"Do you like to fish?" she asked.

There, that helped. Fish. Think about fish.

"Yes. I like to fish." He sounded emphatic—even to himself—as if he was trying to convince her of it.

"Fly fish?"

"Haven't ever tried it, darlin'. But I'd like to."

She sat up so quickly, he almost fell out of bed. "I could teach you."

He smiled. The way her face lit up was adorable. "I'd like that."

She was out of bed, pulling him with her.

"Come on, let's get a move on. The fish aren't gonna wait around all day for you."

"Do I have time for a shower?"

"A shower? Who are you? No, you don't have time for a *shower*, cowboy. Jeez. Little dirt gonna hurt ya?"

Jace laughed out loud. "Nope, not at all. Let's get at those fish."

He'd barely gotten his boots on by the time she was marching off in the direction of the main lodge.

"Where you goin'?" he shouted after her.

"I gotta talk to Red about a couple things before we go. You wait here."

5

Jace sat in the Adirondack chair and pondered his situation. Being with Bree was not something he could've predicted. She'd asked him to stay, last night, but that was it. What about later? After they fished, would she expect him to hop in his truck and drive back to Montana? He sure hoped not. Even if it couldn't be forever, he longed to hold her next to him again. Would she let him?

Bree was walking toward him, fishing gear in hand. He rose to meet her.

"What's all that?"

"Red's gear. He's letting you use it today. He also gave me permission to take you to one of his secret fishing spots, although I doubt it's a secret to anyone who knows Red. Are you hungry?"

Was he? Hungry for her, no question. Hungry for food? Now that she mentioned it, he was.

"Don't want to hold up the fishing trip," he laughed.

"It's okay. Red is having the kitchen put a basket of goodies together for us. I'm sure it'll just be a few minutes until it's ready."

A couple of minutes later, Red brought them the promised picnic basket.

"I made her swear not to tell anyone about my fishin' spot. You gotta do the same," Red teased.

"Cross my heart," Jace answered.

"Same thing she said," Red laughed. "And here she is, takin' someone there already."

"But he's special," Bree said, her cheeks turning pink.

Jace smiled. "Why, thank you, ma'am. You're pretty special yourself."

Red put the basket in the back of Jace's truck.

"I hope you don't mind the trailer sittin' over there." Jace pointed in the direction of where he and Wyatt had parked it next to a few others.

"No, I don't mind. Y'all have a good day out there on the water. Mind you, son, she'll out-fish you."

"That's a given, sir, since I've never fly-fished before."

"Oh, boy," Red answered as he turned and walked back toward the lodge. "Take care of my girl," he added right before he opened the big, wooden lodge door.

"He's taken a fancy to you." Jace walked over so he was close enough to cup the side of her face with his palm.

"I remind him of his daughter." Bree leaned into his hand.

Jace doubted she realized she did it.

"That right?"

"Yes." Bree grew somber. "She passed away a long time ago. She was my age."

"I'm sorry to hear that. One of the guys told me he lost his wife last year, too."

That was news to her. She'd spent just about every day of the last couple of weeks with Red, yet it seemed as though Jace knew as much, or more, about him than she did.

She sighed. She was about to take Jace fly fishing with her. And she was going to teach him how to do it. This could go south very easily. Although, as she had to remind herself over and over again, she was here mourning Zack. Anything she did to help facilitate the grief she needed to force herself to face was ultimately a good thing. Right?

"Where'd you go?" he asked.

"Thinking about Zack. I can't help it. I don't want to help it. I hope you understand."

"I do understand, Bree. And if you've changed your mind about fishin', or about me being here today, you won't offend me."

She wouldn't? Maybe he wanted to leave. Maybe he didn't want to be around a woman mourning her late husband. It had been evident he'd wanted to do more than hold her this morning, but she'd told him she couldn't. Did he understand that it wasn't because she didn't want to, that she just wasn't ready?

"It's up to you, Jace. I know I'm not the best company. If you want to leave…"

His arm moved around her shoulders so he could bring her in close. "I didn't say that, Bree. There isn't any place I'd rather be than with you."

"You're a charmer, aren't you?"

"No, I'm not. I'm just a man who wants to spend some time with you. I'm not tryin' to charm you, or seduce you, or anything else. Just time, Bree, that's all I'm looking for."

"So we're friends. Just friends?"

"For now," he winked at her.

Yeah, he wanted it to be more than that. Of course he did, but he was willing to wait. He had plenty of his own crap to sort through. She wasn't alone in that. There, lingering in the back of his mind, was the thing that he never stopped thinking about—the situation with Tucker.

He'd fallen in love with, made love to, a woman he knew his brother was also in love with. And she'd been with Tucker first. There was something in his psyche that allowed him to do that. It was part of his character, and that wasn't the kind of man he wanted to be.

While it seemed as though it was a lifetime ago, it wasn't. It hadn't been ten years since the accident took the life of the woman both he and his brother had loved. He couldn't blame it on his youth. He wasn't that much older now.

"My turn," she said. "Where did you go?"

"Thinkin' about Tuck. You see, Bree, I've got my own mourning to do. Even though it isn't the same, I've lost my brother."

"I don't think you've lost him. He'll come around. He's just angry, and hurt."

"Thought we were goin' fishin'?" He needed to change the subject, or it was going to be a very depressing day for them both.

Bree pulled away from him and walked to the passenger door of his truck. He held it open for her, wanting so badly to lift her up into the seat, but more, he wanted to kiss her breath away. Maybe he *should* leave today, because resisting her was going to be increasingly harder to do.

Bree pointed to the mile marker on the right. "You turn off here," she said. "And keep going straight down this dirt road for a mile or so."

It didn't look like a road to him. It looked more like a trail that a horse or a human could navigate on foot, not something a truck would be able to drive on.

"You sure?"

She raised her eyebrow at him. "Can't ever trust the girl knows what she's talkin' about, can you, Rice?"

Jace grinned. She was a feisty one. When they'd first met, it drove him crazy. She challenged everything he said, and she also accused him of being controlling. Which, he had to admit, he probably was. At least a little. Not with her though, never with her. This was a woman who knew her own mind and was never afraid to speak it.

It made him crazy with wanting her. He'd seen her softer side, and he craved it. When she let her guard down and let him comfort her, neither one of them needed to be in control.

"Jace? Are you listening?"

"What? No, I'm sorry. What did you say?"

"I said you missed the turnoff. You have to back up now, I don't think there's anywhere for you to turn around."

"Damn. Sorry 'bout that, Bree. I got lost in thought there for a minute." Jace put the truck in reverse, rested his arm on the back of the bench seat, and turned his head to see where he was going.

"What were you thinking about?"

He took his foot off the gas, and the truck stopped moving. "Fishin'," he answered.

"I don't believe you."

He put the truck in park.

"Why are you stopping?"

"Because we gotta get somethin' straight."

"What's that?" She folded her arms in front of her, like she did when she was about to rip into him for something.

"You can't always ask me what I'm thinkin' about."

She lifted her chin. "Why not?"

"You aren't always gonna like the answer, that's why."

She didn't respond, and for a minute, Jace actually thought he'd shut her up. Wrong.

"You're still hung up on my sister, aren't you? That's why you don't want to tell me what you're thinking about. And it's also why you aren't trying very hard to make up with Tucker."

That stung. Sure, there had been a time when he believed he was in love with Blythe. And Bree was never going to let him forget it. Tucker had pulled one of his disappearing acts, and Jace felt it was his duty to be there for the woman his brother had gotten pregnant.

In hindsight, he might've believed that by selflessly stepping in to help Blythe, he would somehow atone for the sins of his past. It had been a ridiculous notion. One he wasn't sure he had been consciously aware of at the time.

But to say that he wasn't trying to make up with his brother, was like a slap across the face. He wanted nothing more than to find a way to get Tuck to forgive him.

"I knew it," he heard her mumble.

"You don't know anything," he growled at her. "You think you're so damn smart. You got it all figured out, don't ya? Well, I tell ya, *sister,* you couldn't be more wrong."

"Uh huh."

When she added self-righteousness to indignity it made him want to hit something. Instead he did the only other thing he shouldn't do.

He grabbed her—there was no other word for it— and pulled her into him. His face was less than an inch from hers. He could feel her breathing accelerate; he could see the panic in her eyes, but neither stopped him.

"This is what I've been thinkin' about, Bree." He pulled her body into his and crushed his mouth into hers. Every other thought left his head, until he heard her whimper.

He broke away from her and sat back. "God, Bree, I'm sorry. I shouldn't have done that."

She had the back of her hand over her mouth, and when he looked into her eyes, he saw them fill with tears.

"Shit, Bree. Dammit. I don't even know what to say."

"It's okay," she whispered.

"It isn't okay." He gently pulled her hand away from her mouth. "Did I hurt you? Jesus, what is wrong with me?"

A tear rolled down her cheek. It made him want to cry himself. "I'll take you back now."

He put the truck into gear and turned to back it up.

"I don't want to go back."

He wasn't sure he heard her right. "What do you mean?"

"I don't want you to go."

"But—"

"Let's fish, Jace. Can we, please, just fish?"

He studied her, looking for some sign that might tell him what she was thinking. He felt like an asshole for kissing her the way he had. How could she be so blind to the fact that he was thinking about her, not her sister? He got nothing. She turned her head and stared out the window.

"I'm sorry, Jace."

"Wait. What? What are you sorry for?"

"Never mind."

"Bree…you aren't makin' a whole lot of sense. Not that I am, either."

"Which is why I want to fish. I don't want to talk, Jace. I don't want to talk about my sister, or that kiss, or…anything. I just want to fish."

He waited to see if she'd say anything more. She didn't.

"Okay, let's fish, then."

He backed the truck up to the point where he could take the turnoff he was supposed to take before.

"This way?" he asked.

"We're almost there," she answered. "Look for a big, red rock and park next to it."

"It's a bit of a walk. I didn't think about that."

Jace bent down and picked up a small branch. He ran his hand over it. "All set. Got my walking stick right here."

She led him down the trail, through the trees, to the tributary Red brought her to the first day they'd fished together.

"Wow," he said when they came out of the woods and he saw the rushing water.

"I know. It's breathtaking, isn't it?" She picked up a rock and turned it over, giving him a chance to take it all in, the way she had the first time she came here. She put it back and picked up another one.

"Whatcha' doin'?" he asked when he saw her do it a third time.

"Looking to see what's hatching."

"What's that mean?"

"Look at the sunlight on the water," she said, speaking softly. "See the bugs on the surface? That's typically what's hatching beneath the rocks. When fish come to the surface to eat, our goal is to present a fly on the water in such a way that the fish will think it's just another bug."

She chose a small dry fly. "This is all we'll need."

Jace leaned in closer to her. He understood the reason she lowered her voice. Fishing was a quiet activity. If you got too loud, you scared the fish away.

He stepped back, and she cast the line. She did it so gracefully, she took his breath away. Her movements were…delicate, quiet, fluid. She gently laid the tiny fly on the surface, and it was immediately snapped up.

She brought the fish in as gracefully as she had cast the line. Bree was as breathtaking as the scenery surrounding her.

She held the fish gently in her hand, removing the fly from where it was caught. She looked over at him.

"I have a ritual. It's a little, uh, embarrassing."

"Go ahead," he smiled.

"I talk to them."

"What do you say?"

"Well...this is one of the bigger guys. So with him, I'll just tell him I'm sorry, and send him back."

"And if it was a little guy?"

"I usually tell them not to tell their mom what happened. And then I ask them to send their dad or their big brother back to me."

If things were different between them, that would've made him kiss her again. As it was, Jace realized that he was going to have to leave soon, or he'd make the same mistake he had earlier. She wanted his friendship, his comfort—nothing more. Maybe she considered him more like a brother; he was her brother-in-law, after all.

They spent the next few hours in the same spot. Jace learned how to cast. He snagged his line, caught his fly on bushes, and caught about a third of the fish Bree did.

He couldn't remember the last time he'd had such an enjoyable day. He even forgot the ache in his leg for the most part. Every so often, he moved it the wrong way, but otherwise, he was so focused on fishing, and on Bree, he didn't notice.

He sat down on a rock and watched her cast again. He'd be willing to bet she'd forgotten he was there. Ten minutes or more passed before she turned to look at him. He hadn't taken his eyes off her.

"Bored?"

"'Bout as far from bored as it gets," he answered.

"We should head back anyway."

"Why should we do that?"

"Honestly? I'm exhausted," she laughed. "Red doesn't usually last this long when we go out. I've grown accustomed to him calling it a day long before I get tired."

"I had a great time, Bree. Thanks for bringin' me here."

"It was my pleasure, Jace. And you're welcome."

They packed up their gear and trekked the mile back to where they left his truck. They stood next to the tailgate and watched an eagle circle above them.

"I should head home," he said.

Bree didn't look at him right away; instead, she continued to watch the eagle. "Do you have to leave tonight?"

"I should."

"I wish you didn't have to."

She still hadn't looked at him, and he wanted her to. "Bree, darlin', look my way."

She slowly turned her head toward him, but kept her eyes closed. He stroked her cheek with his fingers. "Please, look at me."

She opened her eyes and the tears were back.

"I'm about as lost in knowin' what to do when it comes to you as I am when I try to cast a fly." He reached out and circled her waist. When he did, she wrapped her armss around his neck. He kissed her hair, then rested his cheek against it. He breathed in deeply. She smelled like sunshine, and outdoors, and the breeze.

"I'm sorry," she sighed.

"Come on." He walked her over to her side of the truck. "Let's go back. I'll call my daddy and see how things are at home. Then we'll talk some more."

Before she could climb in, herself, Jace put his hands on her waist and lifted her into the truck. It made her giggle, a sound he was quickly growing to love.

"Guess you're stuck with me for a few more days at least," he said when he hung up from talking to his father. "Turns out there might be a bull 'round these parts after all."

"What do you mean?"

"There's a fella buckin' bulls in Stanley this weekend. My understanding is that he's also got an auction in the works. My daddy thinks there might be a bull or two worth me stickin' around for."

Bree wasn't sure what to do with this information. She was glad he was staying. Very glad. But the kiss had changed things, and that was the part she wasn't sure about.

When Jace kissed her, she didn't want him to stop. And tonight, no matter how many times she told herself she shouldn't, she knew full well that she'd do just as she did the night before. It was too tempting, having him on the other side of the cabin's thin interior wall. She'd want him to hold her until she fell asleep, because when he did, the nightmares didn't come. And that wasn't the only reason she wanted him to hold her. It felt good, and right, to be in his arms.

The problem was, he'd want more. And after the heat of that kiss, so would she. But she knew, and there was no denying it, it was a step she wasn't ready to take.

Was it fair to ask him to be there for her when she was also asking him to hold back his feelings?

Jace reached over and stroked her forehead, his finger running over the creases she knew were there.

"Just because I'm stickin' around, doesn't mean you're really stuck with me. I know you're here to spend time on your own. I don't want to intrude any more than I have already. I can always find a place to bunk in town. Is that what's causin' all this worry in that pretty head of yours?"

Bree leaned forward so she could rest her furrowed brow against his chest. "What's worrying me is how much I want you to stay. And by that, I mean stay here, with me."

Jace wasn't sure how to respond. Stay here, with her, as he had last night, in the other part of the cabin, or stay with her in her bed? If he did, would she ultimately regret it? He'd be the detour again. She needed to stay on the road she was on. Even though he didn't know much about grief, he did know there were stages of it she needed to work through. He couldn't let himself get in the way.

There wasn't anything selfless in his thinking though. He wanted her to work through it because he wanted her to be his...all his. As long as part of her still belonged to her late husband, she could never be his completely. This time, with this woman, he wasn't willing to settle for any less than all of her. He was done compromising, done settling, done accepting anything other than it all.

He wanted what his parents had, and what Tucker had with Blythe, and what his friends Billy and Irene had. He wanted a great, all-encompassing love, and from the day he met her, he'd known, somewhere deep in his soul, that Bree was meant for him and he was meant for her. Their timing was off, but that was all. Everything else about them worked. They fit. He could be patient; he could wait until she was ready. She was worth it. He was as sure of it as he was sure of his own name.

"I'll tell you what," he began. "I'll stay, just like I did last night, next door. I'll even hold you until you fall asleep, just like I did last night, but that's it, Bree. I won't allow anything else to happen between us."

At first she looked surprised, then confused. His fingers, which had been running across her furrowed brow only moments before, stroked down the side of her face.

"Bree—" he breathed.

"Don't say it. I'm begging you not to say it." She pulled away from him and started to walk in the direction of the cabin.

He grabbed her arm; there was no way he could chase after her and have any hope of catching her with the shape his leg was in. If she made it all the way to the cabin and closed the door, he might not be able to convince her to let him in.

"*Stop!*" he shouted.

She spun around and glared at him. "Don't you tell me to stop; don't you tell me to do anything, Jace Rice."

"I have somethin' to say to you, and you're gonna listen to me."

"I already told you I don't want to hear it."

"That's only because you think you know what I'm gonna say, and you don't. You don't have any idea."

She folded her arms across her chest.

If he weren't about to tell her how important he thought it was for them to wait until they were both ready, he'd pull her into his arms and kiss the daylights out of her. Instead he took a deep breath.

"You mean a lot to me, Bree, more than you know, or at least, more than you'll allow yourself to believe. When the time is right, I want the chance to see where this thing between us is going. But the timing isn't right. It isn't right for you, but more importantly, it isn't right for me."

He saw her arms relax, even if she didn't drop them completely. Her stiff shoulders softened, as did the glare she'd been giving him.

"I am not proud of what I did to Tucker. In fact, I'm downright ashamed of it. I could blame it on my youth, but that would be taking the easy way out. Instead, I'm gonna take responsibility for what I did, and I'm gonna do whatever it takes to get Tucker to forgive me. In order for me to do that, I have to believe I'm worthy of his forgiveness."

That made her drop her arms.

"There's a lot I need to work on, the same way there's a lot you need to work through. And when we've both done that work, I'd like to come back together and see if this overpowering thing between us could turn into something real. Something lasting."

She looked at him but didn't speak.

"Now tell me, Bree Fox, is that what you were begging me not to say?"

"No, it wasn't," she murmured.

"What was that? I couldn't hear you," he prodded.

"I said it wasn't."

"You were so sure I was going to tell you that I didn't want to make love to you, because I'm in love with your sister. Am I right?"

"Yes, Jace."

"Speak up, woman, I can't hear you."

He was having a hard time keeping a straight face because the look on hers, like she was ready to belt him, was so damn cute. But he knew, if he started to laugh, she just might follow through and slug him. Worse, he might hurt her feelings, and that was something he definitely didn't want to do.

"So, about tonight…"

"Yes?"

"Will you stay?" she whispered.

6

As if she could get him to leave. He hoped that, since he assured her they would not be taking the physical side of their relationship any further, she would relax.

"How would you feel about taking a drive with me?"

"That sounds nice."

He liked that she didn't ask where. He wanted to get her away from the ranch for a little while. Not that he minded the place, or Red, or anyone else who worked there; he just wanted to be alone with her.

They walked to the truck, and he opened the passenger door. Before he could help her up, Bree put her hand on his shoulder and climbed in. Part of him wanted to tell her she had to keep her hands off of him if he was going to honor his commitment to remain just friends with her.

The view of the Sawtooth Mountains, as they drove south, was breathtaking. Jace hadn't spent much time in Idaho and was awed by its beauty. He'd had no idea.

He asked Bree if she'd ever been to Sun Valley, and she shook her head, lost in thought.

Two of his friends from Aspen had opened an Asian-fusion restaurant right off the highway in the main stretch of town. From what he'd heard, it was a popular place and they were doing well. The drive would take them over an hour each way, but they weren't on any kind of schedule.

Even after he'd asked her about Sun Valley, Bree didn't ask where he was taking her. Maybe it didn't matter to her. It didn't to him. He still had to pinch himself, every now and then, just to be sure he wasn't dreaming. He was just happy to be with her—that was the simple truth of it.

Her phone pinged and she jumped. She pulled it out of her pocket and looked at the screen.

"I'm not used to having a signal." She seemed distracted by it, but whatever it was brought the sweetest smile to her face.

"Can I see?" Jace smiled over at her.

"Of course," her smile had gone dreamy as she held the phone up for him to see. The photo on the screen was of their nephew, Cochran. Big green eyes smiled back at him, the same way Bree had.

"He looks like you," she said.

"That's what my dad says. Although I'll remind you, as I reminded him, Tuck and I are twins. So in fact, I think Cochran looks like his daddy."

"No, I disagree. He looks more like you than Tucker."

It felt as though someone was squeezing his heart—the ache, reminding him again that he'd never met his nephew.

"He's amazing, Jace," she said, still staring at the photo on the screen. "He's happy, funny, sweet, and cuddly. Gosh, I didn't realize how much I miss him." Tears filled her eyes, but her smile remained.

"I want to meet him."

"Make it happen."

"It isn't all within my power, Bree."

"Of course it is. You'll figure it out, Jace. I know you will. In fact, I'm counting on it."

"You're counting on it?"

"You told me, once, we'd always be in one another's lives because of this baby. Every minute I've been with him, since the day he was born, I've imagined what it would be like to have you there with us."

Jace didn't know what to say. The vise grip on his heart tightened, if that was possible.

"I talk to him about you all the time. He knows about his Uncle Jace. And someday soon, when he starts to talk in a language we can understand, I know he'll ask about you."

She did it again. Tightened that grip. He couldn't take much more.

"Do you, really?" It was as though he was afraid to say it out loud, so he whispered the question.

"Yes, Jace. I really do. I talk to him about you all the time."

He brushed the tear that leaked out of his eye away with the back of his hand. She was right. Cochran was worth it. He had to figure out how to get through to his brother, no matter what it took. He couldn't stand the gulf that separated them any longer.

His friends' restaurant was everything he'd heard and more. They were both there, and even though it was busy, they found time to sit and talk with Jace and Bree. It was after eleven when he finally noticed the time. The drive would put them back at the ranch close to one in the morning.

When his friends invited Jace and Bree to stay with them, he wasn't sure how Bree would react. They had definitely made the assumption that he and Bree were a couple.

He thought about excusing himself to see if she would follow, so they could discuss it privately, when he heard her accept their invitation. She put her hand over his and said, "We'd love to. Thank you for inviting us."

"You're sure?" he asked her.

"Yes, I'm sure. It's too late for us to drive back tonight."

The four of them stayed up, talking about the fun they'd had growing up in a place like Aspen. Bree loved hearing about Jace and Tucker's antics as boys.

"Did you ever find out who the other guy was?" they asked.

Bree felt every muscle in Jace's body go rock hard. He murmured something unintelligible and said he thought it was time for them to get some sleep. His abruptness did not go unnoticed.

"Are you okay?" Bree asked once they were alone in the guest room.

"It's something I know I have to own up to, but… I'm not sure I'll ever be man enough to do it." He was sitting on the bed, his head in his hands. She sat down next to him and ran her hand over his back.

"You and Tucker need to heal first, Jace. You don't owe an explanation to anyone else. It isn't anyone else's business."

"Isn't confessing part of this, Bree? Isn't that part of making amends, admitting what I did? Admitting what role I played that horrible night?"

"For now, all that matters is you and Tucker."

She stood and pulled the big, fluffy duvet back. "Come to bed," she said to him, as if those were the most natural words to pass between them.

She saw the question in his eyes. They both wore jeans and heavy shirts. They had nothing else with them since they hadn't planned to spend the night. The light on the bedside table remained illuminated, and his eyes remained focused on hers as she unbuttoned her jeans and slid them off.

When she stood and began to unbutton her shirt, she heard him take a deep breath. She expected him to turn, to look away. He didn't. She shrugged her shirt off her shoulders and eased under the covers.

"Jace, come to bed," she said again, reaching her hand out to him.

"Bree—"

"Come to bed."

She kept her eyes focused on his in the same way he had with her. His hand moved to the button on his jeans, and he hesitated, as though he was waiting for her to tell him to stop, but she didn't. Nor did she turn the light, which she could easily reach from her side of the bed, off.

Her hand rested on the bedding but remained outstretched to him. He let his jeans drop to the floor and pulled the covers back on his side of the bed. As he climbed in, Bree slid over and wrapped her arm around his waist, bringing her head to rest on his shoulder.

"I wish…" he whispered.

"Me, too," she answered.

His friends were gone when they woke the next morning, but he found a note in the kitchen, apologizing that they'd had to leave. There was a basket of muffins on the kitchen table and a bag of ground coffee near the coffeemaker.

Bree and Jace moved around each other slowly. They'd fallen asleep easily, given the lateness of the hour, but there remained a tentativeness of things unspoken between them.

Last night had been *different*. She hadn't crept into his bed in the middle of the night, seeking his comfort. This time they'd found comfort in one another. As they waited for the coffee to brew, Jace opened his arms and she filled them. Bree wrapped her arms around his waist and rested her head on his chest.

"Sometimes it's almost too easy," he said.

"I know."

"I have to come to terms with what I did to Tuck, and you have to mourn Zack. And we both have to do it on our own. The sooner we do that, the sooner we can be together."

They made the drive back to the ranch in near silence, but it was a comfortable one.

"When's the auction?" she asked.

"Saturday."

They had three whole days and four nights, and then it would be time for him to leave. Jace no longer felt the need to ask her if he should find a place to stay in town. He knew they would sleep in each other's arms, yet neither of them would let it go beyond that.

They spent the next three days fishing. They talked and tried to dance, but Jace's leg hadn't healed well enough for him to do more than sway with her to the music. They sat on the porch and looked at the stars, and then held each other close as they slept.

The pretense of Jace staying in the other side of the cabin was dropped. He moved his travel bag over to her room, and came and went from her door.

They invited Red to join them at the bull bucking, and he went along enthusiastically. Bree sat, nestled between the two men on the bench seat of Jace's truck.

"Been a long time since I've gone to see anyone buck bulls," commented Red.

"It's become a way of life for me recently," answered Jace. "Although it's been a long time since I tried to cover one myself."

Billy Patterson had convinced him he had more talent as a saddle bronc rider than as a bull rider. Jace had been skeptical at first, but soon believed Billy called it correctly.

He'd spent several months, out on the rodeo circuit, riding broncs, and did well. He almost always ended up in the money, but his heart hadn't been in it.

Settling down on the ranch with his parents had been the best decision he'd made in a long time. He had a knack for recognizing good bucking bulls, the same as his father did. Soon, he hoped they'd be able to add broncs to their list of rough stock.

There was only one bull Jace bid on at the auction, and then made arrangements to pick him up on his way back to Montana in the morning. Red offered to let him bring the bull down to the ranch, but Jace knew the logistics of doing so would be far more complicated than Red imagined.

Bree had a big smile on her face while she watched the bulls and riders. Jace would take that smile away when he left the next day. As hard as it would be to leave, he had to remain steadfast, and he knew it.

They agreed not to make plans as they lay next to each other that night. There weren't any rules about not talking, or texting, or even seeing each other. The only thing they'd agreed on was, come morning, Jace would drive back to Montana, and Bree would stay at the ranch.

Saying goodbye was as hard as they both knew it would be. Jace held on tight, hoping she'd give him just another minute before she pulled away. She did.

"I'm going to miss you, Bree."

"I'm going to miss you too, Jace."

When her eyes filled with tears, he almost lost his resolve. He wanted to tell her to come with him—their troubles be damned. He wanted to assure her they could work through them together, side by side, and come out of it in the same place, the same way they would if they each did it alone, but he'd be lying.

"It is so hard to say goodbye to you," he told her.

She held on tighter. "I don't want to let go."

"Me, either."

Finally Jace knew he had to. He kissed her softly, took her hands from around his waist, and stepped away. The hardest part was turning away from her. He watched her in the rear-view mirror, as he pulled away.

Jace made the trip back to Montana with less than a handful of stops. Once he picked up the bull, he only stopped twice to check on it and rest his leg.

He pulled into the ranch outside Helena a little after nightfall. His house was dark, but his parents' place was all lit-up, like a welcoming beacon.

He got the bull settled into a pen of his own, un-hooked the trailer from his truck, and drove up to see his mom and dad.

His mama was on the porch, waiting for him, when he climbed the steps.

"It is so good to see you," she said, wrapping her arms around him when he got close enough. His daddy stood behind her, smiling.

"Brought back a good bull, did ya?" he asked.

"I sure did."

"And I trust the rest of your trip went well?" his mother snooped.

"We'll talk tomorrow, Mama," he answered. "I'm beat."

"I'll be by in the morning, to make breakfast."

"Nah. I'll come to you tomorrow."

She raised her eyebrows.

"It's all good, Mama. I know you're dyin' to hear, but you're just gonna have to wait until I get some rest."

"You've waited this long, Carol," his daddy added. "A few more hours won't kill you."

"Just might," his mama muttered.

Jace didn't keep his mother waiting long the next morning. He showed up just after sunrise, wishing he'd been up earlier to help his father with the morning chores.

"You're in some trouble," he said to her when he walked into the kitchen.

"By the look on your face last night when I asked about your trip, I know you aren't the slightest bit angry with me, Jace Rice. So don't think you can intimidate me now."

"Can't fool you, can I?"

"How is she?"

"As amazing as she's always been."

"So forthcoming…I have to admit, I'm surprised. I expected you to be more tight-lipped about her."

"No sense. Seems you know more about how I'm feeling than I do. Trying to keep it a secret from you is a waste of time."

She laughed, but quickly grew serious again. "What's next for you, Jace?"

"I have to figure out this thing with me and Tuck. I'm at a loss about how to, but I gotta."

"If she had anything to do with you coming to that conclusion, I'll love her until the day I die."

"Some, I suppose. Mostly she convinced me there were a lot of good reasons I needed to try harder."

"Oh! Before I forget, Billy Patterson called your daddy while you were gone. Said he'd been trying to reach you."

"Wasn't much cell coverage where I was, but I don't remember getting a message from him."

Jace told his mother about his time with Bree, the abridged version of it anyway, and then went in search of his father.

"What did Patterson want?" he asked when he found him.

"Wants to talk to us about partnering with the rough stock."

"In what way?"

"Ben Rice and his brothers want to expand their rough stock business at the Flying R in Crested Butte. Given Billy's experience on the rodeo circuit, and the contacts he has, along with what we're doing here, they think it would be better to partner rather than each of us trying to build it on our own."

If anyone knew about broncs, it was Billy Patterson. It was almost as though Billy had read his mind from a distance. He'd been thinking about expanding their operation into horses while he was in Idaho. He hoped his cousins and Billy were interested in raising bulls too.

"They want us to come to Crested Butte in two weeks," Jace told his father after he ended his call with Billy. "It won't be easy for both of us to go, but if we fly, we can minimize our time away."

"I've been givin' this some thought, son, and I believe it's time for us to hire a full-time ranch manager. Particularly if we can make a deal with Patterson, Ben, Matt, and Will. I can see you needing to be in Colorado on a regular basis, and while I can fill in for you in the short term, I'm gettin' too old to do this kind of work day-in and day-out."

Jace hadn't considered that, even with a full-time staff of hands to help, the ranch work might be too much for his daddy. Now that he was paying attention, he could see the exhaustion on his father's face.

He remembered the conversation he'd had with Tucker a couple of years ago when they went to Crested Butte for Thanksgiving. Tuck said he thought their father was winding down his life. Investing in this ranch was the antithesis.

"I'm sorry, Daddy, I didn't—"

"Stop right there. Partnering with you was my idea, and I knew there'd be hard work involved. I'm still as committed as ever."

"You got anybody in mind? You don't need to talk to me about it. Whatever decision you make, I'll be fine with."

"I've mentioned it to Yance. Seems interested."

"Great. You'll handle it?"

His dad nodded.

Two days later, Bree ventured into the dining hall for breakfast. She hadn't since Jace left, but morning and night, there had been a knock on her door. When she answered, there was a tray of the morning or evening meal, waiting on the table on the cabin porch. She never saw who delivered it but knew it was Red.

"Good morning," he said cheerfully when she walked into the dining room.

"Good morning. Mind if I join you?"

"Nothin' I'd like better."

"Headin' out to do some fishin' today. Wouldn't mind some company."

"I'd like that."

Red eyed her plate and raised his eyebrows.

"I'm okay, Red," she answered without him asking. "You've kept me well-fed the past couple days."

"Let's get out on the water and work up an appetite, then."

He took her to a spot they hadn't been before, and their hours fell back into the rhythm of their earlier days.

Hank hired the ranch manager, and then he and Jace made arrangements to go to Crested Butte.

His mother was going with them, but on their way, she wanted them to take her to Monument. She planned to stay there while Jace and his dad made the rest of the trip.

7

"What would you think about me staying on here a while longer?" Bree asked Red when they returned to the ranch for dinner.

"I figured you were going to."

"Why, Red? Are you some kind of shaman?"

"I wouldn't go that far. But I've been where you are, more than once in my life."

From the first day he had breakfast with her, Bree felt as though she'd been destined to meet Red, that they'd been brought together for a reason.

He hadn't been at the ranch the week she and Zack were here, and she was glad he'd never met her late husband. She wouldn't have felt as comfortable talking about Zack with him if he had.

"I don't think you're ready to go home yet."

"See? How do you know? Seriously, Red, what makes you say I'm not ready?"

"You haven't done what you came here to do."

"What is that? What am I here to do? Because, I have to admit, I can't figure it out. I know what I wanted to do while I was here, but now I've come to the conclusion that it isn't something I can force. It has to happen on its own."

"Then, I'd say you're gettin' closer than you think."

As frustrated as she was with him for talking in riddles, if she was honest, she understood more than she was willing to admit. Wouldn't it have been neat and tidy if she'd simply been able to go to the places she and Zack had been together, cry her heart out, and then move right into the acceptance phase of grief? She knew better.

Early on, Bree had faced the denial phase. Both in denying it happened, and then by denying herself the time and space she needed to grieve.

Coming to the ranch had been about isolation. She'd hoped, by being so, she would be able to push herself through the remaining phases. Maybe that was the problem—she was spending too much time intellectualizing her grief, rather than allowing herself to feel it.

"I have to stop thinking about it so much," she said, not sure if Red was still listening to her.

"I agree."

"Really? First you challenge me, then wait for me to process through it, and then simply agree with everything I say?"

Red looked at her with softened eyes. She waited for him to say something, and about the time she was ready to give up and walk away, he said, "You know what you need to do. Get out of your own way and do it."

"More riddles," she huffed.

"On that note," he rose, "I'm going out of town for a few days. I hope you're still here when I get back, and we have the chance to fish together before you go back to Colorado."

Bree's eyes filled with tears. "Red?"

He stood behind her, put his hand on her shoulder and squeezed. "You're gonna get through this, Bree. Give yourself the time and space to do it. You said it yourself, this isn't something you can force."

He walked away, leaving Bree sitting in the dining room of the main lodge. She'd never felt more alone than she did right then.

Jace and his parents stopped in Casper, Wyoming, for the night, since it was about halfway between Helena and Monument. He called Billy and asked if he could stay at his place in Black Forest. His mom and dad were staying with Tucker and Blythe.

When he pulled into the driveway, his mother argued with him about it.

"You'd make more progress with your brother if you stayed with him rather than here."

"Drop it, Mama. I'm not showing up at their house unannounced."

She kept at him, insisting that they were both being stubborn. Once they saw each other, it would be different, she told him.

He ignored her, climbed out of the truck, grabbed his bag, and walked into Billy's house without looking back. It might mean he'd be stranded there for the night, but he didn't care.

He was feeling the way he'd expected to, like an outsider in a life that had once been his. If he hadn't met Irene at Colorado Black Mountain Ranch that summer, none of this would be happening. His life's chain of events would be entirely different. It wouldn't have changed what happened in the past though, so regardless of how it came about, his role in the accident would've come to light eventually.

Through Irene, Jace had met Billy Patterson, and even though it had been complicated for a while, they'd become close friends.

Two Thanksgivings ago, Jace reconnected his parents with another branch of the Rice family, who they hadn't seen since they were kids. Irene's mother, Liv, had married Ben Rice, and they invited Jace and his family to join them in Crested Butte for the holiday.

That had been when Jace and Tucker met Blythe Cochran, who was now Tucker's wife.

It felt as though that week was a lifetime ago. In reality, it hadn't been two years.

Jace opened the refrigerator, expecting it to be empty. Billy and Irene lived in Crested Butte almost full-time. He should have thought of that before he let his parents leave with the truck. To his surprise, it was stocked with beer.

He sat on the back deck, took in the view of Black Forest, pulled out his cell phone, and called the one person he knew would welcome him with open arms and not an ounce of judgment: Lyric Simmons.

He'd been with Blythe the night they met Lyric, the week before the start of the National Western Stock Show in Denver. Once again, it felt as though that had been a hundred years ago; so much had happened since then.

Blythe and Lyric had become fast friends, and shortly after they met, Lyric hired Blythe to work with her at RodeoChat, a social media-based outlet for the latest rodeo news.

"Jace Rice, how the hell are ya?" was the way Lyric answered his call.

"I've been better, but I've also been worse. How 'bout you, girl?"

"Busy, as always, back and forth between here and Oklahoma. Never a dull moment, right?"

"Right. Hey, uh, I'm in town and wondered if you would like to get together?"

"In town meaning what? Where are you exactly?"

"Billy and Irene's place. In a couple days, I'm headin' down to Crested Butte."

"You see Tuck and Blythe yet?"

"Nah. My parents are stayin' with 'em, though."

"Why aren't you?"

Lyric knew why he wasn't, but it was just like her to poke at him about it.

"Give me a break here, would ya?"

"Yeah, okay. I'll give you a break for now, but we aren't done talkin' about this."

"Right."

"What are you doin' now?" she asked.

"Drinkin' a beer."

"Give me twenty and I'll join you."

"You're a sight," she said as she hugged him hello.

"Better sight than the last time you saw me, I hope."

"I'll say." She stood back and studied his face. "Looks like your nose healed up okay." She tweaked it with her fingers. "How 'bout the rest of you? You healed yet?"

"I'm not sure what you mean by that, but my best guess is the answer is no."

"Heard you spent some time with Bree recently. How'd that go? You get her to loosen up and have some fun?"

"If you know I was with her, I'm surprised you don't know all the details. I would have expected you to get the inside story, Lyric. What happened? You gettin' soft on the investigative side of journalism?"

"Nah, I just wanted to hear what you'd say. I already talked to Bree." She studied him for a minute. "When's the last time you talked to her?"

"Bree?"

"Of course Bree. I know you ain't talkin' to Blythe."

"God, I forgot how you are. I mean, I remember how you are, but I forgot that you don't beat around the bush for even a minute."

"One, I don't know what the hell you're talkin' about. And two, who has time for beatin' around any bushes? Gotta keep movin' forward to shine bright, boy."

"I haven't talked to Bree for a couple of days. Cell coverage is iffy where she is, but you already know that.

You probably also know exactly how long it's been since we talked, so I don't know why you're even askin' me."

"She misses you."

"I miss her too. More than she knows."

"They got anything to eat in this place?"

When Jace told her the only thing he'd found was beer, she told him there was a new place in town she wanted to try. They hadn't been open long, but she heard the food was good.

Jace couldn't believe he'd let Lyric talk him into going to a winery.

"Thought you said you heard the food was good."

"I did. What's your problem? You think a winery can't have good food?"

"More like do they have *any* food?"

"Come on inside, cowboy, and see for yourself. I think you'll be surprised."

Jace was indeed surprised when he walked in, but it had nothing to do with the food.

"Welcome," said the pretty woman with the long red hair. "Is this your first visit to our winery?"

Jace turned and looked at her, tried to smile, but was too stunned to be polite. He walked over to a painting hanging nearby, on one of the walls. He didn't need to look at the tag next to it or the signature; he'd recognize Tucker's work anywhere.

"This is Jace Rice," he heard Lyric say.

Tucker's work filled all the walls of the main room of the winery. He wandered from painting to painting, taking it all in. It was new work, and it was good.

The disparity in the images his brother painted startled him. He recognized the Black Forest area in both the paintings he'd done before and after the fire that had consumed fourteen thousand acres and burned over five hundred homes and other structures to the ground.

"There's more in the other room," the woman said to him. "I take it you haven't seen your brother's new work."

"No, ma'am," he murmured. He hoped she didn't think he was being rude, but he was dumbfounded. He could barely breathe, let alone talk.

"It's good, isn't it?" Lyric followed behind him but let him set the pace.

"It's incredible."

As he rounded the corner into the other room, there was a painting on the far wall that made him stop in his tracks. The image depicted on the canvas was of two men fishing. The view was of their backs, but even so,

Jace could tell the men were relaxed, companionable. Between them, a baby boy played in the sand.

"It's you," Lyric whispered.

Without her saying so, Jace would've known it. Regardless of not being able to see their faces, it was clear to him that the men in the painting were him and his brother.

"And that is most definitely Cochran in the middle."

Jace's eyes filled with tears. *Cochran.* He could have guessed, but he wouldn't have known. He still hadn't seen the boy in person.

"What do you think it means?" Lyric asked.

Jace didn't answer. The question was rhetorical. It meant Tucker missed him. It meant that, in his mind's eye, Tucker could see the three of them—him, his brother, and his son—fishing together.

Jace slowly made his way around the second room, taking in each of the images. Tuck had done a series of horses, and Jace recognized the land in the background. It was Billy's ranch.

"There's one more you should see. It's in the cellar, which is a private room," said the lady.

She took them through a hallway and down a stair-well made of stone.

"This was once the Monument jail," she told him. "Although I don't think the accommodations were as nice then as they are now."

The walls of the room, like the stairwell, were stone. There was an indentation in the southern wall, and bars on what, once, might have been a window.

On the back wall, Jace saw the piece she'd brought him here to see. It was of a rider on the back of a bronc.

"I recognized you from this painting," the woman said. She was right; it was him. There was enough detail for him to know the setting. It was Cheyenne, Wyoming, last July. He'd ridden well there, placed first in fact.

"He was there," Lyric whispered.

"How do you know?"

"I was with him."

He looked into her eyes. "Why are you telling me this now?"

"He made me promise not to tell you then."

"I could've sold this painting ten times or more, but he refuses to let it go," murmured the woman. "I need to get back upstairs, but take your time."

Lyric pulled out one of the ten chairs that surrounded the big farm-style table in the center of the small room.

"Has Bree seen it?"

"No, she hasn't seen any of Tucker's recent paintings. The ones of the fire…"

"Are too much for her?"

"I don't think Bree realized there were ones like this, or the series of horses in the meadow."

"He won't sell it."

"That's what she said."

Jace looked back at Lyric. "Do they even have food?"

"Yes," she laughed. "They have great food. I didn't lie about that part. And I'm starving. Do you mind if I go upstairs and order?"

"Not at all. I'll be up shortly, if that's okay with you."

"Take your time," she smiled.

Jace sat in the chair Lyric had been seated in, and stared at the painting. His brother had been in Cheyenne last summer, but hadn't wanted him to know he was there. He'd painted not only this one, but the one of the three of them fishing. Maybe his mama was right. Maybe they were both being stubborn.

The morning Tucker had realized that Jace was the man he'd seen in the dark that night, with the woman Tucker believed he loved, he'd come after Jace. He'd broken his nose and maybe would've done worse if Jace had fought back. But he didn't. He couldn't. Maybe that was why Tucker had stopped and walked away.

Jace hadn't tried to see him after that. He hadn't explained, or asked forgiveness, or even tried to talk to Tucker about it. He just left. Ever since, he'd been waiting for his brother to contact him. Maybe he was waiting for Jace to make the first move.

Twenty minutes later, he climbed the stairs. Lyric was sitting at a table laden with enough food to feed ten people. And a bottle of red wine.

"I wasn't sure what you'd like, so I ordered everything."

"Everything on the menu?"

"Yeah, it isn't a very big menu."

When they opened their second bottle of wine, Lyric started to talk about her family.

"You know I got a twin too, right?"

Jace knew she had a twin brother. He had a weird name, one Jace knew he should recall, but didn't.

"Yep, how is your brother?"

"Bullet's as much of a hot mess as he's always been. Or more. I been tryin' to get him the hell outta Oklahoma, but haven't had any luck yet."

"Why not?"

Lyric spent the next hour telling Jace her brother's story. When she finished, Jace was thankful his life wasn't as much of a mess as this kid's was, although in some ways it was close.

At twenty-five years old, Lyric's brother had two kids, with two different women. The first, he never married, but supported anyway. The second, he married, but Lyric never knew, from day to day, whether they still were. From what she said, they hadn't been married much over a year, and had spent as many nights apart as they had together.

"What's he wanna do?" Jace asked.

"Ride bulls."

"Yeah?"

"You gonna partner up with Billy? You've got bulls up in Montana, right? Is he gonna raise broncs in Crested Butte, or both?"

"Not sure yet, but how the hell do you know so much about it already? Billy and I have barely talked about it ourselves."

"I got my sources well placed."

"You know enough to have an opinion. What is it?"

"It's ambitious, but it's been done."

"Fair enough. Back to your brother. Does he know how to work with rough stock?"

"I'm sure he could handle it."

"What's he doin' now?"

"Drivin' a truck."

"And you're thinkin' he should move to Colorado, maybe to Crested Butte, and work with me, Billy, and Ben."

"Damn, Jace, you catch on quick."

"Gotta get him over here if you want us to hire him."

"I'm workin' on it. Easier said than done."

They talked for most of the afternoon, out on the winery's patio, with a view of Front Range mountains.

"Can you drive?" he asked.

"Yeah, I stopped drinking a couple hours ago."

Jace looked at the bottle and realized it was still half full. He'd slowed down quite a bit himself.

"Since there isn't much food at Billy's, you wanna come back to the house in the glen with me? I could make us some dinner."

"I'd like that. If you don't mind." He'd missed Palmer Lake and the glen, where Lyric lived, in a house she shared with Bree.

He held his breath when he walked in the front door of the craftsman-style bungalow, and then breathed in deeply. *Bree.* He could smell her perfume, so faint that maybe he only imagined it. God, he missed her.

He looked over at the sofa and thought about the night they'd fallen asleep there, back when they couldn't stand each other. It was the same night he'd picked her up and carried her into her bedroom. And the same night she'd reached out to him and begged him not to leave.

He and Lyric talked late into the night. Jace had forgotten how much he liked her. He regretted that it had been so long since he saw her.

"You wanna stay? You could sleep in Bree's bed. Not like it'll be the first time or nothin'," she poked him.

"Sounds good to me. If you don't mind."

"I don't offer things if I don't want to."

He laughed. He did know that about her.

If he was lucky, Bree's sheets would still smell like her, the way the rest of the house did. It would make his dreams that much better.

He woke with a start right around sunrise. *Tucker.* It had been a long time since he'd felt his twin, but he recognized it for what it was. His brother was anxious, conflicted, and confused. Much as he was.

Today was the day. Jace could feel it. One way or another, he was going to see Tucker, and maybe even meet his nephew.

When he looked at his phone, there were two missed calls, one from his dad and one from Bree. Neither had left a message.

It was early, and he might wake her, but he didn't care. He loved hearing the sleepiness in Bree's voice. If he closed his eyes, he could remember how it felt to wake up next to her and hear that voice in person.

"Good morning," she answered, sounding as sleepy as he thought she would.

"Hey, there, sweet girl. I'm sorry I didn't see you called last night."

"It's okay. Were you out with Lyric?"

How did women know these things?

"I was." He rolled over in her bed and hugged her pillow close to him. "You know where I am right now?"

"You're in my bed, aren't you?"

"Yes, ma'am, and damn—I sure wish you were here with me."

"Me, too," she murmured.

"How are you, Bree?"

"I'm okay. Red left for a few days, so I'm spending time on my own. It's what I wanted. They say to be careful what you wish for."

Red left? Jesus. If he'd known Red was leaving, he could've made arrangements to go back to Idaho before he drove down to Monument.

"Jace? You still there?"

"I'm here. Wishing I was there. I hate that you're alone."

"It's the way it's supposed to be, remember? It isn't a bad thing, Jace. It's a necessary thing. I think he left on purpose."

"Why would he do that?" Maybe Red wasn't as good of a guy as Jace initially thought he was.

"He knows this is what I need. I'm making progress. And I feel really good about it."

"Yeah? That I'm glad to hear."

"How about you? Are you doing what you need to do?"

"Not yet. But when I woke up a little while ago, I could feel him."

"Tucker?"

"Yeah. I know that sounds weird, but I haven't for so long."

"It doesn't sound weird."

"I decided today is the day. I'm goin' over there, Bree. He doesn't have to see me if he doesn't want to, but I can't let any more time go by without meeting Cochran."

"I'm glad, Jace. Really glad. And when you see that sweet baby, would you give him a hug and kiss from his Auntie Bree?"

"You know I will." He took a deep breath. "I gotta ask you somethin'."

"Sure."

"You still feelin' it?" he said it so softly he wasn't sure she could hear him.

What could she say? The last several days had been really hard. She started out feeling sorry for herself and mad at Red for leaving her alone. Once she kicked herself out of that funk, she started to see things more clearly. It was a relief to be alone. And instead of spending all her time crying, she went and did things she and Zack had loved to do together.

She fished, but that wasn't all. She sat on the bank of a stream and read a book that had been one of his favorites. The next day, she drove up to Salmon to see Annie and Dave again. She shed some tears when they asked her if she wanted to sit and tie flies, but soon they were reminiscing about Zack, and laughing.

Her husband had been a good man, who people liked easily. Not long after they'd met, Annie and Dave had invited her and Zack over to their house for dinner. Bree doubted they did that sort of thing with all of their customers.

When they invited her to join them for dinner this time, part of her wanted to turn them down, but she didn't, and she was glad of it.

She ended up staying over, and the next morning, she and Annie went riding—another thing she and Zack loved to do together.

The more days she spent alone, the better she felt. She still believed there was a reason she was supposed to meet Red—maybe she hadn't been as ready to be alone as she thought when she first arrived at the ranch. Or maybe Red was a conduit back to the places she and Zack had been, or to the things they'd done together. Would she have been as brave, facing it alone, as she was, doing it with Red by her side?

What about Jace? That was the question he asked. Was she still feeling the same way about him? Even though she'd spent most of her time thinking about Zack, Jace was always there in the back of her mind. She dreamed about him as often as she dreamed of Zack, and when she closed her eyes and imagined someone's arms around her, it was almost always Jace's.

"I do," she answered, after too much time had passed.

Jace had stopped breathing, waiting for her to answer.

"What about you?" she asked.

"Do you really need to ask?" he laughed.

"Yes, Jace. I do," she didn't laugh.

"It's different for me, Bree. I'm not mourning someone. I guess, I am in a way, but it's different. I'm estranged from my brother, and I need to fix it. Part of doing so is me coming to terms with who I am. But all of this, I could do with you by my side."

"You could?"

"You make me want to be a better man, Bree. I can't explain it, but you do. All my life I've worried more about being liked than being a good man. As long as everyone saw the fun, happy side of me, they'd never know the guilt and shame I carried around with me."

Jace closed his eyes and imagined she was next to him. "You have this way of looking at me, and when you do, I feel as though you can see all the way through me. I can't hide the guilt or shame from you. More, I don't want to."

"I don't know what to say, Jace. I'm flattered that you feel that way; I love that you feel that way. But—"

"No, don't say it."

That made her laugh. "That's usually what I say to you. But I can assure you, you don't know what I'm going to say any more than I do with you. You've proven that to me over and over again."

"You're gonna say I need to do this for myself, not for you."

"Well, damn, Jace Rice, I guess you did know what I was going to say."

"I am, Bree. I'm doing this for me, not for you. You just make me *want* to do it. You understand the difference in what I'm saying, right?"

"I do."

He told her about Tucker's paintings, the ones he'd seen yesterday.

"I wish I'd seen them, Jace. I can't believe how hard I tried not to. I could've…"

"It was better that you didn't. I gotta admit, Lyric threw me for a loop, but it was better the way it happened. I was blindsided, but I think I needed to be."

"What are you going to do?"

"I haven't figured it out yet. What do you think I should do?"

"Ride over."

Two hours after Lyric dropped him off at Billy's, Jace had one of the boarded horses saddled up and was headed across the field to see his brother, Tucker.

8

As Jace rode up, he could see his mom and dad out on the front porch. Tucker, Blythe, and the baby were with them. His father walked toward the railing and shaded his eyes with his hand. Moments later, his mom and dad went inside. Blythe followed them, carrying Cochran in her arms.

Jace held his breath. Would Tucker go in too? Would he shut him out? He felt sick to his stomach waiting to see what his brother would do.

Instead of going inside, Tucker walked down the steps of the porch. Jace reined in the horse and dismounted. He and his brother were still separated by no more than a hundred feet.

"Tucker."

"Jace."

He walked toward Tuck, holding the horse's reins in his left hand. He had no idea what to say. This might have been easier if he'd taken a shot of whiskey before he left Billy's place.

"I saw your paintings yesterday," he said when they were within a couple of feet of one another.

"I know," answered his brother.

"I don't know what to say, Tuck." Jace looked at his brother as tears filled his eyes.

"It's usually me that comes crawling back with my tail between my legs. You've always made it easy for me."

"This is different, Tuck. You never did anything—"

"Of course I did. Every time I left and expected you to clean up my mess, I did something."

Jace saw the same pain he was feeling in Tucker's eyes.

"I can't tell you I understand, Jace. I don't. I'm damn mad at you, and for a while I thought I hated you. But, I don't. I couldn't."

"I would. I'd hate you if you'd done what I did."

Tucker put his arms around Jace, hugging him. "No, you wouldn't. And you wouldn't have let so much time go by either." He released him, but kept one hand on Jace's shoulder. "But then you've always been a better brother to me than I've been to you."

"How can you say that? Tuck, I fucked up pretty bad."

"You did that." Tucker's gaze was penetrating. "But so did I. More than once."

"I was just thinkin' this would've been a hell of a lot easier if I had a drink before I rode over."

"Then it's time we had one. Come on inside. There's somebody I want you to meet."

Bree was out on the water when the text from Jace came through. It startled her since she so rarely had a signal when she was fishing.

In the photo he sent, Jace was holding baby Cochran on his lap and they were both waving at her. Her eyes filled with tears, of happiness for them, but sadness for her. She missed them both so much.

What she couldn't explain was the feeling that came after. If she could put a name to it, it would be dread.

Tucker took Cochran to put him down for a nap, and Jace went back out on the porch by himself. When the door opened, he'd expected to see his brother, instead he saw Tucker's wife.

He stood to hug her. "How are you, Blythe?"

"Better, now that you're here."

"Me, too."

"How are you two doing?"

"Okay. Tentative. Haven't talked too much yet. But it's coming."

"You met your nephew. He's beautiful, isn't he?"

"He is. Couple people told me he looks like me," he laughed.

"Well, you and Tucker are twins."

He laughed again. "That's always my answer."

The door opened again. This time his mom joined them. He opened his arms to her too.

"I'm proud of you, son."

"Thanks, Mama."

"Your daddy is proud of you too. Both of you. It takes a big man to own up to his mistakes. Too many people choose to walk away instead. That would have been as much of a tragedy as the one that started all of this."

Jace wondered when the time would come that he and Tucker would be forced to sit down and talk about it. It had to be soon—he and his daddy were supposed to leave for Crested Butte in the morning. Maybe he should call Billy and tell him they might be delayed for a couple of days.

Blythe was chewing her fingernails, and his mother noticed.

"I'll go back inside now." She squeezed Blythe's shoulder. "Let you two catch up."

"Thanks," Blythe looked up at her and murmured.

"How's my sister?" she asked when Carol closed the door behind her.

"She's good...I think."

"I know you talk to her, Jace. She told me about the time you spent together. You can talk to me about her."

"Yeah, I know. It isn't a secret." He laughed. "*It.* I don't even know what it is."

"You've helped her."

"Have I? I don't have any idea. I was there for her, for a few days anyway, but we didn't talk much about Zack. We talked around him. More about the things they did together than things about him." He took off his hat and ran his hand through his hair. "She tells me she needs to do this on her own. That's another thing I don't know; what *this* is."

"She grew up with Zack. When they met, she was a girl. With him, she became a woman. She expected to grow old with him."

He knew Blythe was right. And he knew Bree was grieving. But how would she feel months from now? Would she still need him? Would she want him in her life?

Even without it being said, Jace knew he was nothing like Zack. Maybe when she came out of her fog of grief she'd want to be with someone more like Zack.

"She needs time," he said. "And space."

"You're right about that."

"I feel as though you're trying to tell me something, in a roundabout way."

"I think you should consider taking a step backwards."

She couldn't have hurt him worse if she'd stabbed him with a knife. "Can I ask why?"

"I don't want to see you get hurt."

"And there's a reason you think I'm gonna?"

"I've seen you do this more than once."

Jace wished Blythe would stop talking. He agreed with her; that was the problem. Jace was the fall-back guy. It had happened with Irene when she was trying to sort through her feelings for Billy, after she found out he'd had a baby with another woman.

Then again with Blythe. For a while he believed he was in love with her. Until Tucker came back. And then Jace was left by the wayside. Again.

Bree was brilliant. She was beautiful, and funny, and could do whatever she wanted with her life. She'd told him about some of the things she and Zack talked about. They'd planned to travel when he was able to take leave again. Most of what she told him didn't sound that appealing. He didn't admit it to her, but it made him question whether they considered the same kinds of things "fun."

When she finished processing through her grief, and was ready to move forward with her life, would she realize how different he was from her late husband and, consequently, leave him in the dust, like Irene and Blythe had?

His world was pretty damn small compared to hers, and he wasn't going to be in the position to change it. If anything, it would get smaller. The larger their operation got, the less he'd be able to be away from it. He'd travel to rodeos and stock shows, but that would be all he'd have time for.

If his daddy had asked his mama to settle down on a ranch when they were younger, he doubted if she would've agreed. The life of a rancher and a rough stock contractor wasn't an easy one. Animals required care twenty-four hours a day, seven days a week—like kids did. He'd be tied to the land in Montana for years, maybe forever. He couldn't envision her being happy with that kind of life.

"I'm what you'd call a 'transition guy.' Is that what you're tryin' to tell me, Blythe?"

"Maybe. Maybe not. Bree is so much like my mom, and I've never been able to predict what my mom will do. I often wonder if she thought she was settling when she married my dad."

"Settling?" That was harsher than he expected.

"Yeah. Then again, I might be full of shit, Jace."

He was afraid she wasn't.

"How did you manage to find me? Did you put a tracking device on my rental car?" Bree asked Red when she saw him walk out of the woods.

"I'm psychic," he deadpanned.

"Right. So, you're back."

"I am. And you're still here."

"It sounds as though you were hoping I wouldn't be."

"Not at all. Before I left, I told you that I hoped you'd still be here when I got back." He sat down on a rock and studied her.

"What's on your mind?"

"Tryin' to get a read on you, that's all."

"What kind of read?"

"How you're doin'."

She was better, or at least, she felt better today. She had no idea what tomorrow might bring.

"How long has your wife been gone?"

"Goin' on two years. But it wasn't sudden with her. I had time to prepare myself, say goodbye, that sort of thing."

"Do you think it makes it easier?"

"I don't know. Both my wife and daughter were very sick. Other than my brother, I haven't lost anybody suddenly, the way you did. When he was killed, I was still a youngin."

"Not saying goodbye—that's the hardest thing for me. I still don't feel as though I have."

"It'll come. You'll know when you're ready."

Red looked off in the distance. Bree sensed there was more he wanted to say.

"What is it, Red?" she finally asked. "I've spent enough time with you to know when you're leaving something unsaid."

"The young man, Jace. What's the story there?"

That was complicated. How did she describe her relationship with Jace? At first it had been love/hate, more hate than love. Then it changed. There was electricity between them. She'd never been so attracted to a man, not even Zack.

When she met Zack, she was fifteen. They waited three years before they made love. When she looked back, it was hard to believe they had. It had been easy between them, natural. She hadn't felt the same sexual charge with Zack that she felt with Jace.

She worried sometimes it was all they shared. They had so little in common, and what they did have, was based more on their families than themselves. If she'd met Jace at a coffee shop, or a bar, or somewhere else, if they'd come together initially as strangers, would anything have come of it?

"I don't know. When we met, there was so much going on with our two families. We were sort of thrown together."

"And now?"

"I can't answer that. I like thinking about him. Part of my reason for wanting to come here was to figure out if Jace Rice was just my way of staying in denial about Zack."

"Uh huh."

"That's all you've got? Come on, Red, just say it, for Christ's sake. Whatever it is, come out with it."

"It isn't any of this old guy's business. Like everything else, you gotta figure it out for yourself."

"You're starting to sound like a broken record."

"How 'bout another trip up to Salmon? I was thinkin' of headin' there tomorrow."

"Hardly a segue, but I'd like that. I spent some time with Annie and Dave while you were gone. It was… good. I mean, it was really hard, but then it got easier."

"Life's like that." Red stood and walked toward the woods. He waved behind him. "See ya tomorrow."

Her conversation with Red was unsettling. It was as though he saw something she didn't. And whatever it was, should be obvious to her.

She had a lot to think about with Jace. The man was…hot. Not the kind of man who usually gave her a second look. Blythe maybe, but not her. And he wasn't her type either.

Maybe things would work out on their own. Maybe she was over-thinking it. Soon she'd go back to Monument and start teaching at the Air Force Academy. The professor she was filling in for was due to have her baby near the end of August. The timing was perfect. Bree would simply fill in for an academic year, and then, the following year, the professor would return. Originally she'd applied for a two-year position, but this worked out better.

She hadn't begun to think about what she might do when her stint was over, but maybe she should.

Jace, on the other hand, knew exactly what he'd be doing. Rough stock. She knew nothing of that life. She loved to ride horses, but that was the extent of it.

She used to go out to Billy Patterson's ranch and watch Jace and Billy practice riding broncs. It was fun to watch, but after a while, she got bored. Rough stock was Jace's entire life; he was raising bulls full-time. Could she feign enough interest in conversations about bull semen to make him think she cared? She doubted it.

"Change of plans, son," Jace's dad said when he came out the front door to where he and Blythe were still chatting.

"What's that?" Jace asked.

"Tucker hasn't had a chance to talk to you about this, Blythe, but what would you think about all of us going to Crested Butte?"

"I'd love it. I haven't seen Renie in weeks."

Blythe and Irene, who everyone but him called Renie, had been best friends since kindergarten. It was hard to remember sometimes; the two were so different.

"What about Lyric?" she asked Jace. "You saw her yesterday. Do you think we could talk her into going too?"

"Maybe. She was talking about getting her brother to come to Crested Butte. This might be a good opportunity."

Blythe called her, and Lyric agreed it was a great idea. Instead of driving with them, she said she'd meet them there. She figured, the only way to get her brother to go would be if she went to Oklahoma and dragged him with her.

"You think this is smart? Putting me and Tuck in a truck, by ourselves, for five hours?" Jace asked his dad the next morning when they were getting ready to leave.

"You can kill each other as easily inside a truck or out," he answered.

"Thanks. That doesn't make me feel better at all."

"Wasn't meant to."

Blythe and the baby were riding in the SUV with Hank and Carol. Blythe made Jace promise that he'd drive the speed limit, because she knew, with the baby in the car, Grandpa Hank wouldn't go a mile over it.

"I don't want to get too far separated from you two," she told him.

Tucker walked up to the truck and put his hand out. "What?" Jace asked.

"Give me the keys."

"Uh, nope. I'm drivin'."

"I hate the way you drive. It'll take us an extra hour to get there with you behind the wheel."

"Which is precisely why he's driving," Blythe told her husband before she kissed him goodbye. "There'll be hell to pay if you get out too far ahead of us," she said to Jace. "Don't you forget it, either."

Tucker grumbled as he walked around to the passenger side of the truck, but Jace didn't miss the smile and wink he gave his wife.

What he'd give to have that with someone. Every time he thought he was getting close, it didn't work out. Was that his penance for the accident? Maybe if he and Tucker could talk about it, if he could say how sorry he was, maybe his life would begin moving in a positive direction, one with love in it.

They were an hour into the drive before either of them spoke. Jace knew they had to talk, but he wanted Tucker to be the one to start the conversation. After a while he decided Tuck was waiting on him.

"How much of that night do you remember?" Jace finally asked.

"Bits and pieces. I remember more about that day. I remember how angry I was with her parents when they told me they wouldn't let her marry me. I had to get out of that house and away from them. When I think back on it, I was just as mad at her. I didn't want to admit it at the time, but it was obvious Rosa didn't want to marry me any more than her parents wanted her to."

Now that they were talking about it, Jace wished they weren't. This was going to be more difficult than he'd imagined, and he imagined it being impossible.

"She played us against each other," Tucker said in the direction of the passenger window.

Jace turned to look at him, but he couldn't see his brother's face.

"I came to the same conclusion," Jace agreed. "When you drove up that night, she was begging me not to end it with her. I figured she was telling you the same thing when she ran toward the truck and begged you not to leave."

"You were wrong about that," Tucker said softly.

They drove in silence a few more miles. "When did it start?" Tuck asked him.

"We were always friends, I mean, all three of us were, since we were little kids. But it changed when we got into high school. She used to talk to me. At first it was about you, and then it wasn't. She knew how competitive we were."

"I thought I wanted to marry her."

"I gotta tell you, up until Thanksgiving Day when I heard you talking to Dad about it, I didn't think you two were that serious. It hit me like a ton of bricks when I heard you tell him what you were planning. I called her while you were still talking to him, and I was furious. The whole day, I couldn't think about anything else."

"How did you end up over there?"

"She called me and begged me to meet her. I agreed, but only to end it with her."

"How did she get you to change your mind?"

"Can't say that she did. You came back while we were still talking about it."

"She told me she was in love with someone else."

"I know, Tuck."

"She was trying to get me to look at her, and I wouldn't. I couldn't stand the sight of her."

"I felt the same way. I never wanted to see her again. I was mad, but I hurt more. I thought I mattered to her."

"You did."

"At the time I didn't think so."

"Her parents came to see me when I was in the hospital."

Jace hadn't heard this before. "And?"

"Her mother told me that Rosa never loved me and that she'd only stayed with me because she was afraid of me. She also told me that Rosa had been in love with someone else for months, but she knew, if she told me who it was, I'd kill him."

"*Jesus.*"

"There was more."

More? Jace wondered what more there could possibly be.

"She cursed me. She said I'd never find love, because I didn't deserve it. I spent a lot of years believing she was right."

That part, Jace understood, because it was the way he was beginning to feel.

"I don't know if I'll ever get over the guilt of what happened that night. She died because of me. There's no denying that part of it."

"It was an accident, Tucker. I'm just as responsible for it happening as you are."

"You weren't driving."

"I might as well have been. I was the reason you were in such a rage, although you didn't know it at the time."

Tucker was quiet again, for a long while. "I understand why you didn't tell me," he finally said.

"I don't. It's unforgivable that I didn't."

"I don't agree, Jace. In fact, if the situations were reversed, I doubt I ever would've told you."

"That doesn't make sense."

"Rosa is dead. We can't go back and undo it. I'll always feel guilty about the accident. I'll always feel responsible for her death, but what happened was just as much her fault as it was yours or mine. More so."

"I can't accept that, Tuck. It was my fault. That's the part I can't get over. A better man never would've gotten involved with his brother's girlfriend. It wasn't casual, I spent more time with Rosa than you did."

"Why didn't I see it, Jace? She was unhappy with me. If she hadn't been, she wouldn't have had time to spend with you. I wonder where the hell my head was the whole time."

Jace had wondered then. Which was why he'd been so surprised when he heard Tucker tell their dad he wanted to marry her. He honestly hadn't believed they were very serious.

"I don't think I spent much time listening to her. She had you for that. I just did what I wanted, what I thought was best for her; I didn't bother to ask her what she thought was best." Tucker rubbed his hands over his face. "I can tell you, Blythe doesn't put up with that shit for a hot minute."

Jace laughed. He knew Blythe well enough to know she wouldn't. She wasn't unlike her sister in that regard. Whenever Jace assumed he knew what was best for either one of them, Bree was the first to tell him he didn't know *jack*.

"I forgive you, Jace."

Jace gripped the steering wheel as tight as he could, and struggled to stop his tears. He'd longed to hear those words, but now that he had, he realized his brother's forgiveness was only part of it. He needed to forgive himself, and he wasn't sure he ever could.

There was no sign of Lyric when Bree walked into the house in the glen. It wasn't surprising. Lyric was almost always off working one part of her business or another. Bree had never met anyone who worked as hard as Lyric did.

The house was stuffy, which told her Lyric probably hadn't been there in days. She walked through the rooms, opening windows.

She unpacked, checked her email, and went to the market to stock up on groceries.

When she came back, she'd run out of excuses. She'd put it off long enough. She had to do it. She had to tell Jace she decided they shouldn't see each other again.

9

It wasn't that simple. She knew she'd have to *see* him. As he said last year, they'd always be a part of each other's lives. Her sister, his brother, their baby. There wasn't any way around it.

At least for the time being, it would be easy. She'd be here for another year, and then she'd leave Colorado. It was a decision she made before she left Idaho, before she said goodbye to Red and promised to come back as soon as she could. That was step one, at least for now. After her year at the academy was up, she planned to return to Idaho and make a life for herself there.

She and Jace might see each other occasionally. Maybe holidays, if he could get away from the ranch in Montana. Otherwise, she'd make herself scarce if she knew he was in town.

They'd both done what they needed to do. She mourned Zack. It wasn't as though grieving ended, she understood that. But she'd made progress. She was no longer in denial; that was the main hurdle she'd overcome.

And Jace? He'd reconciled with his brother, and they were in Crested Butte together, arranging to make a deal to partner with their cousins in rough stock contracting on the Flying R Ranch.

Blythe told her about the plan. She and Jace hadn't talked yet. They'd left messages for each other, but hadn't connected.

The contracting deal had been an easy one to make. Billy had laid the groundwork before they arrived. The initial idea behind the partnership changed, though. Rather than Ben Rice and his brothers going into business with Billy, Jace and his parents, Tucker was added as a partner in the new venture too.

There were barns and a practice pen already in place at the ranch. They'd need to add fencing strong enough to manage the bulls, front and back chutes, and a few other things, but it wouldn't take them long to get the Crested Butte operation running at full capacity.

"Lotta babies around here," Jace said to Billy during dinner at Ben and Liv's.

"Another one comin'."

"Oh, yeah? You and Irene been breedin'?"

"That's a damn crass way to put it, Rice, but yeah, we're havin' a baby 'bout eight months from now. And you know, everybody but you calls her Renie. Hearin' you call her Irene…"

Jace understood without the words needing to be said. Whenever he called her something other than Renie, it was a reminder of when Jace had believed he was in love with her. It probably reminded Billy of the same thing. "Congratulations," he said. "This is big news, 'specially for somebody as old as you are."

Billy scowled at him, then shook his head, and his scowl turned into a grin. "Gotta give Willow a little brother or sister before she gets too big to wanna play with 'em."

Willow was Billy's daughter with another woman who had passed away. Jace heard that *Renie* adopted the little girl soon after she and Billy were married.

Jace looked over to where Renie played with Willow. Ben and Liv's baby girl, Caden, and Cochran were playing too. Willow was a little older than the other two, but they were close enough in age that they would grow up as playmates and friends.

Jace wondered if he'd ever have kids of his own. He hoped so. Maybe even one day soon. He wasn't getting any younger himself—in just a few months, he and Tucker would turn thirty.

He walked out to the front porch and hit redial on his phone. He and Bree had been playing phone tag, and he needed to talk to her.

"Hey, pretty girl," he said when she answered.

"Jace, how are you?"

"Better now that I hear your voice. It's been too long since I have."

"Where are you?"

"At Ben and Liv's. They hosted dinner for the crew. Did Blythe pass on the news 'bout the deal we got goin' down here?"

"She did, and congratulations. Not just about that. I'm so happy you and Tucker have worked things out."

"Yeah," he sighed. "I can't believe I haven't talked to you about it. I sure have wanted to."

When she didn't answer, Jace wondered if their call had dropped.

"Bree? You still there?"

"I'm here, but I'm awfully tired, Jace. Can we talk more tomorrow?"

"Uh, of course we can. You okay, Bree?"

More silence.

"Come on, talk to me. What's goin' on?"

"I've given this a lot of thought..."

Jace felt sick to his stomach. Was she really about to say what he thought she was?

"*Jesus,*" he muttered.

"Jace, please, hear me out."

"What's happened, Bree? I thought we were both workin' out our shit so we could see what might happen between us. You tellin' me I was wrong about that?"

"Here we go, Jace. Do you realize what you're doing?"

"What am I doing, Bree?" Sarcasm dripped from each word he spoke.

"Forget it. Why do I need to say anything at all? As usual, you've got it all figured out. Have a great life, Jace. Maybe we'll bump into each other over the holidays."

This time Jace recognized the silence for what it was. Bree had disconnected the call.

That hadn't gone the way she'd wanted it to at all. She'd wanted to explain that she'd given it a lot of thought and realized how little they had in common. If she'd had the chance to explain, maybe he would've understood. Then again, maybe not.

The first time someone shows you who they are, believe them. It was a quote from Maya Angelou, and this wasn't the only time she was reminded of it. When she met Jace, he was overbearing, unwilling to listen to the opinions of those around him, and generally, a pain in the ass. Just the way he'd been a few minutes ago.

"I gotta get out of here," Jace said to Tucker.

"Hold up a minute." Tucker had Cochran in his arms, and the baby was almost asleep. He handed him to Blythe.

"What's goin' on?" Tucker asked.

"I've been spending some time with Bree. You know, Blythe's sister."

Tucker nodded his head.

"I think she just dumped me."

"Ya think?"

"Nah. I don't think. I know. *Shit.*"

Tucker's head was down. "You wanna run."

"Yeah, I do. Not far though. I just gotta get away from all these babies and all this damn...*happiness.*"

Tucker laughed. "Come on, bro. Let's ride instead."

Jace followed Tucker to the barn. "You think we should ask somebody before we take one of their horses?"

"We're takin' two. And no, we're good."

They didn't talk for most of the ride. When they did, Jace spoke first.

"I brought Irene out here on a day that she was fixin' to run herself." He laughed. "I got dumped that day too."

Tucker didn't respond.

"Come on, Tuck. Say whatever you're thinkin'."

"I got nothin'."

"Really? Nothing? Nothing at all? Or nothing you wanna say?"

"I'm about the last person on earth who should be giving anyone advice about women. It is by the grace of God that Blythe loves me."

"But…"

"Nope. I mean it. I got nothin'. Just about anybody else in that ranch house could give you better advice than me."

Ben walked into the barn just as he and Tucker finished getting the horses settled back in.

"Hey, Ben," said Jace. "Hope you don't mind that we went for a ride."

Ben smiled. "Better than one of ya leavin' town without thankin' my Livvie for dinner."

Tucker laughed. "Exactly the reason I got him on a horse instead of lettin' him get in the truck. Didn't want Liv to think both of your cousins were rude assholes."

"I woulda' come back." Jace grinned. "Unlike you."

"Good to see you two givin' each other shit again."

Jace's eyes met Tucker's. Words weren't necessary. Both felt the connection; it was solid for the first time in a very long time.

"How's Blythe doin'?" Tucker asked Ben.

"Tired. I think she's ready to take a nap alongside Cochran."

"You got a minute?" Jace asked Ben after Tucker left the barn.

"Got nothin' but time out here on the ranch."

"Can I ask about you and Liv?"

"I can talk about sweet Liv all day and all night. She's my favorite subject." Ben smiled again.

Jace doubted he'd ever known a guy happier and more in love than Ben Rice. Except Billy and Tucker, and his dad. Jeez, it seemed as though every guy he knew was happy and in love.

He'd heard most of the story of how Liv and Ben met. He'd also heard that Ben had had to work mighty hard to convince Liv they were meant to be together.

"How did you finally win her over?"

Ben sat down on a bale of hay, closed his eyes, and leaned his head back. "It was fate more than it was me if you wanna know the truth. I just about gave up plenty of times."

Ben stood and rubbed the nose of the horse in the stall closest to them.

"If this horse could talk, he'd be able to tell you how hard it was for me to convince her we belonged together. Isn't that right, Micah?"

Liv's horse nickered as though he understood what Ben was saying.

"She was convinced she wasn't enough for me, crazy as it sounds. The truth was, we both had some cookin' left to do when we first met. Wasn't just her; it was me too. You couldn't have told me at the time though."

"Yeah?"

"Oh, yeah. Once I decided she was the girl for me, I wouldn't take no for an answer. Until I was finally forced to."

"How'd you end up back together again?"

"I'm telling you, it was fate. Every time either one of us gave up, fate would throw us back in front of each other. We both decided we might as well start paying attention."

"You know who Bree is, right? Blythe's sister."

"Yeah, I do. Sad that, losing her husband."

"We spent some time together, but now…"

"Talk about someone who's still got cookin' to do."

"What do you mean?"

Ben continued to rub Micah's nose. "You should talk to Liv about this. Nobody understands better than she does."

Jace remembered hearing that Liv lost her husband before Renie was born, also in a war, also in the Air Force. He supposed Ben was right. Liv could shed a light on how Bree felt, unlike anyone else.

"Think she'd mind?"

"You don't know Liv very well if you have to ask. You said you spent some time together. What does that mean?"

"My mama and Blythe conspired to get the two of us together. Bree was at a dude ranch in Idaho. One that I visited, thinkin' they had a bull for sale that my daddy wanted me to go and bid on."

"No bull?"

"No bull."

"Then what happened?"

"We spent a few days together. Talked about our lives. I credit Bree with helping me realize that I had to do whatever it took to fix things with Tuck."

"What about her?"

"We both knew she wasn't ready for another relationship. I mean, we both wanted it, bad. But, we agreed to wait. When I left Idaho, it was with the understanding that we'd go off, work on our shit, and try to find our way back to each other."

"That doesn't sound so bad. You're workin' things out with your brother. She's doin' what she needs to do. What's the problem?"

"When I talked to her a couple hours ago, I think she was tryin' to tell me she wasn't interested any longer."

"Wait a minute. You *think* that's what she was trying to tell you?"

"I didn't give her much of a chance to talk."

Ben leaned his head back and laughed. He laughed so hard that Jace couldn't help but laugh himself.

"What's so funny?"

Ben leaned over and rubbed Jace's shoulder. "You're a Rice, son. Through and through. Liv's gonna love this." Ben continued to laugh.

"I'm glad you think my pain is so hysterical."

"You know that isn't why I'm laughing. I'm laughing because you sound so much like me. And I'll tell you, you're what? Twenty-nine?"

"That's right."

"I was forty-three before I realized I should keep my damn mouth shut once in a while. You're years ahead of me. Be happy about that."

"I have a feeling it's too late for me with Bree."

"Maybe. Then again, if you think about it, you were crazy about Renie. Am I right?"

"I was."

"And you had a thing for Blythe too for a while."

"Yep. You have a point?"

"When it's right, it works. And when it isn't, it doesn't. If I remember correctly, you were pretty broken up about Renie. Didn't take you long to move on."

"Bree's different," Jace scowled.

"You know, I get the sense she is different."

"I don't want to move on from her."

"Then don't."

When Bree came out of her bedroom the next morning, there was a man sleeping on her couch.

"*Who the hell are you?*" she screeched before she had a chance to think about it.

He rolled over and pulled the blanket up, over his bare chest. "I'm Bullet, ma'am. Lyric's brother. I'm sorry if I scared ya, bein' here."

Lyric came flying out of her bedroom.

Bree held up her hand. "I'm sorry, Lyric. I didn't realize you came back last night, and I didn't mean to be rude to your brother."

"Ah hell, don't apologize to me. I was just about to apologize to you. We didn't get in 'til almost four in the morning. I shoulda' woke you up to tell you he was here."

Bree walked over and held out her hand to the bewildered-looking man on her couch.

"I'm Bree," she said.

He reached out from under the blanket and shook her hand. "I guess I already told you my name. It's nice to meet you, ma'am. Lyric's told me a lot about you."

The three of them stayed in the same place, each waiting for the other to move. It dawned on Bree that Bullet might not have much clothing on under that blanket.

"Excuse me," she said and went into the kitchen. "I'll get some coffee started. Bullet, do you drink coffee?"

"Uh, no, ma'am, but thank you anyway."

Figures, she thought. Bree needed at least two cups of coffee before she could function in the morning. She'd never seen Lyric drink it, and no one had more energy than Lyric did. Bullet was probably the same way.

"Why don't you come with us?" Lyric asked her later, when they were getting ready to leave for Crested Butte.

"Thanks, but I just got home. I haven't seen my parents yet."

"But Blythe and Cochran are down there. Bet you're missin' them. Not to mention Jace."

Lyric came close to talking her into going by mentioning Cochran. But as soon as she added Jace's name, Bree remembered why she didn't want to go.

"You're right. I miss them, but I have to pass. I'll see them the minute they get back."

"Chicken shit," she heard Lyric mumble.

Lyric wasn't wrong. Part of her was afraid to see Jace because she knew her resolve would crumble if she did. Just thinking about him made her want to rewind their conversation.

"Jace Rice and I…" What? She didn't know what to say. They were over before they began. It was better that way. The longer she let herself believe there was a chance the two of them could make something work between them, the more she opened herself up for hurt when it didn't.

"I don't know how you can resist him. He's so damn hot."

Lyric wasn't wrong about that either. He was hot. If she closed her eyes, she could see his sweet smile and those green eyes that seemed to look straight into her soul.

"The things that take you down seem so beautiful from a distance," she murmured.

"What's that?" Bullet sat across from her in the kitchen.

"Nothing, really," she answered. "Just that sometimes it's better to resist, no matter how intriguing the temptation."

"I heard that," he grinned, shaking his head.

"Words you should live by," said Lyric, smacking him upside the head.

"Yeah, yeah," he glared at her.

"Lyric mentioned you had a wife and a baby." Actually two babies, but Bree didn't want to open that can of worms. "Aren't they with you?"

"My wife didn't wanna come."

Oh. Bree didn't know what to say to that.

"She's like that. Ain't nothin' in it for her, and she isn't interested."

"Well, uh—"

"You don't have to come up with nothin' polite to say. I'm sure Lyric told you all about me and my screw-ups."

"I wouldn't put it that way, Bullet." Bree looked to Lyric to rescue her from the very awkward conversation she was having with her brother.

"Yes, you would. And yes, I did. Poster boy, over there, for why you should pay attention in health class when they're tryin' to teach you the importance of condoms."

Bullet turned as red as Bree knew she was. It was too early in the morning for such an embarrassing conversation.

"When did you say you were leaving?"

Lyric laughed. "Let's get on the road, Bullet. We embarrassed *Miss Priss*, here, enough for one morning."

Bree started to say something in her own defense, and then thought better of it. Lyric was right, this conversation was making her very uncomfortable.

"Nice to meet you." Bullet leaned over and looked a little too deeply into her eyes.

Bree fanned her face. "Oh, my goodness. Your sister isn't kidding. You are something."

The smile he gave her was no less devastating than the look before it.

"Warn me next time he's staying over," Bree said to Lyric. "I'll stay with my parents."

Lyric slapped Bullet upside the head again. "You're walkin', talkin' testosterone, bro. You hear ads on the radio for low 'tee'—think they got anythin' for high 'tee?'"

Liv came out the front door of the house and joined Jace where he sat in one of the Adirondack chairs.

"I heard you wanted to talk to me."

"I do. About Bree, if you don't mind."

"She's so much like me," sighed Liv later, when Jace finished giving her the short version of their relationship.

"I don't know what to do. Her last words to me were to wish me a nice life."

"You pushed her buttons by not letting her tell you what she was thinking, Jace."

He knew he did. He couldn't bear to hear her say the words. Just when he'd made progress on one important relationship in his life, the other important relationship took a nose dive.

"What did Ben say?"

"He said we both had some cookin' left to do. Whatever the hell that means."

"Sounds like something Ben would say. And then write a song about later. Good advice, though."

"I can't stop thinkin' about her."

"You and Bree parted ways how long ago? A couple of weeks? Slow down, Jace. Give her time. You and Tucker have made great progress in healing what's between you in no time at all. What she's dealing with is going to take a lot longer."

"I have to see her."

"Oh, dear boy, it isn't as though you have no reason to. If you can't get yourself front and center in Bree's life, then shame on you."

"Between the ranch in Montana, getting the operation going here, building our inventory of rough stock, and then getting out to the rodeos, I don't know when I'll have time."

"There's your answer."

"What?"

"The best thing Ben did for us was give me time to miss him. If it's right, it'll work out. If it isn't right, it won't."

"He said almost those exact same words."

"He's a smart man." Liv smiled up at her husband, who had joined them on the porch.

"Somebody's hungry." Ben handed their baby girl over to her mother. "And I don't happen to have what she's lookin' for."

Jace got up to go inside, but Ben put his hand on his shoulder. "You don't have to go anywhere."

Liv had the baby cuddled up against her with a blanket over her. Jace felt the same pangs of envy he'd experienced earlier.

"You can't force it, but you sure can help it along." Ben smiled. "You're a Rice, after all. And don't you forget it."

10

"What do you mean she's in Crested Butte?" Bree asked her father.

"She left a couple of hours ago," Mark answered.

"But I'm home," she pouted.

"When did you get home?"

"A couple of days ago."

"Did she know you were home? Because I didn't."

"She knew I was coming home."

"She did? When?"

"Well, I didn't say exactly when."

"Ah. So what you're saying is that you're upset with your mother for leaving town when she didn't know you were in town. Is that right?"

Bree hated when her father was right. Not just her father, she hated it when she was wrong and anyone else was right.

"Okay, so she didn't know exactly when I was coming home, but still. How often does she go to Crested Butte?"

"Depends on how you define 'often.' Since Liv moved there, and you and your sisters developed lives of your own, she's in Crested Butte at least once or twice a month."

"*Once or twice a month?* Why?"

Mark put his hand on top of Bree's. "Stop this, and tell me what's really going on."

"I just didn't expect her to be gone." Bree put her head in her hands. Tears threatened, and she wasn't a six-year-old; she was a grown-up. The fact that her mother wasn't home shouldn't make her cry.

"You could always go too. Renie and Blythe are there. I think that's why your mother went. Jump in the car, you won't get there much after she does."

She couldn't, but she didn't want to tell her dad why not. Bree looked over and saw a suitcase near the front door. "Whose is that?"

"Mine."

"Where are *you* going?"

"I'm going to help your sister Brooke and her husband put a deck on their new house. If you don't want to go to Crested Butte, you could come with me."

If there was anything she could think of worse than going to Crested Butte, and seeing Jace, it would be going to visit her older sister.

Tucker was insisting they stop in Santa Fe for the night. Billy and Jace wanted to keep driving.

"The sooner we get to El Paso and pick up the bronc, the sooner we can be on our way back. You are in a hurry to get back, aren't you?" Jace asked him.

"Not in such a hurry that I don't want to sleep."

"Jesus Christ," swore Billy. "Is this how it's gonna be with the two of you? One of you whinin' all the damn time about somethin'?" He pointed to a service station they were about to pass. "Pull in there."

Jace stopped the truck. Billy got out the passenger door and walked back, toward the trailer. When neither Jace nor Tucker followed him, he walked back and pounded on the window.

"Get your ass outta the truck," he yelled at Tucker.

"What's he talkin' about?" Tucker asked Jace.

"No idea."

He got out and walked back to where Billy stood by the trailer.

"What?"

"You wanted to sleep, go sleep."

Tucker opened the door. "Why didn't you show me this before we left Crested Butte? I could've been sleeping comfortably this whole time."

Billy shook his head and glared at Tucker. "Cause I didn't know I was travelin' with somebody too stupid to know the first thing about a rig." He stomped off, back in the direction of the truck, and opened the driver's door.

"Get out," he barked at Jace. "I'm drivin'."

"What the hell was that all about?" Jace asked when he got back in the truck.

"Your idiot brother didn't know he could sleep in the rig. And he's our newest *partner*. This is just fuckin' great. Tell me this, does he at least know the difference between a bronc and a bull, or am I gonna have to explain that to him too?"

Jace laughed. It was the first time he felt like laughing in two days.

"Remind me why we had to bring him along?"

"He's our partner, Billy. He's gotta learn this stuff if he's going to be any help to us at all. You wanna be out on the road all the time? I sure as hell don't."

"Quit bein' such a pussy."

"Wait a minute. What? How am I bein' a pussy? I'm not complainin' about anything." Jace couldn't figure out what had gotten into Billy. Was he pissed at him because of Tucker's behavior, or was he calling him a pussy because he didn't want to be out on the road all the time?

"There's gotta be somethin' Bree likes about you, even if I can't figure out what it might be."

"Where you goin' with this, Billy?"

"You didn't have a shit chance with Renie."

No, he didn't, because she'd been in love with Billy all her life. "What's your point?"

"And Blythe, she's better suited to your idiot brother anyway."

"Again, Billy, do you have a point? Because if you don't, I'd rather you just shut the hell up."

"You scare the shit outta her."

Why hadn't he gone to sleep when Tucker did? Billy was rambling, and he wasn't in the mood for it. What the hell did he know about Bree anyway?

"She's damn smart, I'll tell you that much. Too smart for her own good. Brooke, she was just a bitch. Still is. And Blythe, she was a damn pain-in-the-ass, spoiled brat. But Bree? She was the steady one. Even when she was a little girl. She's just like her mama. Always holdin' it all together."

Jace was stunned. Billy wasn't exactly one to express his opinion about much of anything. If anyone had asked, he would've told them Billy didn't know any of the Cochran girls even existed, for all he seemed to notice.

"I'm tellin' you, she's runnin' scared."

"Okay, let's say you're right. What am I supposed to do about it?"

"Keep right on scarin' her. Best thing for her really. Look at Mark and Paige."

"What about them?"

"When ol' Paige met Mark, he was this bigger-than-life rock star. Travelin' all over the world. Even after he quit, he still rocked *her* world, if you follow."

"Okay, so…"

"I feel damn bad about Zack. That was an awful thing. I didn't know him real well, but from what I did know, he seemed like a nice enough guy. Can't say as I ever saw Bree look at him the way she looks at you, though."

"How's that?"

"Like she's about to be lit on fire."

"Is that a good thing?"

"She's smolderin' for ya," Billy smirked. "And that's a great thing."

"Blythe told me she thinks Bree would feel as though she settled if she ended up with me."

"Don't agree. I'm bettin' she thinks you'll lose interest in her. Protectin' her heart."

"When did you get so philosophical?"

"Just because I don't spend all my time talkin' about stuff, doesn't mean I ain't noticin' it. In fact, I notice more than all of you put together."

Billy had a number of valid points. Especially the part about him being a pussy. Billy might think Bree was protecting her heart from him, but he felt it was the other way around. His heart had been stomped on plenty in the last couple of years. If anyone needed to swathe their heart in bubble wrap, it was him.

Jace had never been intimidated by a woman. Not ever. But Bree Fox sure as hell changed that. One minute she seemed so fragile he was afraid he'd break her. The next, she had him by the balls. That's the way it had always been between them.

"Quit thinkin' about it so much. If you want her, go get her. Simple as that," Billy mumbled.

Was it that simple?

Bree cleaned the house from top to bottom. She went for long rides on her mountain bike. She went fly fishing. She even looked into getting her Ph.D. No matter how busy she tried to keep herself, she was bored out of her mind.

She wasn't just bored; she was lonely. She was home, and everyone else was gone—her parents, her sister, Lyric, and Jace. They were all together too, which only made the loneliness worse.

There wasn't anything she could do about it either. Her isolation was self-imposed. She'd done it to herself when she and Jace last spoke. But had she? Had he given her a chance to speak? When he assumed she was ending things with him, he wasn't wrong. It was what she'd planned to do; he just didn't give her the chance to say it. It wouldn't have ended differently if he had. So, yes, she had done this to herself.

Next week would be better. The academic year would be starting, and she would be teaching at the Air Force Academy. She wouldn't have time to be bored or lonely.

Part of her was scared about being there. Zack had gone to the Air Force Academy. He was buried in the cemetery on the grounds. Everywhere she looked, there would be reminders of him. Would she feel closer to him, or farther away?

Bree closed her eyes and imagined she was with... Jace. Not Zack, but Jace. He was her comfort. Whenever she felt worried, or sad, she thought of him. It was his arms she wished she was in, not Zack's. What was wrong with her?

She opened her book and read the same chapter she'd been trying to get through all day. When she didn't get past the first couple of paragraphs without her mind wandering, she slammed the book closed. She had to find something to get her mind off Jace Rice.

"We'll go ahead of you," Hank said to Jace and Tucker. "I want to spend a day at TZ Bucking Bulls with Billy before your mom and I go back to Montana. Bullet's goin' with us."

When they got back from Texas, Lyric was at the Flying R with her brother, Bullet. Before Jace knew it, the other partners brought him into the fold, not as a partner himself, but he'd be working for them in some capacity. Jace didn't mind. Bullet was smarter than Lyric gave him credit for, and he knew a lot about the rodeo industry.

As a group, they'd decided to take half the broncs from Crested Butte to Montana, and work on bringing more bulls south as soon as they could.

Billy had been talking to his father about setting up another operation in Black Forest. It would be smaller than the ones in Montana and Crested Butte, but even so, Billy's dad would require help to make it work. That's where Jace figured Bullet would prove most useful.

"You stoppin' in on your way home?" asked Billy.

"Just for the night. I'll stay with Tuck and Blythe, and get on the road the next morning."

Billy was chewing on a piece of straw, studying Jace.

"Since when are you the relationship whisperer? I never figured you'd be one to meddle."

Billy grinned at Jace, and walked away.

"That's more like it," muttered Jace.

11

"Can you hold him for a minute?" Blythe asked Jace. "Tucker is unpacking our bags, and if he gets any further along, I won't be able to find anything."

"I can hold him all day," Jace said, taking Cochran out of her arms. "We got a lot of catching up to do, don't we, little guy?"

Cochran reached out and tugged on Jace's hair.

"Ouch," he yelped, which made the baby giggle and do it again.

"First sign you need a haircut," said Blythe, walking out of the room.

"Tell me, little man—you got your Aunt Bree's heart in the palm of your hand—how'd you do it?" Jace murmured to his nephew once he was sure Blythe was out of earshot. "Give your Uncle Jace some pointers, would ya?"

When Cochran leaned in and put his head against Jace's chest, it melted his heart. "You're a charmer, that's what you are. It's that Rice blood runnin' through your veins."

Jace leaned back and closed his eyes. Cochran stayed where he was, his head resting against Jace's chest. It wasn't long before both of them were sound asleep.

That's the way Bree found them when she walked in the back door of the house and through the kitchen. She was about to holler out to Blythe, to see where everyone was, but she was glad she hadn't.

Blythe came around the corner, and Bree put her hand over her mouth.

"Shh. Look," she pointed to Jace and Cochran, sleeping on the sofa.

"Let's go outside," whispered Blythe. "Oh my God, I've missed you," she practically screeched once they were on the porch, and hugged Bree.

Bree hugged her back just as hard. "I missed you, too. And that sweet baby boy. He's gotten so big."

"He's growing up too fast. You have to promise you won't leave again for a long time. As in, not until he's in high school," Blythe smiled.

Bree didn't.

"What?"

"I can't make that promise, Blythe."

Blythe hugged her sister again, even harder. "I know you can't. I wasn't really serious. I just missed you, that's all."

"Um, I missed you too, but I've got to run. I just stopped in to say hello and see when we could get together. Maybe later on?"

Blythe studied her sister, all signs of her previous grin long gone. "Bullshit."

"What?"

"I said 'bullshit.' You didn't just stop in. You came to visit, and now that you've seen Jace, you're leaving."

"Blythe—"

"No," Blythe stomped her foot on the wooden porch. "This is not how it's going to be. Cochran is not going to grow up with one of the two of you leaving whenever the other is visiting. This is bullshit, and I'm not going to stand for it."

"Who are you yellin' at?" Tucker came out on the porch. "Oh, hi, Bree." He hugged her. "You're gonna wake the two of 'em if you don't keep your voice down, and I'm guessin' that's the last thing Bree wants."

"Too late." Jace walked out the front door with the baby in his arms. As soon as Cochran saw Bree, he started kicking his legs and reaching for her. Jace walked over, handed him to her, and looked into her eyes. "Hi."

He knew she wanted to focus all her attention on their nephew, but she didn't look away from him.

"Hi," she answered.

Cochran put his pudgy hands up to her face and broke the spell.

"Hello, my sweet boy." She hugged him close and showered his face with kisses, which made him giggle.

She turned and walked down the porch steps, talking to Cochran all the while. Jace wished he could hear what she was saying.

He turned around and saw both Tucker and Blythe had gone back in the house. He sat down on the porch steps and watched Bree walk around the front yard with the baby. She knelt down next to a whiskey barrel full of flowers and picked one for him. He took it in his hand and put his lips against her cheek.

Jace envied the boy. He envied Bree, too. Cochran was getting more comfortable with him, but nothing close to the way he was with her. She had such a way with him. Similar to Blythe, but different. Jace knew Aunt Bree would always have a special relationship with her nephew. They'd have conversations that no one else would be privy to, and the boy would learn a lot from her.

She looked over then. Her cheeks turned pink when she realized he was watching them. She walked back to where he sat on the porch step.

"I'm sorry," she said. "I didn't mean to take him away from you. I just missed him so much."

"You didn't. I like watching you with him. He loves you, that's for sure."

"Oh, yeah?" She nuzzled Cochran's hair. "I love him too, like no other love I've ever felt."

Jace felt another pang of envy somewhere deep in his belly. Cochran won her love so easily. Would he ever be able to do the same? Lord knew he desperately wanted to know what it felt like to have Bree love him.

The baby was reaching for Jace again. He hesitated, thinking she might not be ready to give him back.

"It's okay. He wants who he wants." She handed him the baby.

He watched her, but her expression didn't change. She was still smiling at the baby.

"He'll change his mind in a minute or two, won't you, baby boy?" She lightly pinched his arm, which made him giggle and hide his face in Jace's chest.

"Peek-a-boo," she said, and went behind Jace's shoulder.

Cochran leaned to where he could see her, and giggled again. Jace kept turning his body so they could continue their game. He was dizzy from spinning around, but he didn't want to stop. There was no better sound in the world than hearing Bree and Cochran giggling together.

"This is how I imagined it would be," she said after they sat down on the grass to let Cochran scoot around them. "Aunt Bree and Uncle Jace."

He knew he shouldn't, but he couldn't help himself. He reached out and tucked her hair behind her ear. "God, I've missed you," he whispered.

She closed her eyes. "I've missed you, too."

He wanted to ask her why she'd pulled away from him, but he didn't. He'd gotten more advice about Bree in the last couple of days than he'd gotten about anything in his life. The person whose opinion resonated the strongest was Liv. She'd told him to slow down and give Bree time. Billy and Ben both told him to go after her, but it was Liv he listened to.

"Everything you told me was right," he said instead. "He's wonderful. And I feel the same way you do. I can't begin to describe the love I feel for him. I've never felt anything like it before."

She smiled, picked Cochran up, and kissed his forehead. Jace leaned forward and did the same. As he was about to pull back, he stopped. She was too close, and he couldn't stop himself. He kissed her forehead too, and then pulled back.

She looked at him. The smile left her face, but the look that replaced it was curiosity, not anger.

He closed his eyes, and willed himself not to speak, not to tell her that he wanted this with her more than anything else in life. The two of them, holding a baby between them, a baby they both loved. Not their nephew, but their own baby. He bit the inside of his cheek in an effort to keep his mouth shut and not let out the words that would scare the shit out of her.

"How long are you in town?" she asked softly.

"A couple of days. We're meeting with a rough stock contractor in Larkspur, and then with Billy's mom and dad. The guys want to start a satellite operation here. We haven't talked about it, but Billy and Renie may want to settle back here full time."

"I doubt it. I know Renie's happy being close to her mom. By the way, I've never heard you call her that."

Jace shrugged. "Hearing all of you call her that has sort of rubbed off on me, and I guess she's got good reasons to be happy, since she's pregnant and all."

"Who is? Renie?" Bree felt as though Jace just hit her. Renie was pregnant? Why did that make her feel… hostility? And envy. "That's wonderful," she said, although she couldn't have meant anything less.

"Billy told me a while back. I get the feeling he wasn't supposed to, so, uh, don't let on you know."

"No, of course I won't. It must be early on."

"He said they'd be having a baby in eight months, so I reckon that's early on," he grinned at her.

"You know enough about it, Jace, to know it is. Even though you may know more about the gestation periods of horses and cattle."

"That's right, little lady. I'm a humble ranch hand." He pretended to tip his hat to her.

Tucker walked out on the porch. "Blythe wants to know how many for dinner," he shouted over to them.

"Oh, good Lord," whispered Bree, "I hope she's not planning to cook."

Tucker was closer to them by the time she finished her sentence. "We're goin' over to the Pattersons' for dinner. Dottie wants to know how many." He winked at her.

"Oh, uh, sorry—"

"Go along, Bree, you haven't seen your sister, or this sweet boy, in ages. I can get somethin' in town."

"Don't you want to go?" She looked wounded.

Jace was glad to see Tucker walking back in the front door. He didn't want witnesses to what was going on with Bree and him.

"Of course I do, but...you know."

"Please, don't avoid me, Jace."

"Oh, darlin'," he stroked the side of her face. "That's the last thing I want to do. Please, don't think that."

"Then go to the Pattersons' with us." Her cheeks turned pink. "Listen to me, inviting you along. They know you so much better than they know me. Maybe I should head back to Palmer Lake instead."

"Now, now, that'll make me feel as though you're avoiding me. You don't want that, do you?"

He wanted so much to tug her closer to him, hold her tight, and never let her go.

Instead, he stood. "I bet Lyric's comin' tonight, with her brother. Have you met him yet?"

"Uh, yeah. He slept on our couch the other night. That was interesting."

"Yeah? Hear tell there's somethin' about the cowboy women can't resist. Don't tell me he's got you under his spell too."

"Don't be ridiculous," she snapped at him. "That's just silly."

"You know what they say when someone protests too much. I'm thinkin' you got a crush goin' on that young man."

"Jace, you can't be serious."

She looked perplexed, and he loved it. Here goes, he thought. He was going to walk away, and then keep his distance. She knew how he felt. He hadn't hidden it, but he was going to show her they could be together, with their families, and he wouldn't stalk her. He'd give her space if that's what she wanted. He prayed hard that Liv Rice was right, otherwise, he might be making the biggest mistake of his life.

"I gotta go talk to Billy. I'll see you later, Bree."

He didn't wait for her to answer, he just walked away. Talk about interesting. He seemed fine.

He was so…easy-going. And relaxed. Why was he so relaxed? And that damn confident swagger of his. He knew how hot he looked, and he used it to his advantage. He was just the sexiest thing…*oh, God, what was she doing?* She was fantasizing about Jace Rice while she played in the yard with Cochran. Thank goodness he didn't try to eat grass, or dirt, or worse—a bug. She hadn't been paying any attention to her nephew. Every thought had been on his uncle.

"Come on, baby boy, let's go find your mama before your Aunt Bree lets you wander off on your own."

Bree walked around to the back of the house, hoping Jace was still in the front. Instead, she came around the corner, only to see Jace climbing into his truck. He waved at her before he started it and drove off in the direction of Patterson Ranch.

It took every ounce of willpower he possessed not to jump back out, walk over, and kiss the daylights out of Bree. Instead, Jace closed his eyes, said a little prayer, and started the truck. Maybe he should skip dinner tonight. Staying away from her, keeping his hands off her, was going to be near impossible.

For the next couple of hours, he had business to take care of, and he hoped to hell he could keep his mind where it belonged.

He was meeting with Billy in the Pattersons' dining hall by the bunk house. Dottie and Bill were serving dinner to the cowboys who worked the ranch, and invited them to join in. He missed Dottie Patterson, not that he'd spent much time with her, but when he had, she always made him feel welcome, and boy, did she give good hugs. Jace was in need of a really good hug.

"Damn time you showed up," Billy smirked at him. "Thought maybe you'd be babysittin' all night."

Jace slugged him. "As if you aren't daddy of the year. Don't give me any shit about wantin' to hang out with Cochran."

"Cochran, my ass. Tucker told me the two of you were with Bree. And you looked mighty smitten."

"Change the subject, Billy. No kidding. The last person I want to be thinkin' about right now is Bree." He adjusted his jeans before he sat down on the bench, which only made Billy throw his head back and laugh.

Billy told him Ty Rinaldo, the guy who raised bucking bulls in a town just outside Monument, was joining them for dinner. Since Billy was pressing hard for his dad to bring more broncs to the ranch, and didn't want to take on bulls too, with TZ Bucking Bulls so close, he thought they could partner instead.

"What about contracting to ranch rodeos?" Bullet asked when he joined their conversation.

"Good question," answered Billy. "What do you know about it?"

"I like the idea of it. More old-school. Buddy of mine did pretty well on bucking horses down in Amarillo earlier this year."

"Told you we should've stopped in Amarillo," smirked Tucker.

Billy rolled his eyes and looked back at Bullet. "Might be interestin' to consider. Both horses and bucking bulls. Probably ain't a lot of contractors who do it all."

With the amount of rough stock and rodeo expertise they had combined, Flying R Rough Stock, the name they'd decided on, would be a new force in the industry. The operation was already so much bigger than Jace ever imagined it would be, and they'd barely started to scratch the surface of what they planned to do.

"Who's in Montana now?" Billy asked Hank.

"Jace and I hired Yance Hatterburn. Best hand Montana ever saw," answered Jace's father.

"Better manager than me and my dad combined," added Jace. "No offense, Daddy," he rubbed his father's shoulder.

"None taken, son."

"It doesn't make sense for you to be up there all the time, Jace," Billy said to him. "You and me got too much work to do on the circuit, gettin' our name out. Gonna be on the road pretty much non-stop." Billy looked over at Renie who was talking to Blythe and Bree, and rubbing her stomach.

"I can't be gone all the time, you know that," Billy shook his head. "I just can't be."

"Nothin' you have to tell me, Billy. I get it." He looked in the same direction and caught Bree looking at him. He loved it when he caught her and she got so embarrassed her cheeks turned pink. Little by little, he'd chip away at that guard she kept snug whenever she was around him. He winked at her, which made her smile, then look away.

"Maybe we can figure out a schedule," Billy was saying. "But at first it'll have to be both of us."

"What can I do to help?" asked Bullet.

Billy looked at him, then at his dad. "We're gonna need you around here for the time being," he answered. "Right, Dad?"

His dad was lost in thought, and Billy seemed annoyed by it.

"You sure about this, Billy?" Bill Senior asked.

"Which part?"

"It's a big start up, and your mama and I aren't gettin' any younger."

"Come on," Billy said to his dad. "Take a walk with me. Let's talk."

Jace was left sitting at the table with Bullet, Tucker, and Ben, when he joined them.

"We need some kind of organizational chart is what I'm thinkin'," Bullet said to them. He pulled what looked like a paper placemat from a diner, out of his pocket. On it were three circles representing Crested Butte, Black Forest, and Helena, Montana.

Under each he had three columns. One was a list of people, the other two were broncs and bulls. Under broncs were two more columns, but off to the side, Bullet had a third column with ranch rodeos written at the top.

Jace took the paper out of Bullet's hand. "We didn't talk about ranch rodeos until a few minutes ago."

"Yeah, I know. I wasn't sure if you'd want to consider it, but I thought it was worth bringin' up anyway."

"Interesting." Jace looked at Tucker and Ben, who were nodding their heads in agreement.

Lyric had definitely underestimated her brother. On the other hand, no one worked harder than her. Stood to reason Bullet would be the same way.

"When's the last time you saw your dad?" Ben asked Bullet.

"Couple weeks ago. Why?"

"He still writin'?"

"Hell, yeah," Bullet smiled. "Every day."

"What would it take to get him here?"

"Say the word."

"Word."

When the conversation between Ben and Bullet turned to music, Tucker got up and walked over to Blythe. Jace wanted to follow, but didn't. He didn't know jack shit about Bullet's dad, or the band he was in, but for the time being, he was going to make it look like it was the most fascinating conversation in the world. Bree was watching him; he could feel her eyes on him.

"I'd love to get together with him and Mark. Shit, how awesome would that be?" Jace heard Ben say to Bullet.

"*Cochran*. That's right, Mark Cochran was the lead singer of the band. I never put two and two together. Damn, my dad would be all over that. He loves that band."

"From what I've heard from Mark, he's always wanted to collaborate with your dad. He was Satin's primary songwriter, right?"

"I've tried to pretend like I know what the hell you're talking about, but I'm lost. Either one of you, willing to explain?"

Ben had the same look on his face Jace saw him get when he talked to his kids.

"Cochran and Satin were two of the biggest heavy metal bands of the seventies. Before your time, but what you don't realize is Bullet's dad and Bree's dad are two of the greatest rock musicians and songwriters of their generation. I'd love to get in a room with the two of them and just watch. Bet it would be magic."

"Well, hell, let's do it," said Bullet enthusiastically.

"Do what?" asked Lyric, sitting down next to Jace.

"Get your dad together with Mark Cochran," Ben answered.

"Hell, yeah!" Lyric stood up and high-fived Ben.

Jace had never felt so out of a conversation he was physically in the middle of, so when Bree tapped him on the shoulder and asked if they could talk, he had two reasons for being the most relieved man in the room.

"What's up?" he asked.

Bree had been watching him talk to everyone but her for the last hour, and she was annoyed.

"I told you I didn't want you to feel as though you have to avoid me, Jace."

"Wait. What? I'm not avoiding you." He waved his arm around the dining hall. "We're both here, with our families."

"But it feels different." She couldn't look at him. If she did, her eyes would fill with tears.

"Hey, come here." Jace put his arms around her.

She rested her head on his chest and wrapped her arms around his waist, and it felt so good.

Jace held on tight and breathed in the scent of her. He hoped it would be a long time before she pulled away. He never wanted to let go. He opened his eyes and saw Liv smiling at him from across the room, and smiled back.

Seeing her reminded him that he had to do this right with Bree, and that didn't mean playing games. It meant giving her the space and time she needed.

Unfortunately, it was the game she was responding to, and he didn't want that. He pulled away, but held on to her arms. Once he started this conversation, Bree was probably going to take it the wrong way. He needed to get her somewhere they could talk, or he could talk, and she'd have to listen.

"Let's go for a ride," he whispered.

She nodded and followed him out of the dining hall.

He opened the passenger door of his truck and put his hand on the curve of her back as she climbed in. He drove down the road to Billy and Renie's place, and parked next to the house.

"Come on." When he held her door open, she jumped out of the truck. "This way." Jace led her around to the other side of the house and up the stairs to the deck that wrapped around the back.

He lit the patio warmers and pulled two of the Adirondack chairs closer together.

"We have a lot to talk about," Jace said when they sat down. "Both of us. There was something you wanted to tell me a couple days ago, and I didn't do a very good job of listening to you. Wanna try again?"

She folded her arms in front of her. "You sure you want to do this?"

"Wanting to do this and wanting to hear what you have to say are two different things. Yeah, I want to do this. Will it be hard for me to listen? Sure will, but I'll do it anyway."

Bree wasn't prepared for this. When they'd talked, the other day, she'd planned what she wanted to say. Now she couldn't remember a word of it.

"It was something Red said to me while I was still in Idaho. It made me think about you and me."

Jace was quiet, his eyes focused on her mouth.

"Is this real, Jace, or are we just keeping each other company until someone better comes along?"

"That's what Red asked you?"

"No, he just made me think. He asked what our story was. When I started to tell it, everything became clear to me."

"Go on."

"You said it yourself. You're a detour. You don't want to be a detour, Jace. I can't let you be. And I can't let myself go down that road. It's as much self-preservation as anything else."

"Stop talking about roads and detours, and just tell me how you feel."

She probably didn't deserve for him to make this easy for her.

"You're…you. And I'm…me."

He smiled. "Profound, Bree. Yes, you're right on both counts."

"Shut up," she smiled back. "I'm trying to make a point, although I'm not doing a very good job of it."

"I'm listening, Bree."

He was. He was staring at her, and he was listening. She needed to choose her words carefully.

"I'm afraid." Wait—that wasn't what she'd wanted to say. Why did she?

"Keep talkin', Bree."

"Think about it. I mean, I just lost my husband. Or when we met, I had. And you were so…wrapped up with my sister, and Tucker. You didn't even like me, Jace."

"I've told you before, I liked you more than you liked me."

"Maybe. But you have to admit, we didn't like each other. Not at all. And then, all of a sudden, we were…"

"What?"

"You know, thrown together. I was hurting, drowning really. And you were distraught over Blythe and Tucker."

She wished he would say something instead of just letting her talk.

"I'm not saying there isn't a physical attraction, at least for me."

"Come on, Bree, you know there is for me, too."

"But, when it comes down to it, I doubt I'm your type, Jace."

"My type? This will be good. What's my type, Bree?"

"Someone more like Renie, or my sister. Young, pretty, fun."

"And you're old, ugly, and boring."

"Essentially."

"Get over yourself. Blythe is your sister, not your granddaughter. I don't need to tell you you're right; you're not pretty, you're beautiful, and—"

The look on her face stopped him mid-sentence. She thought he was bullshitting her. She didn't believe him, and nothing he said would change her mind.

Instead of saying more, Jace stood and pulled Bree out of her chair and into his arms. He put his hand on the back of her neck and kissed her the way he'd wanted to since this morning. He pulled her against him, so she could feel exactly how attractive he found her.

He backed her up so she was against one of the floor-to-ceiling windows separating the deck and the inside of the house, put his hands on her bottom, and lifted her up, so her legs were around his waist.

His lips trailed from hers, down her neck, and she weaved her fingers in his hair. She could stop him, pull away, but she didn't.

One hand held her against him, and he unfastened the buttons on her shirt with the other. His lips trailed down further, until he grazed the skin where it met the lace of her bra.

"I need you, Bree. Do you hear me?"

"Yes," she answered. It came out between a whisper and a gasp.

He put his other hand around her, and carried her, holding her as close as he could, and opened the door he knew Billy always forgot to lock.

Once inside, he lowered her onto the leather sofa in front of the fireplace. Only her eyes moved, as she watched him cross the room. Her shirt was mostly open to her waist; she didn't make an attempt to cover herself. He lit the fire and came back to where she was, grabbing her legs and turning her so her back rested against the arm of the couch. He lowered himself and nudged her legs apart with his knee. He unfastened the remaining buttons on her shirt, pulled it apart, and then cupped her breast through her bra.

"Stop me," he murmured before his lips traced the lace against the skin of her other breast. "Stop me now, Bree."

"I can't," she pulled him closer.

"We're gonna make love, Bree. Tell me now if that's what you want."

"I want it so much."

He pulled away from her, but only so he could slide his arm under her knees and behind her back. He lifted her from the couch and carried her toward the master bedroom.

"Wait—"

"Are you stopping me?" he asked.

"Downstairs."

Right. Billy and Renie were in town, and he and Bree were in their house. He turned toward the staircase.

"I can walk—"

"No."

Before she could say anything else, he covered her mouth with his.

He pushed the door open with his leg and laid her on the bed. He reached over and turned on the lamp that sat on the bedside table. The way she'd looked the night they spent in Sun Valley—he wanted to see her that way now.

"Take your clothes off, Bree."

She rolled to the other side of the bed, turned the other lamp on, and then stood and faced him. He watched as she slid the shirt off her shoulders. Her fingers worked the zipper of her jeans, and she slid them off her hips, her eyes never leaving his. She stood before him in her bra and panties, waiting.

"All your clothes, darlin'."

When she unfastened her bra and let it drop to the floor, Jace took a deep breath.

She wrapped her fingers under the sides of her panties, shimmied them down to her knees, bent her leg, and stepped out of them. "Your turn," she whispered.

He pulled the pearl snaps on his shirt open, and shrugged it off as he watched her climb onto the bed. Her eyes still hadn't left his. His hands lingered at the top of his jeans, waiting to see if she'd say anything, as she had that night.

"Come to bed, Jace," she smiled.

Those were the words he wanted to hear.

Bree closed her eyes when Jace lifted the blanket to crawl in next to her. He slipped his arms around her body and his tongue inside her mouth. Their kiss was soft at first, then it deepened, lengthened, growing more urgent.

His hand slid to her breast, cupping it, harder, until he could feel her heartbeat quicken underneath.

She moaned softly, the way she did in her sleep—a sound he loved. He felt his control slipping away; he couldn't be gentle with her any longer. He had to take her.

"Open your eyes and look at me," he growled.

Bree looked up at Jace, heat pulsing through her veins as she watched his eyes wander over her body. His mouth followed. The way he used it made her purr.

When Jace slid inside her, Bree felt her body imploding. Every part of her trembled as he brought her to the brink of bliss, and then eased off, only to take her back to the edge again. He did this over and over until she gripped his shoulders, digging her nails into his back.

"Please," she begged him. "Please, Jace."

He stopped instead and dragged his hungry gaze over her body again. "I want you to remember this moment," he leaned down and whispered into her ear. "And who made you feel this way."

His mouth fastened on hers, hard, and he began to move again, taking her body back to the precipice. If he stopped again, she'd flip him over and take what he was unwilling to give. This time, though, his buildup wasn't gradual. He forced her to the brink and pushed her over with the strength of his body.

She tried to rip her mouth from his, so she could breathe, or gasp, or even scream, but he was relentless. With one hand, he held her, kissing her roughly, owning her, possessing her. As the wave of pleasure slowly rolled to a quiet stillness, she looked into his eyes. His gaze penetrated the same way his body had.

"What?" She tried to hide her face in his shoulder, but he wouldn't let her.

"No hiding from me. Let me see it."

"See what?" She tilted her head slightly, just not far enough that he could look into her eyes.

"The look you had on your face when you came, sweetheart. I could get used to seeing that look. I want to see it, again and again." He lowered his lips to hers, this time softly, gently, lovingly—not with the hunger he'd had just a few minutes ago.

He ran his tongue over her bottom lip, and grazed it with his teeth. "Bree," he murmured. "Open your eyes, darlin'. I want you to see me, and no one else."

Would he see regret? Or sadness? Had she been thinking of Zack when their bodies were joined together? Did she imagine Zack's hands caressing her body, instead of his?

The look on her face when she came was one he'd never forget. Or the sound of her begging him, not Zack, to bring her there. He couldn't wait to see that look in her eyes again.

He forced himself to look, to see what her eyes said now that their passion was spent. What he saw reignited the fire in him. He whipped the pillow from beneath her head, so she lay flat on the mattress. This time she didn't close her eyes.

Instead of letting his gaze wander as it had before, he kept his eyes on hers. Waiting, watching, wondering. When he saw her heat match his, he kissed her. Her soft moans reverberated in his mouth. Her lips were warm, willing, eager. He let his kiss linger, drawing out the exquisite feeling of being this close to her.

When her hand caressed the side of his face, he shuddered. How long had he waited to feel her hands on him?

"I want to touch you," she said. "Everywhere."

He groaned and rolled onto his back, letting her take her time exploring his body. Her fingertips swept from his Adam's apple, across his shoulder, and down his arm. Her touch was so soft it almost tickled.

When she ran her lips across his sternum, he groaned again, willing himself to give her this time to explore, and not ravage her body the way he was so tempted to. He ran his fingers through her hair, weaving it so he could stop her if he needed to. And soon he would, or she would unman him.

"What are you doin' to me, Bree?"

"Exploring," she murmured. "Learning." She ran her lips down his torso. "Memorizing."

Jace closed his eyes and took a deep breath, letting Bree continue her exploration.

12

When he woke the next morning, she was gone. He couldn't have been asleep more than an hour.

He thought about the things she said yesterday afternoon, her words confirming his fears, and even the power of their lovemaking couldn't drown their message.

You're a detour. You don't want to be a detour, Jace. I can't let you be. Those words played over and over in his head. He was so tired of being a detour. He wanted to be the main road, the right road to take, the one that always brought the girl home. He needed to tell her so.

He got out of bed and pulled his Wranglers up over his hips. He left the top button undone, and climbed the stairs in search of Bree.

He smelled coffee, and then realized he and Bree were probably not alone in the house. *Shit.* He'd gotten so used to Billy and Renie being in Crested Butte when he stayed here, he hadn't given any thought to them coming home last night.

He came around the corner and found Bree sitting in the kitchen, with Renie. They both turned toward him when he walked into the room.

"Shirt might be nice, Jace," she said with a smug look.

He ignored her and walked straight to Bree. He stopped behind her, leaned down, and kissed her neck. "Good morning, darlin'."

"Don't mind us, *the people who own the house,*" said Billy, coming around the corner, carrying Willow. "Might want to consider there's a child in the house, dude."

"Uncle Jace!" squealed Willow. She wiggled out of Billy's arms and came running toward Jace.

He picked her up and twirled her in the air.

"Did you sleep here, Uncle Jace?" she asked when he set her down.

"I did. Did you?"

"Mama said I could sleep with her and Daddy last night. Right, Mama?" Willow looked at Renie.

"I did, sweet girl. We had our own slumber party. Just like Uncle Jace and Aunt Bree did."

Willow looked over at Bree. "Hi, Aunt Bree," she waved.

Bree thought she'd die of embarrassment. She'd spent a little time around Willow, but not that much. She knew the little girl considered Blythe her "aunt," too.

Renie was so casual about it all. If it were her daughter, Bree doubted she'd be so forthcoming about the "slumber party."

Willow walked back over to Billy. "Time to say hi to my baby," she told him. She led him by the hand, and they both walked over to Renie.

"Good morning, baby," Willow whispered against Renie's belly. "Your turn, Daddy."

"Mornin', baby," he said.

"Do it right, Daddy. You have to give baby a kiss."

Billy lifted the bottom of Renie's shirt and kissed her belly. Willow did too.

Billy stood and looked straight at Jace. "Not a word," he mouthed at him.

It was all Jace could do not to laugh.

He leaned back down, closer to Bree. "How are you this morning?" he whispered.

"Mortified. How are you?"

"Tired. Really tired. Thinkin' I should drive us over to Palmer Lake, so we can get some rest."

"We have a meeting with Ty Rinaldo today, *Romeo*," Billy grunted at him.

"What do you need me for?" Jace kissed the back of Bree's neck. "You can handle it, Patterson. You…" he kissed her neck again, "and Tucker…and Ben…and your dad…and Bullet." Jace kissed her neck between each name he spoke. "Don't need me…"

"You're right," Billy said with disgust in his voice. "Bree, get him outta here, would ya? Before he corrupts my wife and daughter, and makes me sick to my stomach."

"Gladly," she answered and led Jace back downstairs.

"Is there a way out down here, so I don't have to go back up there and embarrass myself again?"

Jace smiled at her, but didn't answer.

"You didn't help matters any, standing there in the kitchen, kissing the back of my neck."

Still he didn't answer but instead put his lips on her neck, just below the curve of her chin.

"Jace," she sighed. "You need to stop this."

"Your words say I should," he went back to kissing her. "But your body and the tone of your voice are tellin' me somethin' else altogether, darlin'."

She put her arms around his shoulders, and thought about pushing him back down on the bed. Wait. *What was she doing?*

"Take me home," she whispered instead.

Jace wasn't showing any sign of stopping, so she pushed away from him.

"Okay, okay. You wanna pick your car up first?" He asked the question but was unbuttoning the top buttons of her shirt rather than waiting for her to answer.

"If I say we can leave my car at my sister's house for now, will you stop what you're doing and drive me home?"

He looked into her eyes. "As long as you don't button up that shirt on the ride home, you can probably convince me."

"What? Are you crazy? I'm not walking outside with my shirt wide open."

He put his arm around her and swooped her up. "I'll carry you with your shirt wide open, then."

"Jace," she couldn't help but smile. "Put me down and put your shirt on. And your boots."

When he put her down and smiled, Bree thought she'd lose her footing. Did he know how disarmingly gorgeous he was? And it wasn't just when he smiled.

They'd been back at Bree's for a couple of hours at least, and must've fallen asleep. Jace tried to ignore his ringing phone, but whoever it was called over and over again, until he finally picked it up.

"Yeah?"

"You and me are havin' dinner with the Rinaldos tonight. I'm bringin' Renie. You bring Bree."

"I'll ask her—"

"Don't ask her, bring her."

Jace hung up, shaking his head.

"What was that about?"

"We're invited to have dinner with Ty Rinaldo and his wife tonight."

"Okay…well, uh…"

"We are, as in you and me. Billy and Renie too."

"Why would I go?"

Jace pulled her into him and cupped her bottom with his big hands. "So you can spend more time with me, darlin', that's why."

She rested her hands on his shoulders. "It isn't as though I bring much to the table…so to speak. I think I'll take a pass, Jace."

He let go of her and turned to look out the window. The rock that just landed in the pit of his stomach was quickly growing into a boulder.

"We're back to I'm me, and you're you," he shrugged. "That what you're tryin' to say?"

"Essentially."

He remembered her using that word before too. "Time for me to mosey on down the road, then, I guess." If she was going to treat him like a cowpoke who wasn't good enough for her, he might as well act the part.

"Jace—"

"What, Bree?"

"We're so—"

He held up his hand. "I hear ya, sister. No further explanation necessary." He reached around her waist, pulled her up against him, and looked into her eyes. Her lips were so close, so tempting. "Good enough to share your bed, but not quite good enough to share a meal with. Got it."

Her eyes were open wide, her pupils dilated. That's right—he turned her on; she wanted him. He could carry her back into the bedroom and spend the rest of the day there with her. But when it came time to leave for dinner, she'd push him out the door.

He let her go and made his way past her, into the bedroom. He pulled on his boots and picked his shirt up off the floor.

"Don't leave like this," she said from the doorway. He didn't answer. He walked past her again, not allowing himself to even look at her, and out the front door.

Bree heard the truck start. She wanted to follow him out the door, ask him not to leave, but she couldn't bring herself to move. The truck was idling. Was he going to change his mind and come back inside? She held her breath until she heard the sound of tires on the gravel. He wasn't coming back.

It took her a few minutes to realize she couldn't have followed him if she wanted to. Her car was still at Tucker and Blythe's place.

"Can you come pick me up so I can get my car?" she asked Blythe later.

"Of course, I could even bring it over, but why didn't Jace bring you back with him? He was just here a few minutes ago."

"It's a long story."

"Uh oh."

"I don't feel like talking about it right now."

"I'll see if Tucker will follow me over, that way you won't have to drive me back."

A half hour later, Bree heard a car in the driveway. When she looked out, it was her car, but her sister wasn't in it: Liv was.

She opened the front door just as Liv walked up the porch steps.

"Hi. Uh, thanks for bringing my car back." Bree looked past Liv to see if anyone had followed her over.

"I told Ben I'd text him when I wanted him to pick me up. I want to talk to you, Bree."

Bree stood back and held the door open for Liv. "Please, come in. Can I get you anything?"

"A cup of coffee would be nice, if you have some made."

"Cream and sugar?"

"Just cream."

Bree went into the kitchen, poured a cup of coffee, got the cream out of the refrigerator, and set it in front of Liv.

"What do you want to talk to me about?"

Liv patted the couch. "Come and sit down with me."

Bree sat next to her and clutched one of the throw pillows in front of her, like a shield. Liv grabbed it and threw it across the room.

"What are you doing?" Bree gasped.

"We're going to have a very frank and honest talk, Bree. No hiding, even behind pillows."

Bree's cheeks turned pink. She picked up her coffee and took a swig, rather than a sip. "I probably should've added some brandy to this," she muttered.

"Probably." Liv turned her body so she was facing Bree, and took Bree's hands in hers.

"Honey," she began, "you know that I know what you're going through."

Bree blinked her eyes, trying not to cry.

"I'm not here to talk to you about Zack; I'm here to talk to you about Jace."

"Why?"

"Because it's time you stopped using your dead husband as a shield, just like you were using that pillow, against moving on with your life."

Bree opened her mouth to argue, but decided to hear Liv out instead.

"You're so much like your mother," Liv laughed. "You've got it all together. You know the answer before anyone else asks the question. But when it comes to seeing what's best for yourself, it's harder to have accurate situational awareness."

Bree thought Liv sounded like Zack. The next thing she'd say would be that Bree needed to get a vector on things.

"Look at me," she said to Liv. "How long can this thing with Jace last? Let's be honest."

"Why can't it last?"

Bree looked at the ceiling. "Because we're so…"

"So…what?"

Bree laughed. "Because I'm me, and he's…him."

"You've lost me."

"I'm a buttoned-up intellectual who has had sex with exactly two men in her life. The second of which was only yesterday."

"And Jace?"

"Jace is a hot cowboy who conveniently falls *in love* with women who he knows very well aren't *available*." Bree made the sign of quotation marks to emphasize her words.

"You believe it's intentional?"

"Of course it's intentional." She rolled her eyes. "Come on, his radar is uncannily accurate."

"He's using you, is that what you're saying?"

"I'm convenient. I've never seen two people thrown together in a more convenient way than Jace and I have been."

"He cares about you, Bree."

"And I care about him, but what does that have to do with anything?" Bree shook her head. "In two weeks I'll be teaching at the Air Force Academy, and Jace will be...I don't know what he'll be doing. Raising livestock? Can you really see *me* mucking stalls?"

As soon as Bree said the words, she regretted them. "I'm sorry, Liv. That wasn't what I meant."

Liv didn't say anything, and with every moment of silence, Bree felt worse. She hadn't meant to insult her.

"Tell me how you see him."

"Him who? Jace?"

"Of course Jace. Who else would I be talking about?"

"He's a good man..."

"No, deeper. If I didn't know him, how would you describe him to me?"

Bree smiled. "Well, first of all, he's hot as all get-out."

Liv laughed. "You sound just like Lyric."

"It was intentional."

"What else?"

"He's a cowboy, through and through. A *real* cowboy. I used to go out to Billy's and watch the two of them buck broncs."

"And?"

"He's honorable. When I said he's a good man, he really is. He's kind, and he cares about his family." Bree stopped talking and put her face in her hands. "He's as patient as he is stubborn, and he certainly thinks he knows what's best."

"Sounds familiar," winked Liv.

Bree smiled. She deserved that. Liv had known her and her sisters since they were little girls. Bree had always had a reputation as a know-it-all. She was definitely the best student among the three girls. Brooke got married right out of high school; who knew what might've become of Blythe if she hadn't met Tucker. But Bree had known she'd go to college, and not just for a regular degree. Even without them talking about it, there had been an assumption between Zack and her that she'd continue her education until she had her Ph.D.

"That's Jace. Let's talk about you now."

"What about me?"

"Your mom and I have had many conversations about how much you're like her. It isn't just her; you're like me too."

"I am? I mean, uh, thank you."

"You're so independent. When Zack was alive, you let some of your independence go. You relied on him. The two of you made decisions together. Now that you don't have him to talk to, you believe you're left alone to make decisions."

Bree shrugged. "In a way, I suppose."

"Let's talk hypothetically for a minute. Say you decided to try to make things work with Jace. What would it look like?"

Bree stood and looked out the window. "That's just it. I can't imagine it. Not long-term anyway."

"Try harder. Close your eyes. Tell me what you and Jace look like together."

Bree closed her eyes and let out a heavy sigh. "I can't, Liv. I can't see us together."

"Because you don't want it?"

"Whether I want it or not, it's impossible."

"Why?"

"I'm here, at least for the time being, and he's God knows where. He's everywhere. It isn't as though he's just going back to Montana. He'll be on the road most of the time."

"Uh huh."

"What?"

"I'm challenging you, Bree. Spend some time imagining what your life might be like with Jace. What if there were no right or left margins? What might it be like?"

Bree heard someone pull in the driveway. Liv stood. "That'll be my Ben."

"I thought you were going to text him."

"He's amazing that way, knowing what I need, or that I need him, before I know myself." Liv winked at Bree.

"Oh, and by the way, I'm throwing another challenge your way. Go to dinner tonight. They're meeting at the Villa at seven. Join them. I think you'll be surprised by what you learn if you do."

A few hours later, Bree decided to accept Liv's challenge. She walked over to the Villa. It wasn't a long walk, and after dinner, she'd be better off not having her car. It would give her an excuse to invite Jace back to the house.

She pulled the heavy front door open and waited for her eyes to adjust. She looked into the bar area and saw Billy and Renie, but Jace wasn't at the table with them. She looked around and saw him standing at the bar, but he hadn't seen her. He was too distracted by the blonde cowgirl whose every word he seemed to hang on.

She'd seen that look on his face before, earlier that morning, right before he'd talked her back into bed. It hadn't taken Jace Rice twenty-four hours before he moved on to his next conquest. It was just as Bree had expected it to be.

She slunk out before anyone saw her. At least she hoped no one had. *How humiliating.* Everything she'd thought about Jace Rice was true. Even the things she hadn't said. Jace was a cowboy, all right. A cowboy who could easily have a different girl in his bed every night of the week. She'd been the Friday night girl. The blonde at the bar would be Saturday night's.

She could no more hold Jace's attention than she could muck out a stall. It wasn't that she thought she was above it. Liv misunderstood, and Bree hadn't tried to explain what she really meant. She couldn't see herself doing it, because she didn't know how.

If Blythe had been the one to walk into the bar, in her place, she would have sauntered up to Jace, insinuated herself between him and the blonde, and staked her claim on her man. Bree could never have done that.

Instead of going home, she walked over to the bar on the corner. They'd have live music tonight. Maybe she'd run into someone she knew. It wouldn't be unusual in the small community they lived in. She just had to be sure she sat somewhere that she wouldn't have a view of the front door of the Villa. The last thing she wanted to see tonight was Jace leaving with the blonde.

A few minutes after they ordered, Ty got a call on his cell phone. In addition to raising bulls, he was an EMT with the local fire department. He wasn't on duty, but there'd been an accident, on the highway, severe enough that they were calling everyone in to help. He wouldn't have time to stop at the fire house, he told them, he'd have to go straight to the scene. He looked over at his wife.

"Go," she told him. "I'll get home. *Now go.*"

He raced out of the restaurant. His wife got up and went to the bar. She didn't cancel his order, but asked them to pack it to go, so he could eat it later, when he got home. Jace walked over to where she waited.

"We'll get you home," he told her when he joined her at the bar.

"Thanks," she said. "Part of being the wife of a local hero," she laughed.

"Oh yeah? A hero, huh?"

"Well, he's my hero. Always has been, always will be."

The look on her face made the boulder in Jace's stomach double in size. Why couldn't he find someone who thought of him that way?

Bree couldn't help herself. She looked. The sun had set, but there was enough light left that she could see Jace hold out his hand to help the blonde onto the passenger seat of the truck. She also saw the *sweet* smile she gave him when he did. She felt sick to her stomach. She threw a twenty on the bar, waited for the truck to pull out of the parking lot across the street, and walked home.

13

Billy called another meeting. This time he wanted to map out their schedule. Jace could've saved them all a lot of time by telling Billy in advance to just put his name in any slot that needed to be filled.

He was the only one of them without any reason to want to stay home. Billy and Renie had each other and Willow, with another baby on the way. Tucker and Blythe had each other and Cochran. Ben and Liv had each other and Caden. Matt and Will didn't have any kids, but they had wives. He didn't have anyone.

How ironic that he'd invested in the ranch because he wanted to get off the road. Instead, he'd be back on it more than he had been before.

"You don't have to do this," said Renie, cornering him in the kitchen.

"What's that?"

"Be a martyr."

Jace shook his head. "Here I thought you were comin' to thank me for taking more on so Billy could be at home more often. Instead you call me a martyr."

"Good ol' Jace. Nothing ever bothers him. Never flustered, never a hair out of place."

"What are you gettin' at? If you've got somethin' to say, just say it. Quit with all the bullshit, *Irene.*"

"No one asked you to spend more time out on the road than everyone else."

"No, no one did. I offered. It isn't as though I have any reason—"

Renie put her fingers on his lips. "Quit feeling so damn sorry for yourself, Jace. If you want a reason to stay home, make it happen."

Billy drove one rig, with the bulls. Jace drove the other, carrying the broncs. They were headed back to Montana, from Crested Butte, and hadn't planned to stop in Monument, until Bill Senior called his son and told him Bullet left the night before for Oklahoma. Some kind of emergency with one of his kids.

"Detour," Billy told him when he called his cell—a word Jace hated.

They pulled into Billy's place two hours later, unloaded the bulls into the various pens, and then took the broncs over to Billy's parents' place. Tucker met them there and helped them unload.

"Bree's at the house," Tucker told Jace when they finished.

"Does she know I'm here?"

"Wasn't sure you'd want her to know."

"Yeah, you're right. Good call. Sorry I'll miss seeing Cochran though."

"Blythe said she'd bring him over when Bree left."

"That's nice of her."

"Jace—"

"Save it, Tuck. I've been on the road, I'm beat, and I don't feel like listening to anything you're about to say."

When Jace turned around, Billy stood behind him. "Don't start," he barked at him. He walked away, but turned back around.

"It wasn't so long ago that your lives were as shitty as mine is now. Just because you got what you wanted, and your lives are turnin' out better than mine, doesn't mean you get to lecture me. I won't listen to either one of you. Got it?"

Billy walked away, shaking his head, but Tucker stood his ground. Jace could feel what he was thinking; he didn't need to hear it.

"You're right," Tucker said instead.

Bree was in her second month of teaching at the academy, her second month of wondering what had possessed her to take this on. Everywhere she looked, she saw Zack. It wasn't the cadets as much as it was the officers.

Every single one of them reminded her of Zack. Most of them knew who she was, and if they didn't today, they'd know tomorrow. She could tell. The look on their faces changed as soon as they did. One day, they'd smile and say hello; the next, they'd say hello, they might even smile, but their eyes changed. They became clouded with pity.

Every morning, she dreaded making the eight-mile drive from Palmer Lake. She'd park, go to her office, teach, go back to her office, and drive home. Some days she'd stop at the cemetery and sit in the car. She didn't get out. She didn't walk over to Zack's tombstone. She'd close her eyes and wish she was living a different life.

She'd think about the time she spent in Idaho, when she was trying so hard to mourn her dead husband. How ridiculous. All she would have had to do was come here. Every day, she walked around in a state of mourning. Every day, she was reminded of her profound loss.

There had been a time when she and Zack talked about coming back to the academy. So many grads did. In fact, the current superintendent was a grad—a woman, and a three-star general. She was the first woman named superintendent of the prestigious institution. The commandant was a grad too. He was a one-star, and a pilot. The head of the department where she taught was a grad too. He was a colonel.

Some of them had been deployed. Some had even served in Afghanistan. They'd come back though. Unlike Zack.

Sometimes she'd let herself imagine what it would have been like if he had. He would've been down at the airfield; she would've been up on the hill during the day. Maybe they would've met on the terrazzo for lunch, in the shadow of the iconic, landmark chapel.

There would've been parties they would've gone to together. She would've joined the spouse's club. And when they had children, they would've gone to school on the academy grounds.

That's what they would've done if Zack had come back. But he hadn't.

Bree was babysitting tonight, so Tucker and Blythe could have an evening out to themselves. When she walked in the back door of the house, Tucker was waiting for her in the kitchen.

"Hi," she said softly. "What's wrong, Tucker?"

"Come, sit down," he said.

Bree's hand covered her mouth, her eyes filled with tears, and she started to shake.

He walked over to her and put his arms around her. "I'm sorry, Bree. Relax. Nothing happened. Everyone is okay. I wasn't thinking. Come. Sit." He pulled her over to the table.

She couldn't stop shaking. He sat down next to her and put his arm around her shoulders. "I'm so sorry," he said. "I should've thought this through."

"Just tell me what it is, Tucker."

"It's Jace, honey. I'm worried about him." He rubbed her back when she put her head on his shoulder.

"Why?"

"Can't explain it, but I think it has something to do with you."

Jace was losing the ability to differentiate one town from the next. And traveling with rough stock was much different than traveling as a saddle bronc rider. As a rider, he'd pull into town, pay his entry fee, cover a bucker or two, and more often than not, collect a check. Afterwards, he'd grab something to eat and a beer with the other cowboys, get a good night's rest, and in the morning, head to the next town.

Now he pulled in, unloaded bulls and broncs, made sure they were fed and secure, and then he'd head to the motel, get a few hours of sleep, wake up, and tend the stock again.

Other than the towns, the only other thing that changed was his travel partner. Billy, Tucker, and Ben rotated shifts. Ben's brothers were responsible for the bulls and broncs that stayed behind in Crested Butte, and Bullet and Billy's dad covered the ones in Monument. Jace's dad, along with their ranch manager, Yance, handled the stock still in Montana.

The end of the season was in sight, although it wouldn't last long. Once the Professional Rodeo Cowboy Association's, or PRCA, National Finals were over, around mid-December, they'd have three or four weeks before the first events would start up again with the Professional Bull Riders, or PBR.

He didn't remember what it felt like to sleep in his own bed, or eat a home-cooked meal. He did go "home" between events, sometimes to Crested Butte, sometimes to Monument, less often to Montana. And while he did get a home-cooked meal when he was in either place, he was usually so exhausted that he'd unload the broncs and bulls, eat whatever was put in front of him, and then fall asleep on the closest unoccupied bed.

The only good thing about his perpetual exhaustion was that he was often too tired to dream. When he did, his dreams only plagued him.

On the road, driving the endless miles between events, he'd get lost in thought, and his mind would drift back to the night he'd spent with Bree. The memories were so vivid. He could remember how her lips felt, trailing over his bare body, or how it felt to be buried deep inside her. He could picture the look on her face when they made love, and hear her soft moans of pleasure.

When he and Billy were on the road, Billy would go back to the hotel to call Renie after dinner, and Jace would go to the bar. There, he would meet cowboys he knew from his time on the circuit, but being around them made him feel like an old man. Most of them were in their early twenties.

There were plenty of girls, but they were just as young, if not younger. Once or twice, he'd agreed to a dance, but nothing more than that. Holding them in his arms felt wrong. They'd rub themselves against him, and that felt worse. Sometimes he'd get so disgusted he'd walk away, leaving them standing on the dance floor alone.

Eventually he stopped going to bars. When Billy, or Tucker, or Ben went back to the hotel, so did he.

"You're a grouchy *sonuvabitch,* you know that?" Billy said to him one morning at breakfast. Jace didn't answer. He kept eating. "Take a few weeks off. Go home."

"I'm good," he answered.

"Bullshit," Billy snapped.

"Drop it."

When Billy didn't, Jace got up, threw a twenty on the table and walked out of the restaurant.

Billy caught up with him, and Jace felt like punching him.

"We gotta talk about Thanksgiving," Billy said. "We were scheduled in Nebraska, and I've pulled out."

Thanksgiving. As soon as Billy said the word, he knew what was coming next. Crested Butte. The whole family. Not just his family and Billy's, but Bree's family too. Which meant Bree would be there.

If he thought he was miserable now—he'd be willing to take the bulls and broncs to Nebraska alone to avoid spending Thanksgiving in Crested Butte.

It was like a damn Disney movie, being around all of them. He and Bree would be the only two people there who weren't happily married, with at least one child between them and others on the way. It made him sick to his stomach just thinking about it.

Bree *would* be there, wouldn't she? As much as he prayed she wouldn't be, the other part of him, his heart, prayed she would be. He knew, down to the day, how long it had been since he'd seen her. Did she? Did she think about him at all? Or had she moved on?

The last he'd heard, she'd be teaching at the Air Force Academy. That was before the school year started, but he didn't have any reason to believe she would've done something different. If she had, he wouldn't have known. No one talked to him about her. And he didn't ask.

There was one other person he longed to see as much as he longed to see Bree. He hadn't seen Cochran since September. He'd been on the road, and had missed his first birthday.

He could've gone, but that would've meant Billy and Ben would've had to be on the road at the same time, and Jace didn't want them to have to be.

Bree had been there; his mother showed him the pictures. She looked good. In every picture, she had a smile on her face. In most, she was gazing at Cochran, and he could see the love she had for their nephew. But he saw something else: the haunted look. He'd seen it before, back when she first got word that Zack had been killed in action. It would creep in at other times, when she was lost in thought and he knew she was thinking about her husband.

Was anyone paying enough attention to notice? Was Blythe, or her parents, or Lyric? Was Bree haunted in silence? He hoped not.

What was he doing? Why did he always make his way back to worrying about her? She didn't need him. She'd made that clear. And here he was, the idiot who thought he saw something in her eyes that no one else did. She'd get a kick out of that. He had no idea how he would face her on Thanksgiving, after her dismissal of him the last time they were together.

Bree was glad Tucker opened the back door when he saw her coming. Her arms were full, and she didn't want to set any of the packages down in the snow.

"Can you believe this weather?" he asked when she got inside.

"It's either ninety degrees or snowing. Autumn in the Rockies, right? Have you heard whether Monarch Pass is open?"

"Last time I checked, it was, and the weather is supposed to get better, not worse."

"There's Aunt Bree," said Blythe, staying close to Cochran, who ran to his aunt.

He started walking right after his first birthday and spent most of his time either falling or bumping into something. He probably wouldn't have as many scrapes and bruises if he'd walk. Instead, he ran everywhere he went. Tucker laughed about it, but it wasn't Tucker who bandaged up the majority of his boo-boos, amidst heart-wrenching tears.

Bree scooped him up and showered kisses all over his little face, which made him giggle and kiss her back.

"Bwing pwesents?" he asked, eyeing her packages.

Bree sat him down on the floor. "There might be a couple for Cochran, but the rest are for Caden and Willow, okay, baby boy?"

He nodded his head and studied the pile of packages with awe. "Fow Caden and Willow," he repeated, a little pout forming.

Bree set the other boxes aside until she unearthed one with Cochran's name on it and scooted it in his direction.

"This one is for you, sweet boy," she smiled at him.

"Open?"

"Yes, you can open it."

Blythe started to intervene, but Tucker put his hand on her arm. "You know how she is, let her be," he whispered.

Bree looked up at them and was relieved to see her sister and Tucker smiling at her. She loved spoiling her nephew, and would have been devastated if they told her to stop.

"Look, Mama," said Cochran. "Dada twactah." He pointed to the green miniature of Tucker's John Deere tractor. He climbed on and rode it around the kitchen.

"There are as many for him as there are for Caden and Willow. I just want to spread them out over the weekend."

"Aren't you going to be here for Christmas?" Blythe looked as though she might cry.

"Of course I am," answered Bree. "These are *Thanksgiving* presents."

Tucker put his arm around Bree's shoulders and kissed her cheek. "What are we going to do with you?"

"Let me be. Isn't that what you told Blythe to do?"

"Can I put these in the truck?"

"Yes, please, and I've got a bag in the car. I'll follow you out."

Tucker held out his hand for her keys. "I've got it," she heard him say as he walked out the back door and closed it behind him.

"I have news," Blythe said when Bree turned back around.

"Yeah? What's that?"

"Jace is coming."

Bree took a deep breath. This wasn't unexpected news. She was glad he was. She hated to think he might not spend Thanksgiving with his family. Especially if his not doing so had anything to do with her. That would've broken her heart.

"There's more…"

Oh, no. Was he bringing someone with him? Why hadn't she thought of that possibility? And she was here already; it wasn't as though she could suddenly change her mind about going.

"I just thought you should know, since you're going to be in the car with us for five hours, and we might have to stop a lot."

"What?" She hadn't been listening. What was Blythe talking about?

"It's early, but I took a test this morning, and it's official. I'm pregnant again."

Bree let out a cry of glee and put her arms around her sister. "Oh, Blythe, that's wonderful. I'm so happy for you. And for me—another baby to spoil!"

Bree looked away, hoping that, when she looked back, the look of pity on Blythe's face would be gone. If this was her destiny, to be the world's greatest aunt instead of a mother herself, so be it. No amount of pity would change the cards she was dealt.

14

Bree sat in Liv and Ben's kitchen and looked out at the view of the ranch. Everyone had something to do but her. Until their mamas put them down for naps, Bree had had the babies to play with, but now that they were sleeping, she didn't know what to do with herself.

Blythe was resting. The five-hour drive from Monument to Crested Butte wore her out. Tucker and Ben were out in the barn, tending to the livestock. She had no idea where Liv and Renie had disappeared to, and didn't know when her parents were arriving.

She pulled her iPad out of her bag and opened an e-book, but she couldn't focus enough to read. No one had said when Jace and his parents would be arriving, and she didn't want to ask. The thought that they might be driving into the ranch at any moment was an inescapable distraction.

"There you are," said Liv, joining her in the kitchen.

"Where was I supposed to be?"

"Nowhere. It was so quiet I thought maybe you were resting too."

"No," Bree answered wistfully. "I have more time to rest than you all do."

"Be careful what you wish for," Liv winked.

"Was I wishing for something?"

"Have you talked to Jace?"

Bree didn't appreciate Liv's implied segue between wishing for something and asking her about Jace. In fact, it annoyed her.

"I don't have any reason to talk to Jace." Bree stood and slammed the cover closed on her iPad.

Liv rested her hand on Bree's shoulder. "Yes, you do. If nothing else, the two of you are friends. I know you care about him, and I also know he cares about you. If there are two people who need to talk to one another, it's you and Jace."

"There's something you should know, Liv. I accepted your challenge that night. I walked over to the Villa, to join Jace for dinner. He was otherwise engaged, chatting up a pretty girl at the bar. As for being friends, Jace Rice is my brother-in-law. He's not my friend."

"You know it isn't that simple. As for what you saw that night, there is always the possibility that it wasn't what it seemed. I stand by what I said a minute ago—you and Jace care about each other, and you do need to talk."

Liv was grinning. *Grinning!*

"You'll see for yourself soon enough. Whatever you're picturing between Jace and me exists solely in your imagination."

"I'm not the only one who sees it, Bree."

"Soon you'll all realize there isn't anything to see." And when they did, maybe they'd stop pestering her about him.

She hoped they weren't doing the same thing to him.

"I hope you're hungry. We're going to a wonderful new place in town, called the Sunflower. It's a farm-to-table restaurant."

She wasn't hungry, and she had no interest in going along. "I'll stay here, if you don't mind."

"I do mind." Liv pulled Bree back over to the table. "Sit."

Bree sat.

"I'm not letting you hide out this weekend."

"Just because I don't want to go to dinner doesn't mean I'm hiding out."

"Does your mother let you get away with this crap? Because I can tell you, if I was spewing the bullshit you are right now, she'd be all over me about it."

Bree looked up at Liv, and saw she was smiling again.

"I'm glad you think this is funny—you with your idyllic life, married to a man who thinks you walk on water. And your grown, beautiful, also happily-married daughter," she waved her hands around. "Not to mention all this. It's easy to cajole me when you have it all, isn't it, Liv? How about you leave me alone instead, and while you are, remember what the last couple of years have been like for me."

Bree's eyes filled with tears, and she wished she could take back every ridiculous word that had just come out of her mouth, but it was too late.

"I'm sorry, Bree, but the last person who is going to indulge your self-pity is me. I've lived the life you're living now for twenty years. I won't sit back and watch you live it for half as long."

"It was different for you."

Liv raised her eyebrows. "Please, elaborate."

"You had Renie."

"Ah, I see. I wasn't all alone."

Bree stared out the window.

"It changed for me when Renie went to college. I suppose that was when I really started feeling sorry for myself. I was a forty-year-old woman, with what looked like a very dull life ahead of me. That's what your mother saw, a woman believing her life was over. Can you imagine the tragedy that would have been?"

Bree nodded her head but still hadn't turned to look at Liv.

"The only thing worse I can imagine is a twenty-seven-year-old woman believing her life is over, when really, it has barely begun."

"Let me ask you this. Be honest. If Ben died today, would you start over? Would you put yourself out there, believing you were going to find someone else?"

Liv didn't answer right away. Instead she walked into the kitchen and poured herself a glass of wine.

"It would be very difficult to think I could find someone after Ben. You're right about that. But from the outside, looking in, I see things so differently. I understand your mother's frustration with me, why she pushed me so hard to get back out there and live a life less isolated. Watching you, I want to grab you by the shoulders and shake some sense into you."

"I need more time," Bree said quietly.

Liv put her arm around Bree's shoulders. "I know, sweetheart. Just be careful how much *more* turns into."

The place where they went for dinner wasn't very big. When they walked in, Bree wondered if they would have room to accommodate everyone in their party. When she overheard one of the owners welcome Liv and Ben, and then saw him turn the open sign to closed, she realized theirs would be a private party.

"They opened, tonight, just for us," Liv explained. "They're usually closed between mid-October and Thanksgiving."

"Nice of them," Bree murmured.

"It's that kind of place," Liv answered. "Crested Butte I mean. It's one of the reasons I love it so much. No matter where we go, we know everyone, and they know us. It's kind of like Monument."

Bree understood what Liv was saying, but didn't necessarily love it, the way she did. More often than not, Bree wished she could be anonymous, invisible, even. She wanted to go to the grocery store, or out for a cup of coffee, and not have anyone recognize her, or start a conversation with her, or ask how she was.

"Where's that handsome brother of yours tonight?" she overheard the pretty blonde who'd just walked in ask Tucker. The woman looked familiar, but Bree couldn't place her.

She wasn't able to hear Tucker's response, and was glad. Thank God Jace wasn't there, and she didn't have to endure the humiliation of seeing him with another woman. She turned around and willed the evening to be over quickly, so she could escape back to the privacy of Liv and Ben's place.

Bree felt the cold air when the door opened. "Speak of the devil," she heard Tucker say.

He was here.

"How's it feel to be off the road for a few days?" Ben greeted Jace. "If anyone's earned it, you have."

"Yeah, yeah, whatever. I'm not workin' any harder than anyone else," Jace grunted.

She couldn't help herself; she had to turn around and look at him. Jace shrugged off his coat, and Bree watched as the pretty blonde leaned in and whispered something in his ear. It made them both smile. Suddenly she realized where she knew the woman from. She was the one who had left with Jace that night at the Villa.

When Bree stood, she almost knocked the table over. She stomped off toward the back of the restaurant where she hoped she'd find a back door. There would be cab service in Crested Butte, wouldn't there?

No luck on a back door, but there was a restroom she could hide out in for a little while at least, until someone else needed to use it.

If only she hadn't agreed to come to Crested Butte for Thanksgiving. It wasn't as though she had other options, but the way she was feeling, staying home alone would've felt better than this did.

Too soon, she heard a soft rap on the door.

"Bree, are you okay?"

Dammit. What was Jace doing on the other side of the door?

"Be right out," she said softly, hoping that, when she opened the door, he would be back in the midst of his family and had forgotten she was there. Instead, when she opened the door, he was leaning against the wall, arms crossed in front of him.

"Hi, Jace." She tried to scoot past him to let him have access to the restroom.

"Hey, wait," he said and grabbed her arm. "Where are you runnin' off to so quick?"

"I, uh, figured you were, uh, waiting to use the, uh…"

"No, Bree," he leaned in close to her. "I was waiting to say hello to you. You skedaddled back here so fast, I didn't have a chance to speak to you when I came in."

"Well, now you have. Shall we go back and join the others?" She tried to wrench her arm away from him, but he held on tight.

"Wait a minute."

"What, Jace?"

"Come here," he pulled her back, closer to him. "How about a hug for starters?"

He hugged her, but she did not return his embrace.

"It seems there's someone else here anxious to hug you, Jace. Why don't you trap her in the hallway instead of me?"

Rather than answer, he pulled her close again and covered her lips with his.

Bree wanted to resist him, but it was impossible to. She'd never been able to resist him.

"Oh, sorry—"

Bree broke their kiss in time to see the blonde turn and walk in the other direction.

"Bet you didn't want her to see that."

Jace pulled back and looked into Bree's eyes but wouldn't release his grip on her. "What's that mean?"

"She's been waiting for you to get here, and don't think I missed the exchange between the two of you when you arrived."

"Sounds like somebody's jealous," he nuzzled her hair and breathed in deeply. "Bree," he sighed.

"Stop it." She tried to push him away, but he was determined not to let her go.

"Come here," he said and pulled her around the corner, and out to the patio.

"Oh, sure, here's the back door. I couldn't have found it earlier," she muttered.

"What's that?"

"An escape, a way out, so I didn't have to witness the reunion between you and your hookup girl." Her cheeks flushed as she said it.

"My hookup girl? I thought you were my hookup girl." He brushed his lips over hers. He had her backed up against the outside wall, his hands on either side of her. "Let's see…the last time you and I were together, we hooked up pretty good, from what I remember." Right before she'd let him know that was all he was good for.

"I figured, with both of us stayin' up at Ben's, it'd be a good opportunity for me to scratch any itches you might be feelin'."

He tried to kiss her again, but she managed to twist away from him. "Are you serious?"

"You know me, Bree. Good ol' cowboy, ready and willin' to take care of you. Somebody you don't need to worry about having dinner with afterwards."

He saw her eyes fill with tears before she swung the door open and stormed back inside.

He could hear the words coming out of his own mouth, and even he couldn't believe he was saying them. What was wrong with him?

He walked in behind her and tried to stop her before she got into the dining room, but he was too late. She'd grabbed her coat and was talking to her mother and Liv. He watched her walk out the front door. Her father followed.

"That was fast." Billy stood in front of Jace. "Gotta be some kind of record. You weren't here five minutes before you got her so mad she left."

"Leave me the hell alone, Patterson."

"Yep, you got your ways; I got mine. Course mine are workin' a lot better than yours are. For example, take a look at that pretty girl." Billy motioned to where Renie stood by the front window. "She's carryin' my baby, more than ready to welcome me into those warm arms every night."

"Shut up," Jace answered.

"Wanna know what I'd do?"

"Not particularly, but I get the impression you're gonna tell me anyway."

"Follow her."

Jace stood his ground.

"Warm arms, every night, that's what I got. Yep, I'm a lucky man."

"Bree isn't interested in me. There's the difference. No point in me chasing after somebody who isn't interested in being caught."

"What's going on?" Mark asked Bree when they got outside.

"I'm not feeling very well, Dad. Can I take your truck? Can you and mom ride home with someone else?"

"Sure, but if you aren't feeling well—"

"Now, Dad, please. Just give me the keys." Bree could see Jace through the windows of the restaurant. He was talking to Billy, but there was still a chance he'd try to follow her. She had to be gone if he did.

Her dad followed her gaze, reached into his pocket, and handed her his keys. "Turn left at the corner." He pointed north on Elk Avenue. "It's about halfway up the second block."

"Thanks," she waved as she broke into a run in the direction he pointed her in.

"Dammit," Jace growled when he got outside.

Mark put his hand on his arm. "Let her go," he said before he went back inside.

Bree swore when she saw the red flashing lights in the rear-view mirror. She always forgot about the ridiculous speed limit in downtown Crested Butte. Was it even possible to drive fifteen miles per hour? She had to have been going three times that fast.

"License and registration," the police officer said without looking at her when she rolled down the window. He glanced up just before she turned her head to dig through her purse.

"Wait," he said. "Are you okay?"

This would be worse. Not only was she speeding, she'd also been crying. He'd probably add public endangerment to her speeding ticket.

"Ma'am, I asked you a question. Are you okay?"

Bree wiped her tears away with the back of her hand. "I'm okay. Sorry, Officer, uh, Akerman. I..." What could she say? She'd just been propositioned by a man she'd already slept with, but the way he talked to her made her cry?

"Listen," he said. "I'm not going to write you a ticket tonight, but I don't think you should be driving when you're upset."

She brushed at her tears again, the ones she couldn't seem to stop, and opened the storage compartment between the two front seats. Her mom would have tissues stored in there, wouldn't she?

Bree found a pack, pulled one out and blew her nose. When she looked back at the policeman, he was smiling.

"I'm about to take a break for dinner. Why don't you join me?"

"Uh, well—"

"I could insist, you know. Either have dinner with me, take a few minutes to collect yourself, or I'll write the ticket after all, but that's probably a federal crime.

How 'bout you just join me, and neither one of us will get in trouble?" He winked at her.

"You are a policeman. I mean, that looks like an official police car," she muttered.

He pointed in the direction of Elk Avenue. "I'm gonna pull around your truck and park over there, behind that building. I'm hoping you'll follow me and have dinner with me. If not, I'll understand."

Bree watched in the side mirror as he got back in the police car, turned off the swirling red lights, and drove toward the building he'd pointed at. She followed.

There were two open spots, so she pulled in next to him. She looked around to make sure there weren't any "no parking" signs she'd be in violation of. When she opened her door, he was standing next to it.

"Hope I didn't startle you." He held out his hand to help her out of the truck. "My name is Kaleb, by the way."

"Nice to meet you. Bree Fox," she took his hand and climbed out of the truck.

"Hope this place is okay with you. Food is pretty good."

She looked up and saw they were going into a place called the Company Store.

"It's not that anymore," he pointed. "It's called the Secret Stash now. Pretty good pizzas, or salads if you're, ya know, more health conscious."

The hostess led them to a booth. Kaleb excused himself just as she sat down. "Be right back," he said.

Bree studied the menu. The last thing she expected to be was hungry, but she was suddenly famished. She wondered what the people at the other tables would think, when Kaleb came back, about her having dinner with a cop. She supposed they had to eat too, right?

She almost didn't recognize him when he did come back. "Uh, you changed your clothes."

"I wasn't completely honest…" He looked so sheepish Bree couldn't help but smile.

"That doesn't sound good coming from a policeman. I mean, are you a policeman?"

"Yeah, I was honest about that part. It's the dinner break part that wasn't the complete truth. I'm actually done for the night. I thought, if I told you that, it might scare you off."

"And you just happen to keep a change of clothes here, at the restaurant? I have to admit, I'm beginning to get a little scared," she laughed.

He laughed too. "It isn't lookin' too good, is it? My sister owns this place, and I bartend sometimes. I keep a change of clothes here so I don't have to drive home in between my shifts if time is tight."

"Are you bartending tonight?"

"Nope. I'm off for the rest of the weekend actually. Policing and bartending."

"Oh."

"I just keep digging myself deeper, don't I?"

Bree laughed again. "You're okay. I'm guessing just about everybody in here tonight knows you. Am I right about that?"

"Maybe one or two don't," he smiled.

"Nobody tried to catch my attention and warn me off while you were changing, so I suppose I'm safe enough."

"Good. Now that we've settled I pose no threat, tell me more about yourself, Bree Fox."

They shared a pizza and a pitcher of beer. At first Bree was hesitant to have a drink, but Kaleb promised he'd get her back to the ranch. He'd have someone follow with her truck if necessary.

"Do you know where the ranch is?"

"Of course I do. Everybody knows the Flying R. Everybody knows the Rice family for that matter."

"My family and the Rice family are kind of intertwined. My sister is married to Tucker."

"Can't say I know Tucker. I do know Matt, Will, and Ben though."

"My mom and Ben's wife are best friends. They have been since I was nine years old."

"You mean Liv? She's great. Who's your mom?"

"Her name is Paige. Paige Cochran."

"And your dad is…Mark Cochran?"

"That would be him."

"But you're Bree Fox." He reached over and touched her left hand.

"I was married," she began.

Kaleb waited for her to continue.

"My husband was killed in Afghanistan."

The expression on his face changed to one Bree was familiar with. "I'm so sorry," he said.

"Thanks," she answered. "I really don't like to talk about it. If you don't mind."

"Of course I don't mind. I guess you're in town for Thanksgiving. Big gathering over at the Flying R?"

This time, Bree's expression changed. She didn't want to talk about Thanksgiving either. Kaleb was going to quickly figure out he was the normal one between the two of them. Bree was a walking, talking hot mess.

15

They talked through pizza, and then dessert. Bree was just about to suggest it was time for her to go home when Kaleb stood.

"Come downstairs with me," he said, pulling her by the hand.

"What's down there?"

"It's called the Red Room," he raised his eyebrows when he said it, and Bree laughed.

"It's part of the Stash. Sort of. It's another restaurant, more of a bar, though. My sister owns it now too, but it used to belong to Matt Rice. It was a sushi place."

"Lobar?"

"That's it. Have you been there?"

"Sure, once or twice. I didn't realize Matt sold it."

"From what I hear the Rices are getting heavy into rough stock contracting, and Matt didn't have the time it takes to run a restaurant anymore."

"Do they still have The Goat?" Bree loved going to the bar, especially when Ben's band, CB Rice, played.

"I don't think they'll ever sell it. It's been in their family forever. That place has been around so long it practically runs itself."

Kaleb swept the heavy brocade drapery, at the bottom of the stairs, aside, and Bree couldn't believe her eyes. The space had been transformed, and it was beautiful.

"My sister hand-beaded the bar with one of her friends. It took her about two hundred hours to do it."

Bree looked closer. It was magnificent. The entire front length of the long bar was intricately beaded on top of the same brocade fabric the draperies were made from.

There were symbols and shapes, even names, worked into the pattern.

Kaleb pointed to one. "This guy, Novak, was a buddy of ours who died in an avalanche. And here," he pointed to another name, "'Eleanor,' that's our mother's name."

"It's so beautiful." Bree was tempted to run her fingers over the beading, but resisted.

Kaleb took her hand and led her away from the bar. "Let's sit back here," he said.

There was a fireplace surrounded by cushions in the back room.

"Looks comfy." Bree wondered how many times he'd refilled her beer over dinner. She'd lost count. She sunk down onto the bench seat and closed her eyes.

Kaleb sat next to her and put his arm around her shoulders.

"You look relaxed," he murmured.

"Hmm? Yes, I am relaxed. Which I didn't think was possible earlier."

"And less sad," Kaleb leaned closer. "Anything you want to talk about?"

"No, but it wasn't anything important. I was being silly. Goes to show how unimportant it was, considering I'd all but forgotten it."

"I'm glad to hear it."

Kaleb tightened the arm he had around her shoulders, and pulled her closer to him. With his other hand, he caressed her face and looked into her eyes. "I want to kiss you, Bree."

Instead of answering, she leaned forward and kissed him. Her head was swirling as she opened her mouth under his. This was so unexpected, but, oh, so welcome. She rested her hands against Kaleb's chest, loving the hardness of his body beneath the sweater he'd changed into earlier. The police officer clearly took good care of himself. Bree ran her hands over his strong shoulders and down his powerful arms.

She leaned back, just slightly, against the cushion, and Kaleb followed, the weight of his body, resting against hers.

"*What the hell?*"

Bree jerked away from Kaleb and looked up into Jace's eyes.

"*Bree? What the hell?*" he said again.

She wiped the back of her hand across her lips and looked at Kaleb.

"Someone you know?" he whispered softly. He didn't look bothered by Jace's outburst. In fact, he had a grin on his face.

"Yeah, I know him."

"Big brother?"

"Uh, no."

"Oh, sorry to hear that." Kaleb's grin widened.

Jace hadn't moved. His hands were on his waist, and he was staring at them. Kaleb moved away from Bree and stood.

"Kaleb Akerman," he said, extending his hand to Jace.

Jace didn't respond.

"And you are?" Kaleb asked.

"Jace Rice," he spat out between clenched teeth. "How the hell do you know Bree?"

Kaleb turned and looked back at Bree, his smile broadening. "I had to arrest Bree, earlier this evening, for speeding. And here, in Crested Butte, we take beautiful women to dinner rather than to jail."

Jace looked confused. And pissed. Bree couldn't stop herself from giggling.

"He's kidding. Well, sort of. I mean, he did pull me over for speeding." Bree giggled more.

"Jace, did you find her?" she heard someone say. The blonde from earlier came out from behind him.

"Bree? I'm going to ask one more time. What the hell is going on?"

She shrugged and closed her eyes. When she did, her body weaved a little, landing her up against Kaleb.

A man who also looked familiar stood next to the blonde. "I think she's drunk," he said to Jace.

Who were all these people, and why did they care whether she was drunk or not?

Bree's head started to feel too heavy to hold up, and she was overly warm. Maybe if she moved away from the fire a little bit. No, that wasn't helping any. Fresh air—that might help. When she stood, she was glad Kaleb was still as close as he'd been. She gripped his shoulder in an effort to get the room to stop spinning. It didn't work. She weaved again, and Kaleb pulled her back down onto the cushions. Except, instead of landing on a cushion, she landed on his lap. He held her tight, and it felt so good. She rested her head against his shoulder.

"How the hell much did you give her to drink?" she heard Jace growl through her haze of temporary happiness.

"Go away, Jace," she heard herself say. "Go back to Blondie over there, and jus' leave me alone."

"Did you hear that? She's slurring her words."

She opened her eyes and saw Jace moving closer to her.

"I'm taking her home," he said, trying to push Kaleb away.

"Uh, no. You're not." Kaleb put one arm under her knees and the one around her shoulders tightened. He picked her up as though she didn't weigh a thing.

The room was spinning again, just a little, so she closed her eyes and rested her head on Kaleb's shoulder.

"Give her to me," she heard Jace demand.

"Jace—" That must have been the blonde, thought Bree. Serves the bitch right. That made her giggle again.

"Bree, are you okay?" That was Jace's voice.

No, she wasn't okay. At least not with him. Kaleb? He was another story. She was perfectly okay with Kaleb. Maybe if Jace went away, Kaleb would kiss her again. She'd like that. She moved her head just enough that her lips could brush against Kaleb's neck. She kissed him there and heard him take a deep breath.

Instead of moving from where they were standing, Kaleb sat back down. That was unexpected, but Bree didn't care.

He turned his head and kissed her again. Yes, that was what she wanted. She kissed him back. When she thought he might pull away, she put her hands on each side of his face to hold him where he was.

"Jace, what do you want to do?"

That sounded like the blonde again. Maybe she'd be able to get Jace to leave. And if he left, Kaleb might keep kissing her. In the meantime, she'd rest her head on his shoulder again. Maybe close her eyes and take a little nap while they waited for Jace to leave.

"Look at her," Jace shouted. "She's passed out. What did you do, drug her?" He was fighting mad now. He'd never seen Bree have more than a drink or two. Now here she was, passed out in the arms of a stranger. What had happened in the last couple of hours?

"Hey, bro," a woman pushed passed Jace. "What ya got goin' on here?"

"Nothing, Kalie. I think the altitude and alcohol hit her a little hard."

"See it every day, don't we? Cab is out front. Do you know where she's staying?"

"She's staying with me," Jace stepped forward. "I'll get her home."

"The hell, you will," answered Kaleb. "You're welcome to follow, but I'll be taking Bree home, and I'll be the one to make sure she gets there safe and sound."

"Oh, Jesus," Kalie groaned. "Just get out of here before this turns into something more than it needs to. And you," she said to Jace, "I want to talk to you for a minute."

Jace didn't have much choice other than to follow her, since she had a death grip on his arm.

"I don't know who you are, but I don't put up with people causing trouble in my bar."

Ben walked up behind Jace. "Hey, Kalie, what's goin' on?"

"Do you know this guy?"

"Sure do. This is my cousin, Jace." Ben turned to Jace. "Jace, meet Kalie Akerman. She bought this place from Matt."

Jace didn't care who bought what from anyone. He turned to look for Bree, and didn't see her or the guy who'd said he was a cop. He bolted for the door, trying to catch them, but when he got to the top of the stairs, he saw the cab driving away. His truck wasn't very far, so he ran toward it. Right before he jumped in, he turned and looked back across the street.

"Go," shouted Ty. "Ben will give us a ride back to the ranch."

"Thanks, Ty, and sorry about this." Jace closed the door and sped off in the direction he'd seen the cab go in.

Bree's head was throbbing. She slowly opened her eyes and looked around the room. It took her a minute to figure out where she was, until she saw the framed photos of Ben's son Jake, sitting next to his baseball trophies.

The room was mostly dark, but even the small amount of light shining through the slats of the blinds hurt her eyes. She'd get up to close them, but she was afraid she'd get sick to her stomach if she tried to stand.

She closed her eyes tightly and tried to recall what had happened the night before. She remembered bits and pieces...getting pulled over...Kaleb asking her to have dinner with him.

Kaleb. Oh, he was handsome. She wondered what had happened to him. She had a vague recollection of him carrying her inside, whispering to her the whole time.

"I got you, baby," he'd said.

Had she dreamed it? She hoped not. If she had, it might mean she dreamed kissing him, and that part, she wanted to be real. He was a good kisser. She'd like to kiss him again.

She heard a knock at the door and opened her eyes again. "Go away," she answered.

The door opened and Blythe walked in. "Oh no, it's worse than we thought." When Blythe laughed, whoever was behind her, laughed too.

Bree put her hands over her ears. "Do you mind? First you bang on the door, now you're screeching at me. Can't you just go away?"

Lyric came around Blythe. "You're bad off, ain't you, Bree? Bangin'? We hardly even tapped on the door."

"Stop your cackling," Bree implored.

"Here," a voice said. Bree opened her eyes and saw her mother standing over her.

She looked at the glass her mom was trying to hand her. "What is that?"

"Dad's secret recipe hangover cure."

"What's in it?"

"Oh, baby," her mother laughed. "You don't want to know. Drink it down, and give it a half hour or so. Try to rest, and I'll come back to check on you later. Now drink."

Paige pushed the glass in Bree's direction. If she drank that, she'd throw up for sure. She shook her head.

"Trust me, baby," her mother pushed. "If you can get it down, you'll feel a thousand times better than you will otherwise."

Her mom was almost always right, and considering she felt as though she was going to die, a thousand times better than dying sounded pretty good. She plugged her nose and guzzled the drink without taking a breath. Her stomach churned and growled, but after a minute or two, she didn't feel as though she needed to throw up.

"We'll leave you now." Her mom was shooing Blythe and Lyric out of the room. "Get some rest, baby."

"Thanks, Mom," Bree whispered just before she drifted back to sleep.

When she woke, her mother was sitting on the side of the bed.

"Hi," she said when Bree opened her eyes.

"Hi. What time is it?"

"A little after two. You slept longer than I thought you would."

Bree sat up. Too quickly. And then lay back down.

"Two? Isn't dinner in a half hour? I need to get up. But, oh, God, I don't think I can."

"No one expects you to, sweetheart. We've all missed a Thanksgiving or two in our lifetime. This year is your turn."

"Oh no, I can't believe it. I'm mortified." Bree rolled over and put her head in the pillow.

Paige rubbed her back. "Don't be, everyone has been where you are at least once. Get some more rest, and tomorrow, you can have leftovers."

"Does everyone think I'm beyond pathetic?"

"No, Bree. Everyone thinks you had too much to drink last night. And as soon as you're ready, they all want to know about the mountain man who so gallantly delivered you home last night."

Bree peeked up at her mom. "Everyone?"

"No, sweetheart, not everyone. If there is anyone more miserable than you are today, it's Jace. His ailment doesn't appear to be a hangover. His is more, uh, the effects of fury."

"Fury?" Bree gasped.

"After the third person asked him if he knew the man who brought you home, yeah, it turned to fury."

As perverse as it felt, knowing Jace was furious, Bree was able to drift back to sleep with a smile on her face.

"You didn't see her," Jace said to Blythe. "She was so drunk she passed out."

Blythe studied him, but didn't answer.

He leaned forward. "Did you hear me?"

"I heard you, Jace, and you can lower your voice. I'm sitting right next to you."

"Okay, so, like I said, she was really drunk."

"You upset her, and she reacted."

"Wait. I upset her? I did? How did this become my fault?"

"Telling her she was your hookup girl? Asking her if you could scratch her itch? Bet you didn't think anyone heard you, but I did."

He put his elbows on the table and his head in his hands. "I don't know what got into me. I was an asshole. I admit it."

Blythe got up so quickly, Jace had to grab her chair before it tipped all the way over and hit the floor.

"Where are you going?"

"Anywhere you aren't."

"Blythe, c'mon. I'm trying to talk to you about Bree."

"I don't feel like talking to you, Jace."

He followed Blythe into the other room. "Wait. Please, Blythe. I'm sorry."

When she sat down on the sofa in front of the fireplace, he sat next to her.

"I knew this was going to be a rough weekend," she said. "But I had no idea it would start out this badly."

Jace didn't know what to say. He knew it would be awkward, but this was way beyond that.

"When did you get here?" Jace kept his voice soft, hoping he'd be able to get Blythe to forgive him. He needed her to talk to him.

"Yesterday morning."

"Do you know the guy she was with?"

Blythe closed her eyes. "No, I don't, but Ben does."

"Is he really a cop?"

"Yep. Ben said he and his sister own property in Crested Butte, too. Something about a restaurant."

"Yeah, I met her last night too. I think she was about to threaten me within an inch of my life, but then Ben stepped in."

Blythe raised her eyebrows.

"How is she?"

"Really hungover. And embarrassed."

"She didn't want to eat?"

Bree hadn't been at the table when the rest of the family had Thanksgiving dinner. No one had said anything about her absence. At the time, he thought maybe he should've skipped dinner too.

"I don't think she had much of an appetite."

Jace leaned forward and put his head in his hands. "What have I done?"

Blythe patted his back. "I think she's more embarrassed than anything else."

"She shouldn't be. It's my fault. You're right."

"Wait a minute. I didn't say it was your fault. I said you upset her and she reacted. She's responsible for her own behavior, Jace."

"What's the difference, Blythe? If I hadn't said what I did, she wouldn't have ended up shit-faced last night."

"And if you weren't torn up about her, you wouldn't have said it in the first place."

"Hi, sweetie. How are you feeling?"

Bree was leaning against the wall by the fireplace. She had on a Crested Butte sweatshirt that was at least three sizes too big for her, and what looked like pajama bottoms. Her face was pale, which made the circles under her eyes look darker. He wanted to smooth her hair back from her face and help her back downstairs, to bed. She looked as though she could use several more hours of sleep.

"I'm sorry. I didn't realize—"

"Wait, don't go." Jace jumped up and followed her.

She stopped in the kitchen. "I can't do this now, Jace. Can we, please, talk tomorrow instead?"

What could he say? She looked green, and her eyes filled with tears. He wanted to talk to her, but he couldn't force her to do it now.

"Sure, darlin'," he leaned in and kissed her forehead. "You go get some sleep."

When Jace came back in the other room, Blythe was studying him.

"I've never seen her like this," she sighed.

"Losing someone is hard. I can't imagine how hard when it's someone you expected to spend your life with."

"I think this is more you than Zack."

"Please, don't say that."

"She doesn't know how to handle your relationship."

"What relationship? From where I sit, your sister doesn't want much to do with me. It's been true since the day we met. Every so often, the ice melts enough that she leans on me. And then she comes to her senses again."

"You make it sound as though she's using you. She isn't like that."

"You've watched it, Blythe. You even warned me. I'm a warm body when she needs one next to her. Otherwise, I don't measure up to Bree's standards."

"Why do you let yourself get into these situations?"

"So you agree?"

"Not completely, but watching what's going on with the two of you breaks my heart."

Jace turned so he could look in Blythe's eyes. "Who does your heart break for? Her or me?"

"For both of you."

Jace nodded his head, stood, and walked out the front door. He didn't know where he was going, he just knew he didn't want to spend the night in the same house as Bree Fox.

16

She must have lost her mind. Here she was, at another Rice family night out. This time her mom and dad had forced her to go along. Given she missed Thanksgiving dinner, they insisted she join the family gathering Liv and Ben were hosting at the ski area.

Since the weather was unseasonably warm, Liv made arrangements to close off Mountaineer Square, at the base of the mountain, for a private party. They'd set tables around the open fire pit, surrounded by heat lamps so they'd be warm when the sun set.

The party wasn't limited to family, Ben and Liv invited friends from town too. Bree was surprised to see Kaleb and his sister walk up and say hello to Ben.

"How are you doing?" her dad asked.

"Better. Not that I plan to drink anything other than water tonight."

"Good plan." He put his arm around her shoulders. "I'm glad your mom talked you into coming."

"That's one way to put it. Some of the credit swings your way too."

"Haven't seen the cowboy tonight. In fact, I haven't seen him all day."

"The cowboy? As if there's only one? We're surrounded by cowboys." Bree surveyed the crowd. Most of the men, her father included, wore cowboy hats and boots. It wasn't just their attire either. They were cowboys by profession. Her father didn't fit in that category, but most of the others did.

"Jace."

"I know who you meant, Dad. I haven't seen him either." She hoped he wouldn't be here tonight. It might be selfish of her, but the last time she and Jace were at the same place at the same time, it hadn't ended well for her.

So far she'd managed to avoid Kaleb. She didn't plan to all night, she just didn't want him to get the impression he was her date. Every so often their eyes would meet, and she'd smile, or wave, and then walk in the other direction, or join another conversation.

As long as Jace Rice didn't show up tonight, she might be able to get through the evening without embarrassing herself for the third time that weekend. She crossed her fingers and said a silent prayer. It wouldn't hurt to cover both bases tonight—superstitious and otherwise.

Minutes later, Jace's truck pulled up, and he wasn't alone. There, in the front seat of his truck, was the blonde. Maybe her plan to avoid alcohol hadn't been such a good one.

It was too soon for this scene to be playing out again. She found herself looking for another escape route. Would someone at the front desk of the lodge be able to call her a cab?

When she turned back around, Jace was standing behind her.

"Hi, uh, Jace." She tried to walk around him.

"Hey, wait," he said and grabbed her arm. "Where are you runnin' off to?"

"I can't do this, Jace. I can't believe you brought a date."

"A date? What are you talking about?"

"Please, don't do this."

Jace looked out at the crowd on the square. "I'm here with my family, and your family. And you."

"What about—" Bree stopped herself. She didn't want to ask who had been in the truck with him when he pulled up. She'd find out soon enough, and not give him the satisfaction of knowing she cared as much as she did.

"What about who, darlin'?"

"Never mind." She looked down at his hand, which still held her arm. "Please, let me go."

Rather than let go, Jace pulled her closer—close enough to kiss her.

Out of the corner of her eye, Bree saw the blonde, walking toward the fire pit. "Her," she said, pointing.

"Who?" he looked into the crowd of people. "I don't know who you're talking about."

"The blonde." Bree cringed at the sound of her own voice. "Listen, this isn't any of my business, at least I don't want it to be."

"That blonde? The one wearing the black leather jacket?"

Bree looked again. "Yes, that blonde."

"Do you see the guy sitting in the chair beside her?"

"What about him?"

"That's her husband, Ty Rinaldo. Didn't you meet them at Patterson Ranch the night we all had dinner there?"

The man did look familiar. She didn't remember ever meeting the woman.

"Oh, wait, she wasn't there. She was at dinner the next night. The night you refused to join us."

"You mean she's…"

"Ty's wife? Yep. Come on, I'll introduce you." Jace took Bree's hand and walked toward the fire pit.

"No, wait." She pulled her hand back. "I'd rather not."

Jace looked over and saw Kaleb-the-cop sitting on the other side of the fire pit. "Yeah, me either. Wanna get outta here?"

Bree hesitated, but when she nodded her head, Jace led her to the parking area.

"Where are we going?" she asked when he drove into town and parked on a side street just off the main drag.

"You'll see." He opened the door. Bree jumped out, and he took her hand. "It won't be too crowded in here yet," he said. "And we can talk."

"What is this place?"

"It's called the Dogwood Cocktail Cabin." Jace led her inside and to a table in the corner.

They hadn't yet sat down when a pretty woman approached them. "Is that Jace Rice?"

He felt Bree stiffen.

"How the hell are you, cowboy?" When the woman threw her arms around Jace's neck, Bree tried to pull away, but he wouldn't let go of her hand.

"Ayla," he said, "have you met Bree Fox?"

The woman extended her hand. "I don't think so, but you look familiar."

"Bree's sister is married to Tucker."

The woman's eyes wandered to where Jace had a firm grip on Bree's hand. She looked back up at Jace and smiled, then turned and winked at Bree.

Bree cringed and tried again to pull away.

"Huh uh." He leaned closer and whispered in her ear. "Ayla and her husband are *both* good friends of mine."

Bree rolled her eyes as Jace moved so she could slide into the booth first, letting him trap her there.

Jace spoke to Ayla and pointed at the menu. "She'll have this, and how 'bout you bring me one of these."

"What if I didn't want a drink?" she asked when Ayla walked away.

"You do."

"You're such an arrogant asshole sometimes—"

Jace stopped her from talking by covering her lips with his. "I missed you, Bree," he breathed.

She pushed against him. "I thought you wanted to talk."

Now that he had her this close, talking was the last thing he wanted to do, but he had to. He had a lot he needed to say.

"I'm mad at you," he began. Probably not the best approach, but the only place he could think to start.

"You're mad at me? Really?"

He expected to see anger in her eyes, instead he saw hurt.

"Do you want to know why I'm mad at you?"

"You're not giving me any choice, are you?"

"I'm mad at you because you wouldn't go to dinner that night."

"I did go."

"What do you mean? I was there, and you, were not."

"Yeah, actually I was. I felt bad about saying no, so I walked over to the restaurant. When I walked in, you were at the bar, talking to someone. So I left."

He didn't remember talking to anyone that night, other than Ty's wife. *Oh.* "You saw me talking to Nancy."

"I don't know who Nancy is."

"Ty's wife." He stroked her cheek with his finger. "I wish I'd known you were there."

"Here you go," Ayla interrupted, setting their drinks on the table.

"I really don't want to drink tonight, Jace. I—"

"No alcohol."

"Huh?"

"There isn't any alcohol in these drinks, is there Ayla?"

"Nope. No alcohol, buddy." Ayla winked at Bree again before she went back to the bar.

"Are you hungry?" He started to get up from the table to order food, but stopped when Bree put her hand on his arm.

"You know I don't like it when you do that," she told him, but in her eyes, he saw the beginning of a smile. She was softening up, letting go.

"Sorry," he smiled back at her. "We'll wait until Ayla comes back, and ask for a menu."

Bree took a sip of her drink. "What is this?"

"It's a chai apple cider."

"What are you having?" she eyed his glass.

"Hot chocolate, with habanero whipped cream."

"You don't feel like drinking either?"

"Nope, I don't." He wanted a clear head tonight. He couldn't afford to make any more mistakes where Bree was concerned.

She took a sip of her cider. "This is good," she said softly. "And you're right, I'm famished. I guess it would be okay if you ordered for us."

That wasn't easy for her, but she said it anyway. Jace smiled.

"Can I ask you something?"

"Of course you can, darlin'."

"Do people talk to you about me?"

"People?"

"You know what I mean. Liv, Ben, Lyric…"

"Yeah, they do. But it isn't only them. Billy can't seem to stop himself from giving me advice. He's become the relationship whisperer."

"Billy?" she giggled.

"Right? I started callin' him that, thinkin' it would shut him up. No such luck."

"Do you think this is real, Jace? Are we together right now because it's convenient?"

She'd gotten right to the point and pushed his most sensitive button, the root of his insecurity. But what choice did he have? Drunk or sober, busy or idle, even sleeping, his mind drifted back to her, without fail.

"You are anything but convenient. It's damn hard for you and me to be in the same place at the same time. All I know for sure is I can't get you off my mind. *Can't.* And I don't want to."

"It worries me," she admitted.

"That I can't stop thinkin' about you?"

"No, that I can't stop thinking about you either."

He smiled, leaned over, and kissed her. "I'm happy to hear that, Bree."

"But, Jace—"

He put his finger on her lips. "Shh, now. What do you say we set aside our doubts, just for now, and pretend we're back in Idaho, just you and me? All the months in between then and now don't matter. Let's go back to who we were then, and have a nice, quiet, simple conversation."

"But—"

He tried to stop her again by kissing her, but she turned her head away. "Stop. I need to say this."

"Go ahead."

"It isn't the same. We can't go back. I can't go back."

"Why not?"

"Because we hadn't made love then, Jace. Everything is different now."

"I get your point. So, we don't have to go all the way back to Idaho. Instead, we can just be here. Now. And instead of talkin' about *us*, let's just *talk*. Tell me how you've been. How's the academy?"

They spent the next two hours talking, and Bree didn't hold anything back. She hadn't told anyone else how hard being at the academy was for her.

"I love being with Cochran. Now, with another baby on the way—"

"Wait. What? Tucker and Blythe are having another baby? Jesus, Tuck didn't tell me."

"I probably shouldn't have said anything. Blythe told me before we left Monument. She just found out. I'm sorry."

"Nah, don't be sorry. I'm sure Tucker will say somethin' when he thinks the time is right. He and I haven't had much time to connect on this trip."

"I'm sorry about that, too."

Jace put his hands on either side of her face. "Will you listen?"

She nodded her head.

"There isn't anybody here this weekend that I wanted to see more than you."

Bree nodded again, and then she yawned.

"Are you ready to go back to the Flying R?"

"Do you mind? I'm so tired."

The house was quiet when they got back. Jace lit the fire and sat down on the sofa.

"Everyone asleep?" he asked when she came back upstairs. She had changed into the same oversized sweatshirt and pajama bottoms she had on the night before.

"I don't think everyone is back yet. Blythe is, she was getting Cochran to sleep."

She sat down on the hearth of the fireplace, pulled her knees up in front of her, and rested her head on her arms. "We haven't talked about the other night. I owe you an apology. At least, I think I do." She closed her eyes. "Just the fact that I'm not sure, must mean I do."

"No, you don't."

She didn't open her eyes.

"Please, come over here and sit with me."

She raised her head and looked at him.

"Please, Bree."

It took her a minute, but eventually she unfolded her legs. Her feet were bare, and when she sat down and drew them up on the sofa in front of her, Jace rested his hand on them. Her toes were like ice. He stood and pulled a blanket off a nearby chair and covered her with it, tucking it under her feet.

"There," he murmured.

"You're too nice to me."

"No one in this house would agree."

"It wasn't your fault, Jace. I didn't mean to get drunk. I just hadn't eaten all day." She shrugged her shoulders. "I know better, and that's a lousy excuse. I drank too much. It's that simple."

"Why did you?"

"It isn't what you're thinking. It wasn't because of you."

He studied her face. "You sure about that?"

Bree rested her head against the pillowed back of the sofa. Part of her wanted to call him out on his arrogance, tell him that everything that happened in life, hers or anyone else's, wasn't about him, but their earlier conversation had been nice. She didn't want to start an argument with him. The truth was, most of her actions were in reaction to him. She'd be lying if she said otherwise.

"Bree?"

"I was upset. I didn't like seeing you with another woman."

"I didn't like seeing you with another man, either. Especially not seeing you kiss him."

She put her hand on her forehead and groaned.

"Can I get you anything?"

"Water would be good." She kept her eyes closed but felt him get up from the sofa. The air in the room cooled without him next to her. She drew the blanket closer, willing him to hurry back.

"Here, drink this." Jace unscrewed the cap and handed Bree the bottle of water.

"Thanks."

He sat back down and pulled her closer to him.

"How much longer will you be in Crested Butte?" she asked.

"At least until Tuesday. Billy has meetings sched-uled most of the day Monday." Jace shook his head and laughed.

"What's funny?"

"Just Billy."

"How are things going with the rough stock business?"

Better than they'd ever imagined. Word was out that their bulls and broncs were rank. That's what mattered most. He and Billy were the front men of the business. As a former saddle bronc national champion, Billy Patterson had his foot in doors most rough stock contractors would never have.

They decided, earlier in the day, about who would go to the National Finals Rodeo next week. They agreed it would take the whole crew to represent Flying R Rough Stock properly. They wouldn't have rough stock in the finals this year, but they were optimistic that next year they would. The trip to Las Vegas this year would be more about seeing and being seen.

"What's it like?"

"NFR? Crazy," he sighed. "A big, damn party."

"Is it always in Las Vegas?"

There'd been talk, the year before, about moving it to Florida, but eventually a deal had been reached to keep it in Las Vegas a few more years. Jace couldn't imagine it anywhere else. "Sure is. Where it belongs, too."

"You're looking forward to it?"

"Part of me is. Part of me isn't."

"Why?"

"That life…I'm gettin' a little too old for. Come here, girl." He gently moved her so her back rested against him. He shifted, turning enough that his legs were on the sofa and she was nestled in front of him. He wrapped his arm around her waist, pulled her closer, and tucked a pillow under her head.

He looked over and saw her water bottle was empty. He should have thought of that before he'd gotten them both so comfortable. She needed to rehydrate, especially at this altitude.

When he saw Blythe peek around the corner, he caught her eye and pointed toward the bottle sitting on the coffee table. She understood and brought two more and set them down.

"She's out," she whispered.

He already knew she was. He'd spent more than one night close enough to her to know the way her breathing evened out when she fell asleep. He longed to slide his hand under her sweatshirt and feel her warm skin, but didn't. He shifted, so if she woke, she wouldn't feel what being that close to her was doing to him. He closed his eyes and willed sleep to come to him, too. It didn't take long before it did.

"Shh," followed by a giggle woke him. He opened his eyes and saw Liv tiptoeing past them, warning Ben to keep quiet. When Jace opened his eyes, Liv waved. Ben waved too, mimicking his wife. He put his finger in front of his lips, as if to say they'd be quiet.

He tried to move his arm from around Bree's waist, but she clung to him. He leaned down and kissed her shoulder through her thick sweatshirt.

"Jace?"

"Yes, sweetheart?" He hadn't realized she was awake.

"Do you think anyone would mind if you came downstairs with me?"

"No, darlin', no one will mind at all." *Least of all me.*

Why did she keep doing this to herself? She woke up in bed with Jace again this morning. It wasn't that she didn't remember asking him to sleep with her last night, after they'd fallen asleep together on the sofa, again, it was just that, each time, she vowed it couldn't happen again.

He shifted and pulled her closer. She closed her eyes, knowing she wouldn't be able to fall back to sleep, not with him pressed against her. So many nights she'd fallen asleep imagining he was holding her as he was now. She'd let her mind drift, imagining his hands on her body, his lips always followed…in her dreams.

His arm was draped over her, his hand close enough that she could run her lips over the fingers she so often imagined bringing her body pleasure. She couldn't resist. She kissed his hand, and then brushed her lips over the back of it.

Before she knew it, she was under him. He urged her legs open with his knee, holding himself over her with his powerful arms. He leaned down and ran his lips over the pulse points in her neck, murmuring her name as he made his way lower.

Her arms went around him, urging him closer than he was. She wanted him as close to her as he could be. She wanted them to be one.

Instead, he continued moving further down her body, soft lingering kisses making a trail lower, and lower. Her body arched against him. Yes, this had been part of her dream too. Jace loving her with his lips, his tongue. She closed her eyes, trying to focus on how it felt to have Jace take her to a place she'd never been, not even with Zack.

"Bree," he breathed. "Baby, I need you. Do you know how much I need you?"

"I need you too."

This is the last place he'd expected to be, and more, the last thing he expected to be doing. He rolled away from her. "Shit."

"What?"

"Bree, darlin', I, uh, don't have anything with me, sweetheart."

"You don't?"

Her voice was so soft, so sweet, he could just eat her up. "I'm sorry, sweet girl."

She sighed. If he didn't know better, he might've thought it sounded more like a huff than a sigh.

He raised himself up on his elbow so he could look at her face. Sure enough, she was pouting. He leaned over and kissed the down-turned corners of her mouth.

"I can try to find some."

"What? No. God, Jace, please, tell me you're joking."

"Okay, I'm joking. Sort of."

"It's bad enough that everyone knows you slept with me. They don't need to know you *slept* with me."

"*Almost* slept with you, baby."

She nudged against him, until he was on his back. She rested her head on his chest.

"Jace?"

He recognized her lilt of insecurity. "Yes, Bree."

"Is it bad that we always do this?"

"No, honey. It isn't bad. Nothing this perfect could ever be called bad."

"But—"

"No, no buts. I love sleepin' next to you. I love making love to you. I'm not going to let you tarnish it by labeling it with the word 'bad.'" He raised up and turned so he was on his side, facing her, and she was facing him.

"Bree, I care about you. It's more than that, and I think you know it. We do this because it feels right. I've never once regretted waking up with you in my arms. Never once."

"I haven't regretted it either, Jace. That isn't what I meant. Not really. It's just that we aren't together, yet we always end up *together*."

Why weren't they together? Why couldn't they be together? Whenever he thought they could be, she pushed him away. Each time she did it, his first instinct was to push back. He assumed she didn't want him, not the way he wanted her, but what if he was wrong?

"How much longer until the academy is on break?"

"For the holidays? Another two weeks. We're back a week, and then there are finals. I'll be done by the middle of the following week."

She'd be finished right before the end of the rodeo finals in Las Vegas. He'd have a break then too, until the beginning of January. He took a deep breath and prayed she'd give him the answer he was looking for.

"I'd like to spend Christmas with you this year."

"Oh." Bree's eyes looked everywhere but at him. He watched her struggle with what to say. He was close to pulling away from her, when she answered.

"Where will you be?"

"Wherever you want me to be."

"In Palmer Lake?"

He closed his eyes tight and willed himself not to let the joy that was building inside his chest escape. He was as happy as any time he'd ever been in his life.

When he opened his eyes, she was watching him.

"Are you okay?" she asked.

He smiled. "I've never been better."

"I don't want to miss Christmas with Cochran."

"We'll figure it out when I get back from Las Vegas. Okay?"

"Okay."

"And, Bree?"

"Yeah?"

"You're gonna have to break things off with Officer Friendly."

"Who is Officer Friendly? Oh. Wait. Oh, God. Kaleb."

"Yeah, Kaleb."

"I don't have to break things off with him. I mean, there's nothing to break off. It was just dinner."

Jace pulled her closer to him. "I don't want him to arrest me when I go into town, later, to buy condoms."

She blushed and looked down, hiding her face from him. "Jace," she breathed.

"Don't hide from me, Bree."

17

Bree unlocked the door to her office and put the coat back on that she'd taken off when she entered the building. Her office at the academy was cold from sitting empty for a week. She reached down and turned on the space heater that sat under her desk.

She waited while her computer powered up, inserted her access card, and entered her password. Her security level at the Air Force Academy was relatively low, but everyone who worked there needed some level of clearance.

She closed her eyes and leaned back in the chair while she waited. The rest of Thanksgiving weekend with Jace was like a dream. It was the same as it had been between them in Idaho, when things were comfortable and easy.

No one commented on her and Jace sharing a bed— why would they? They were consenting adults. She expected her dad would; he was usually the one who said what everyone else was thinking. He seemed preoccupied though, and not his usual self. If there was inappropriate humor to be made, her dad was all for making it. Not so this weekend.

Bree wondered if he was worried about her, and spared her his usual torment. It wouldn't really be his style, but maybe he was one more person for her to add to the list of her pitiers.

She decided she'd call him soon, and invite him to dinner, just the two of them. She'd let him know she missed his incessant teasing, as hard as it would be to say those words out loud. But she did miss it. When she was little, her mother told her and her sisters that their dad teased them because he loved them. She didn't doubt her father's love for her, but she wouldn't mind him acting more like himself with her.

The ringing office phone startled her. "This is Bree Fox," she answered. Often phone calls coming in were from people who didn't realize the permanent professor was on leave.

"Ma'am," the voice on the phone began. "We have a package for you in the mail area. Would you like us to deliver it now?"

"For Bree Fox?"

"Yes, ma'am."

"I can come and get it."

"No, ma'am. As I said, we can deliver it now."

"Come in," she said when she heard the knock on the door a few minutes later. When it didn't open, she realized the airman making the delivery probably had his or her hands full.

"Hello, ma'am," the airman said when she opened the door. "Where would you like me to put this?"

She pointed to a table near her desk and thanked him on his way out.

Bree looked at the return address. It was from an APO, a military address.

She reached for a letter opener, and then a pair of scissors, to get the well-taped package open. She removed the tissue paper covering the contents and found several manila envelopes.

She opened the first, and reached for her chair. It held letters from Zack. There were at least a dozen in this one alone.

Bree pulled the second envelope out of the package and opened it. Inside was a notebook. Skimming through the pages, it looked as though it was full of notes, also in Zack's handwriting.

She stopped there. Bree didn't want to see what else was in the box, at least not right then. She put the letters back in the first envelope, the notebook back in the second, and returned everything to the box.

Should she have wine or something stronger? She couldn't decide. The box had been sitting in the middle of her living room for two days, near the couch. She thought about putting it in a closet and looking at the contents later, after she'd had time to prepare herself. But would she ever be ready?

She wasn't much of a whiskey drinker, but the bottle sitting on the counter was too tempting. She poured a couple of fingers, sat on the sofa, and stared at the box.

Zack's belongings had already been returned to her. This box was unexpected. She hadn't decided yet whether it was also unwelcome. After two more shots of whiskey, she reopened the first envelope.

"Dear Bree…" the letter began. She took a deep breath, already anticipating what it would say, like how much he missed her, or maybe something about them starting a family. Instead, he talked more about "the mission." He said he wished she understood how important this was to him—it wasn't a job, he wrote, it was his life.

She only read one letter, before moving on to the envelope containing the notebook. She read the first few pages of what she soon realized was Zack's journal. One she knew nothing about.

Her cell phone rang, but when she saw it was Jace calling, she let it go to voicemail.

A few minutes later, she made a call to someone else.

As silly as it seemed even to himself, Jace was nervous. It wasn't his first trip to the National Finals Rodeo, but it was the first time he had this much at stake.

It wasn't until they checked into the hotel that Billy told him they'd be roommates. It didn't bother him, he was just surprised that he wasn't rooming with Tucker. Then again, Ben and Billy had never been great fans of one another.

It stemmed back four years, when Billy won National Saddle Bronc Champion at the NFR. For some reason, Ben got it into his head that Billy and Ben's now wife, Liv, were an item. Nothing could've been further from the truth. Billy had been in love with Liv's daughter, Renie.

It didn't matter how illogical it was, Ben never had much good to say about Billy, and the feeling was mutual.

"Don't understand why the hell we couldn't have had our own damn rooms," Billy mumbled. "We got money problems nobody told me about?"

"It's not that," Ben answered. "We were lucky to get the rooms we did. Everything was sold out months ago."

Tucker was off to the side, on his phone, probably talking to Blythe. Jace had called Bree and left a message, the day before, but hadn't heard back from her. Maybe she hadn't gotten it. It wasn't like her not to call him back, at least not lately.

He walked in the opposite direction of where his brother stood, and hit redial on her number. The call went straight to voicemail.

"This is a pleasant surprise," Red said when he answered Bree's call.

"Do you have a minute?" she asked.

"For you, I've got all the time in the world."

"You're always so nice to me."

"What can I do for you? Or are you just calling to shoot the breeze?"

"I'm not. I, uh, need to get away, and was wondering…"

"The ranch is closed up tight for the season…"

As she feared.

"But you can stay over at the lake house with me. If you wouldn't be too uncomfortable."

"That's so generous of you, Red. I don't want to impose."

"You should know, I don't offer if I don't want to. I'd love to have you visit."

"Thanks…" Her voice trailed off.

"Do you want to talk about whatever it is, now?"

She didn't; she couldn't.

"The semester ends in a few days, and then winter break lasts until the first week of January."

He told her she could stay as long as she wanted, and offered to pick her up at the airport in Hailey, so she didn't have to rent a car.

"I need to ship something up to you, something I don't want to bring on the plane."

"Are you sure you don't want to tell me what's on your mind?"

"I can't," she couldn't say any more. If she tried, she knew she'd start to cry, and then he'd worry more than she was sure he already was.

"If you change your mind and want to talk, you know where to find me."

"Thanks, Red."

Bree knew it was a lot to ask. It wasn't as though Red was family, even though it felt like he was. She'd never known her grandparents—they all passed away before she was born, but she imagined the way she felt about Red would've been how she'd feel about them.

She taped up the box and drove to the Palmer Lake post office. She hadn't read more than she did the first night, and once the box was gone, she'd be free of the temptation to keep reading.

She still had another call to make, and it would be far more difficult than the one she made to Red.

They were four days in and Jace was exhausted. Endless meetings filled their days, and at seven, the competitive events began. The after-parties started at ten and went on until two or three in the morning.

The Flying R crew didn't stay at any of the parties very long, although showing up was expected of them. Bullet and Lyric were the only ones who stayed until the wee hours of the morning. Bullet was there to help Lyric with RodeoChat, along with his stock duties.

"How're you doing?" Ben asked Jace while they waited for a cab to take them to an after party. "You're a helluva lot younger than me, yet you don't seem to be having too much fun. All this partyin' getting to you?"

It wasn't the partying Jace was having trouble with, it was Bree. He hadn't been able to reach her, and from what Tuck said, Blythe hadn't seen much of her, but when she had, she seemed fine. Jace feared he'd landed in a seat on the same roller coaster he'd had with her in the past.

If she was going to pull away from him every time they weren't together, there wasn't any chance a relationship would work between them. No matter what, he'd have to travel, in the same way Billy, Tucker, and

Ben had to. They didn't want to be away from their wives and families, but none of them had a choice.

"Jace?" Ben was waiting for a response.

Before he could answer, his cell rang and Bree's number showed on the screen. He breathed a sigh of relief. "I need to get this," he told Ben, who waved him off.

"I was just thinking about you," he answered.

"You were?"

"Yep, but I always am, so I'd say that no matter when you called."

"Jace, I need to talk to you."

She'd started one other conversation this way. He couldn't accept this was a repeat. "Bree, tell me what's goin' on, darlin'." This time he'd listen rather than jump to any conclusions. He'd learned at least that much.

"It's about Christmas."

"Christmas?"

"I've had a change of plans. I'm not going to be home for Christmas."

"Okay. Tell me what's goin' on." Jace was trying hard not to allow any emotion to creep into his words. If he could keep it light, just listen to her, maybe this wouldn't circle down the drain.

"I'm going away."

"What about Christmas with Cochran, and your family?" And me?

"Something has come up, and I'm going to Idaho."

Her voice caught.

"Tell me why."

"It's something I need to do. I don't know if I can explain."

"Come on, darlin'. Don't shut me out. What's this about?"

"Zack," she hesitated. "It's Zack."

There were questions he wanted to ask. What did she mean? Why did she have to go to Idaho? He waited for her to continue, but was met with silence.

"Can I call you?" he asked.

"I don't think that's a good idea. I need to go now, Jace."

NFR had barely begun and Jace was already exhausted. Endless meetings filled his days, and even though the competitive events were just getting started, the all-night parties had started a week ago. Jace watched as men and women spilled out of the hotel's shuttle. The buses ran non-stop from one rodeo event to another. Once one emptied, the line of people waiting would pile on, headed where the last people came from. The line was long, full of cowboys and cowgirls, most feeling as tired as he was. He focused on one couple specifically.

The man stood behind the woman, his arms around her waist. She leaned back so her head rested against his chest. Jace watched as the man lowered his head and kissed the woman's neck. Her eyes closed, she smiled, and then turned her head. When she did, the cowboy kissed her. She turned in his arms, and their kiss deepened.

He should look away; their moment was private, even if they were in public, but he kept watching. When their kiss ended, she rested her cheek against his chest. The cowboy's arms tightened, pulling her closer. Jace sighed, envying their moment, their closeness, their love.

When he turned to go back into the hotel, no longer interested in going to tonight's party, Billy was leaning against the wall, watching him. His hat sat low on his face, but Jace could see his eyes. He wasn't smirking, the way he often did. Good thing. Jace wasn't in the mood to take any of Billy's shit today. He had enough of his own.

He was tempted to turn around, catch a cab to the airport, and head back to Montana. He'd spent the last few days counting down to the day he'd be with Bree again. Instead of winding down, the count had just spiraled up.

"Hold up," Billy said when Jace walked past him.

Jace ignored him, walked straight to the bar, and ordered a shot of bourbon. He downed one and shoved the shot glass in the bartender's direction. "Keep 'em comin'."

Billy stood next to him at the bar, but didn't say anything. After Jace's third round, he turned the shot glass over. Getting drunk was pointless; it would only make him feel worse.

"I want out," he said, without looking at Billy.

"You're out."

"That simple? Huh. Must be I'm not as important to this whole venture as I thought."

"You're important as any of the rest of us, but nobody's gonna force you to stick with this if you don't wanna be here."

"I can just walk away?"

"Sure ya can. We all can. Nothin' tyin' any of us to this deal, except money."

"I walk away, I lose my money. Fair enough."

"Hell, no. I'll buy you out. I got no problem doin' that. None of us would screw you outta your investment."

"All right, then." Jace held out his hand, but Billy didn't shake it.

"We'll do it after the first of the year. Cleaner that way from a tax standpoint. Plus it'll take that long to draw up the paperwork."

"If that's that, I'll go pack my stuff."

"Where ya headed?"

"Home. Back to Montana."

"Home, huh? Your operation up there is still part of all this. Or you plannin' on askin' your mama and daddy to buy you outta that, too?"

Jace hadn't gotten that far. He hadn't expected Billy to accept him walking away from the rough stock business without an argument. Maybe he should give up the place in Montana, although that wouldn't be fair to his parents. They'd partnered with him because he needed them to, not for themselves. They couldn't sell now and expect to make any money on the deal.

He couldn't make a good decision to save his life—his stupid, pointless life.

He took off his hat and ran his fingers through his hair, pulling it with the weight of his tension. "Hell, if I know," he finally answered.

Billy motion to the bartender, who set two shot glasses in front of them and poured. Jace studied the glass in front of him.

Billy threw the shot back and waited for Jace to do the same. He was already light-headed from the three shots he'd had when he walked up to the bar. He wasn't sure he could stand another one. He pushed the glass in Billy's direction.

"Good decision," Billy said before he downed the second shot.

"You know what I don't understand, why you give a shit."

Billy motioned for the bartender again, this time holding up only one finger. Jace waited while Billy downed his third shot. Now they were even.

"I owe you."

"What for?"

It took Billy a while to answer. Usually, he didn't have much to say, and when he did, he took his time saying it.

"Renie and I woulda ended up together no matter what. But what you did, that day, took balls. I'll never forget it, and I'll likely never repay it."

"I didn't tell you anything you didn't already know. Looking back on it, I was a damn arrogant jackass for calling you."

"Doesn't matter." Billy was studying the last couple of drops in the shot glass. Jace wondered if he was going to order another. "All that matters is you cared enough to do it. You're a better man than I am, and for that, I owe you."

"You don't owe me nothin'." Jace turned to walk away, but Billy grabbed his arm.

He waved his other hand in the direction of the casino. "I've been part of this rodeo circuit for a hell of a lot of years. You don't see any cowboys walkin' up, offerin' to buy me a drink. You know why that is?" Billy didn't wait for Jace to answer.

"It's because I kept to myself. I know these guys, but even after years of travelin' to the same places, week after week, I would betcha not a single one of them would call me a friend." Billy looked straight at Jace. "But I'd call you a friend, a damn good friend."

"I appreciate you sayin' that, Billy—"

"I'm not finished. I don't know what the hell is goin' on with you, but whatever it is, you're not thinkin' straight."

"It's not important."

"Not important? Only one thing it can be, then. Bree's got you in a tizzy. Wants you by her side day-in-day-out, that it? Yep, that's how it is when you're in love."

"Nothing could be further from what's happening. Whatever was going on with Bree and me, isn't any longer. She's decided to go to Idaho for Christmas. You see, she and I planned to spend it together this year. I don't think you make a spur of the moment decision to cancel holiday plans when you're in love."

Billy shook his head. "You've got it all wrong, partner."

18

Red was quiet on the drive back from the airport. Bree didn't mind; she didn't feel like talking either. It was cold and snowing, and she hadn't been able to get warm since she got on the plane that morning. Her body involuntarily shuddered, and she wrapped her arms more tightly around herself.

"What's in the box?" he asked after more than an hour on the road.

"Things that belonged to Zack. Letters mainly, and I found a journal."

"I see."

"I started to read the letters the day the box was delivered, but I stopped. I hope you don't mind me coming here to do it." Suddenly she felt like a huge imposition.

"I appreciate the company," Red smiled.

Bree smiled back, and then lost herself in the beauty of the Sawtooth Mountains. Their craggy spires, covered with snow, reached into the blue Idaho sky, as though they were yearning to grow taller still, to touch heavens that remained always out of reach.

"I didn't ask if you had plans for the holidays."

"I get my share of invitations from the ranch manager and his family, and some of the boys you met at the Stanley bakery."

"Do you accept any of them?"

"Not so far."

"Why not?"

"My wife passed away a couple of years ago. I wasn't good company."

"And this year?"

"Something told me I should stay home this year, too."

"You don't have to, I mean, if you're doing it for me. I could go back to Colorado."

Red reached over and patted her mittened hand. "Let's take it one day at a time."

She nodded, and lost herself again.

"I don't understand why you need me in this meeting, I'm out of this after the first of the year."

"Ben and his brothers are meeting with the Wrangler people. I can't very well send Bullet into a sponsorship meeting."

"You can handle it on your own."

Billy glared at Jace. "You got somethin' more important to do this mornin'? 'Cause the way I see it, Flying R Rough Stock has been payin' for your entertainment the last few days. You can step up and go to this meeting with me. Plus, we might get a free breakfast out of it."

Jace followed him into the elevator and down to the restaurant in the lobby.

"Tristan?" Billy asked the woman standing near the entrance, looking at her cell phone.

"Yes." She shook Billy's hand. "Billy Patterson, right? And this is?" she looked in Jace's direction.

"This here is Jace Rice, the other founding partner in Flying R Rough Stock."

Jace shook her hand and wondered what Billy was up to with an introduction like that.

"I'm Tristan McCullough, with Lost Cowboy," she said.

"It's a pleasure to meet you, Tristan. I like what you've done with your brand, admirable marketing strategy."

Tristan bowed her head, just slightly, and he saw her cheeks pinken. "It's more than a strategy," she told him. "It's my father's way of life. My grandfather's, too."

Billy deferred to Jace throughout the meeting, and he had to admit, he enjoyed it. Sponsorship was something Jace understood from his days as a competitive skier.

Flying R Rough Stock planned to contract stock to rodeos, but also to sponsor rookie cowboys and cow-girls. They had to be careful with bull and bronc riders, but sponsoring participants in the timed events, along with barrel racers, wouldn't be a conflict of interest. Partnering with Lost Cowboy allowed them to help promote the riders they wouldn't otherwise be able to.

"Pretty girl," Billy said when Tristan excused herself to take a phone call.

"Yes, she is." Billy's motivation in getting him to the meeting became obvious.

Jace wasn't blind. Tristan was more than pretty; she was stunning. She was tall and thin, with long, dark, brown hair, and big brown eyes. She had been a competitive barrel racer, but once her family started their clothing business, she said it became her true passion.

As beautiful and interesting as Tristan was, she wasn't Bree. There had been plenty of buckle bunnies who tried to catch Jace's attention the last few days, but they weren't Bree either. She was all he could think about, all he wanted.

"Hey, fellas," Bullet sat down at the table, uninvited.

Lyric stood behind him, taking it all in.

"Who y'all meetin' with?" she asked.

"Tristan McCullough—"

"Lost Cowboy," she interrupted. "I'd like to get a Twitterview with that girl. Think y'all can put that together for me?"

Jace laughed. Lyric never quit. Wasn't she as exhausted as the rest of them were? Looking at her, you'd think she just stepped off the plane, enthusiastic as ever.

"Here she is," said Billy when Tristan came back to the table.

Lyric took it from there, and Jace was glad their business had concluded. There'd be no getting a word in edgewise once Lyric got started.

"Who is she?" Bullet asked, leaning in close to Jace.

"She represents a brand that's going to sponsor riders, some in partnership with Flying R."

"Ya think she'd sponsor me?"

"Uh, I don't know." The look on Bullet's face was equal parts hopeful and lustful. Jace didn't want to rain on the cowboy's parade, but he was afraid Tristan McCullough was way out of Bullet's league.

Bree stared at the box. There it sat, on the dresser in the guest room.

When Red pointed out the cabin to her, last summer, she hadn't gotten a good look at it from across the lake. In fact, what she'd seen through the woods, that day, wasn't the cabin at all, it was the boathouse.

The cabin stood higher on the hill, almost impossible to see from the lake.

The main floor was comprised of a large great room, with a wall of windows that looked out over Pettit Lake and the Sawtooth Range. It was as though the dense trees surrounding the cabin magically opened to the perfect view.

The kitchen was expansive, with a vintage Magic Chef combination range. It had ten gas burners, five small oven compartments, and three warming trays that ran along the bottom. Bree had never seen anything like it. The design was brilliant. Why didn't they make ranges like this anymore?

A wooden, winding staircase led to the second floor where there were five bedrooms, three of which had doors that opened to a deck overlooking the lake.

The bathroom closest to the guest room had a black, claw-foot tub, and a raised, dark wood, tall tank, and pull-chain toilet that had a black porcelain base, like the tub. The sink was the same black porcelain as the toilet and tub, and was set in a cabinet made of dark wood. It was one of the most beautiful bathrooms Bree had ever seen.

The guest room was feminine looking, despite the use of dark wood and black accents. The bedding and curtains were made from the same cream and black-colored French toile fabric. Upon closer inspection, Bree saw there were three distinct scenes woven into the fabric.

In one, a woman and child were gathering flowers. A man, carrying a hay rake, walked with them. In the background, other people were cutting hay. A second scene showed a man on a ladder, next to a grape arbor. The final scene showed a mill, and a woman and child stood on a bridge, looking down at the water.

Bree ran her hands over the bedding, plump with down filling. Her gaze lingered on the box on the dresser. She closed her eyes and willed herself to sleep. After fifteen minutes, she was still awake. She couldn't avoid it any longer. She was here to read whatever she found in the envelopes, and it was time she got started.

She found a Hudson Bay wool blanket in the cedar chest near the door leading out to the deck. The snow had melted, and the sun had dried the wood enough that she wanted to sit outside. She slid her feet into the furry, ankle-height slippers, also sitting by the door, and wrapped herself in the blanket. She opened the door, carrying Zack's journal with her.

She opened the cover and found a date, along with a volume number, written on the first page. Zack's handwriting filled every page. He'd started this journal a few days before his last deployment. There was no end date, but the volume number was fifteen.

In all the years she'd known Zack, she'd never known he kept a journal. She went back inside and pulled the remaining envelopes out of the box. There were fourteen in addition to the one that contained the letters, and the one she'd pulled the first journal out of. Each one contained another journal. The last manila envelope contained volume one. The date showed Zack had started the journal when he was a freshman in high school, two years before she met him.

She put the journals in order and started reading. It was filled with entries about schoolwork, girls, and family, as you might expect from a teenage boy.

The second journal was much harder to read.

May 3
An angel visited our church today.

May 10
The angel came back, with her family. They're joining our church. I invited her to come to our youth group meeting.

May 17
She came! Her name is Bree, and she is the most beautiful girl I've ever seen.

Bree closed the journal, and then closed her eyes. She remembered meeting Zack when her parents visited their new church for the first time.

"Dinner?" asked Red, standing in the doorway.

"Dinner?" she responded. "Already?" Bree looked at the time on her phone. How had she lost track of so many hours?

"I didn't want to interrupt, but...you didn't eat breakfast, or lunch." His eyes studied hers. "You need to eat, Bree."

She ran her hand through her hair. She hadn't even showered today. "I can make something—"

"No need. I've already made something. Join me whenever you're ready."

"You wanna talk about it?" Tucker asked Jace when he found him at the bar.

"Which *it*?"

"Let's start with you wanting out of the rough stock business."

"I don't know, Tuck. The whole reason I went to Montana in the first place was to get off the road. Now I'm on it four times as much."

"Maybe we can work out a compromise. You were the one who insisted you would go out on the road twice as much as you needed to be."

Jace turned away from the bar and scanned the casino floor. "I'm drowning, Tuck."

Tucker put his hand on Jace's shoulder. "I know you are, but I didn't feel it until the last couple of days. What's changed?"

"Same thing that always changes."

"Bree?"

"Not just Bree. Women."

"Tell me what happened."

Jace told Tucker about his phone call with Bree, and about her change in plans for the holidays.

"I've been countin' the days, Tuck. Literally countin' them. All I've been thinkin' about is the next time I'll see her, and now I don't know when that'll be. I'm goin' back to Montana from here. I need a few days to get some perspective."

"Good idea. We'll see you back down at our place for Christmas though, right?"

"I don't know, Tuck."

"Fair enough. The door will be open."

"You wanna talk about it?" Red asked Bree when she sat down at the dinner table.

"It's as though I'm getting to know him all over again."

Red nodded. "Maybe you're not getting to know him again, maybe you're getting to know him for the first time."

"How do you know this stuff? I swear you're clairvoyant."

Red shrugged his shoulders.

"I received the box a couple days before I called you. It was…unexpected."

"What's in it?"

"Letters. Most written to me and never sent. But there are also journals. They go back to when Zack was in high school. I don't know who had them, or why they sent them to me."

"Someone in his family?"

"It's an APO return address, so it wouldn't have been his parents, or his sister."

"Have you asked them?"

"I haven't."

"Why not?"

"I don't know, to be honest with you. I haven't told anyone about them until just now. You're the first."

Red got up and took his plate into the kitchen. "Ready for seconds?" he asked. "There's lots more."

"Sure, it's really good, Red. I haven't had chicken and dumplings since I left home for college. Is it homemade?"

"Yes, ma'am. My mama's recipe. Hits the spot on a cold winter night, like nothin' else."

"Mmm. Comfort food." Bree stood and looked at a photo hanging on the wall of the dining room. "Who's this?"

"My daughter," he answered without looking up.

"She...uh..."

"Looks like you, Bree? Yes, I agree."

"Wow, I mean, there is a resemblance, right?"

"A strong resemblance."

"Red?" He still hadn't looked up from what he was doing.

"That morning, when you walked into the ranch dining hall, I could've sworn you were her, tellin' me it was time to come home to Jesus."

"I don't know what to say."

"Nothin' to say. Whether you look like her or not, doesn't matter. You and I had a connection that first day."

"We did," she agreed.

"Somethin' brought you to the ranch. Somethin' made me offer to take you fishing," Red looked up at the ceiling. "Not sure what or why. Not likely to get an answer, so I don't question."

"I felt that way too. Like I was supposed to meet you."

"You were."

"Thank you, Red. You've done so much for me."

"No thanks necessary. I was supposed to meet you, too. This isn't one-sided."

"Why do you think? I mean, it seems obvious why I was supposed to meet you. You've helped me more than anyone. But why me, for you?"

Red sat back down at the table. "Not a lot of reason for an old guy like me to get up in the mornin' if I'm not needed."

"I don't know what—"

"Say no more," he held up his hand. "You're welcome here any time. Now, what do you say we watch a movie? I have quite a collection. I take 'em from the ranch library, and then I forget to return 'em."

Bree laughed when Red pointed to his collection of DVDs. There was a stack, up against the wall, almost as tall as she was.

The next morning, Bree took a journal with her when she went downstairs for breakfast. The dates on the title page included Zack's final year as a cadet at the Air Force Academy. He proposed to her the day he graduated. Bree wasn't sure she wanted to be alone when she read this one.

A couple of hours, and many tears later, the tone of the journal changed. Zack was headed to his first base, and several of the pages were dedicated to how he felt about serving in the military. Most of what was written, Bree had understood fundamentally, at the time. What surprised her was Zack's depth of passion.

October 12
Many question the meaning of life. I do not.
I know, without question, what my calling is.
I was put on this earth to protect and serve
my country. It is not a responsibility I take
lightly, nor do I pay lip service to it, as many
I serve with do. More than being Bree's hus-
band, more than being a son, or a father, I am
a soldier.

She and Zack had talked about his commitment to the Air Force on their way to Yellowstone. It was the same trip that brought them to Idaho for the first time.

"It's something I should have told you before we got married," he'd said then.

She'd told him she understood his passion, but when she read his journal entry, she realized she really hadn't. If he'd told her then that he believed it was more important than she was, she might've reacted differently. Maybe when he said it, she'd disregarded it as the ramblings of an idealistic young man.

They'd argued about it more than once in the course of their marriage. Zack volunteered for more things than Bree thought were necessary. He didn't do it because it was necessary to his career, he told her—he did it because it was necessary to his soul.

Zack volunteered to help coach the academy track team, when he was stationed at Peterson Air Force Base. He also volunteered with the Wounded Warrior Program. At the time, he told her she didn't understand. He'd been right. She understood now, but only after reading his journals.

She walked out on the porch and looked out at the lake. It was warm today, warm enough to go for a walk.

"Hey, now, there's a pretty girl," Red said, coming around the corner of the house.

"Hey, Red. I was just thinking about taking a walk. Join me?"

"I'll do ya one better. How about a ride?"

They took the truck to the ranch, and Red called the barn on their way over. "Hey, Wyatt, can I talk you into saddlin' up a couple horses?"

He smiled at Bree when he hung up. "Perks of bein' the boss."

"All that time, I thought you were just another ranch hand."

"I like to keep a low profile around the guests."

That made Bree laugh. "I'll say."

They rode a trail south, through the woods.

"How's reading?"

"No easier, but no harder either. There are things about Zack I never knew. Or maybe I knew, and I just didn't understand."

"I learned a lot when my wife got sick. There were times I felt the same way you are now."

"How so?"

"I never realized how much she held inside."

Red reined his horse in. "It had been years, you see. For years, she kept her feelings bottled up, and I did nothing to draw them out of her. Instead of leaning on each other, we dealt with the grief of losing our daughter each in our own way."

"How would you have done it differently, if you had to do it over again?"

"I don't know. I would have tried harder to get her to talk about how she was feeling."

"How?"

"I asked her once, you know, how I could've been a better husband."

"What did she say?"

"She told me to figure it out for myself."

Bree nodded. It sounded like something she'd say.

"She told me to look inside myself, maybe I'd find I had been the best husband I knew how to be."

"Did you?"

"In some ways, I suppose I did."

"Is there a lesson for me in what you're saying? I feel that way whenever I'm with you."

"There is."

"But you aren't going to tell me what it is."

"Nope."

"Yeah, I didn't think so."

19

"He needs a break," Jace overheard Billy say to Ben and Tucker. "And we're gonna give it to him."

"Of course we are," answered Ben. "We'll all have a break until the beginning of January. Unless we try to get into the New Year's Eve Extreme Bull Bucking up north."

"We're not, and we're also givin' Jace the whole month of January off. As far as I'm concerned, this isn't negotiable."

Jace couldn't decide whether to let them know he was within earshot, or turn around and walk away. Evidently, Billy hadn't taken his resignation seriously.

"Guess you heard all that," Billy said, walking up behind him.

"Yeah, I did. Taking a month off might not change my mind about leaving the partnership."

"I hear ya. Let's address it again after the holidays. But I'll tell you this, ain't none of us gonna be worth a damn if we keep runnin' ourselves ragged. We don't have to do it all the first year, ya know."

"What are you thinkin'?"

"I'm thinkin' you should head home early. Now, in fact. Then, we talk again after Christmas and figure out where we've bit off more than we can chew, and where we can scale back."

"Fair enough."

"After I heard you bought the Beiman place, first thing I thought was ol' Jace and I are gonna partner in buckin' bulls and horses. It wasn't this three ranch circus. Originally, I saw it as you and me partnerin' up. Nobody else."

"I don't get it."

"What's to get?"

"Why me?"

"We already had this conversation," Billy chewed on a piece of straw. "Ain't gonna have it again."

"Come January, what happens if I still want to bow out?"

Billy motioned for Jace to follow him over to the bar. "Let's get you back on track before we talk about any of it."

He held up two fingers, and the bartender brought over two shot glasses and a bottle of bourbon.

"Get things settled with Bree before anything else. It's either gonna happen or it ain't. But you can't keep goin' like this. If you don't think you can make a life with her and be a partner in the Flying R, then we'll move forward without you."

Jace threw his shot back and motioned to the bartender for another. "Sometimes I think you were captured by aliens, and they left mister sensitive behind when they went back into the galaxy."

Billy pulled his wallet out. "You see this?" He showed Jace a photo of Willow. "My life wasn't worth shit until this little girl came into it." He showed Jace a second photo, of Renie holding Willow on her lap. "And this? This here's my dream come true. This is what life's about. It ain't about stayin' on a bull or bronc for eight seconds. It ain't about winnin' a gold buckle, or havin' a big bank balance. It's this, right here." He pointed at the photo again, and then handed it to Jace.

"If there's a chance you can have this in your life, you gotta take it. You'll regret it every day, for the rest of your life, if you don't."

"Bree isn't interested."

"Bullshit," Billy shook his head. "If you don't take another single bit of advice from me ever again, take this one. It ain't time to give up yet."

Jace threw back another shot.

"Where's she at?"

"Idaho."

"Why?"

"No idea."

"Why'd she go there before?"

Jace told Billy the short version of why Bree went to Idaho last summer.

"When we were together at Thanksgiving, I thought she was ready to move forward." He never would've made love to her if he thought she wasn't ready.

"Somethin' happened."

"What?"

"Don't know, but it's gotta be somethin' big for her to stay away from home for Christmas. Bree lives and breathes for baby Cochran."

December 20
Our first Christmas as husband and wife, and
Bree and I aren't together. She's angry with me
about it, but she knew this was how it would
be when she married me.

She did? Bree remembered the conversation she and Zack had had when he told her he couldn't be home for Christmas. He couldn't take leave while at pilot training. She didn't understand. He was in Texas, not overseas. She'd offered to come to him, but he told her not to.

She remembered that week, and how much they'd argued. There were several entries written between December 20 and Christmas Day.

December 25 - Christmas Day
Only someone with no sense of their own
purpose could be so closed off to the needs and
beliefs of others. How could I have been so
wrong?

Bree slammed the cover of the journal closed and threw it across the room. The door to the bedroom was open just enough that Red, walking by, witnessed her display of anger. She heard the door creak and saw he had opened it enough to stick his head in.

"Everything okay?"

Bree crossed her arms in front of her. "No, it isn't. He thought he was the only one with doubts. He wasn't. I had doubts, too."

"Came up to tell you I was headed into town. Good time to take a break?"

When Bree stood, she knocked the pile of envelopes to the floor, from where they sat on a foot stool. She bent down to pick them, and when she stood, her eyes were filled with tears.

Red took the envelopes out of her hand, set them on the bed, and put his arm around her shoulders.

"Let's get you away from this for a couple hours. Change of scenery will do you good."

They drove south from the ranch, rather than north. Red almost always went north. The only time she'd traveled south was with Jace, when they went to Sun Valley.

Her mind raced with memories of the arguments she and Zack had in the few years they were married. How many times had he accused her of not understanding him? Now she knew he'd been right. At the time, she'd agreed that she didn't, but what she meant was she didn't understand his ambivalence to her when he was deployed.

"He was so different when he was on leave. He would relax. We would have fun. That's who I thought he was."

"And you were wrong?"

She nodded her head. "Very wrong."

Jace pulled into Helena a little after five. Since his parents were still in Monument, he decided to stop and get takeout Italian food. Once his belly was full of homemade pasta and a couple of glasses of Chianti, he fell into bed and slept for twelve hours.

When he woke, late the next morning, he called the ranch manager, Yance, and asked him to come up to the house when he had a break in his day.

Jace hoped Yance would tell him everything was under control, after which, he'd fall back into bed and sleep for another twelve hours, guilt-free.

Two days later, Jace felt as though he'd finally caught up on sleep. Since they bought the ranch, his focus had been on operations, and then on the rough stock start-up.

He hadn't spent much time in his house other than to eat and sleep. Even when he injured his leg, he kept active and spent most of his time outdoors. He walked from room to room, taking a longer look at the shape it was in. He pulled up a corner of the carpet in the main room, and discovered hardwood floors underneath. Three hours later, the carpet from the first floor of the house was in a pile outside.

When he pulled it up, he found tracks at each of the entryways to the living room. He went out to the barn, returned with a crowbar, and removed the molding around the wide doorway. Under it, he found two pocket doors. The wood of the doors matched that of the floor. And apart from where the carpet had been tacked to the wood, the floors were in good shape. It wouldn't take much to repair and refinish them.

There were two staircases in the house, a narrow one in the back, and a larger, grander one near the front door.

Jace climbed the stairs to the landing and studied the wood on the wall. It wasn't drywall. It looked more like shiplap.

Starting at the lower corner, he used the crowbar to loosen one of the boards. He could see there was something underneath. Little by little, he loosened and removed the boards. When he finished, he stood back and studied the five foot wide by eight foot tall stained glass window that the shiplap had covered.

Four circles, like something you would see looking through a kaleidoscope, overlapped slightly in the middle of the window. The focal point, though, was the silhouette of a woman, which overlapped the kaleidoscope circles. The starkness of it was so dramatic against the bold primary colors used in the patterns of the circles, it almost looked three-dimensional.

The window had been boarded over on the outside of the house too. If it was warm enough the next morning, he'd remove those boards as well.

With the dawn of the next couple of days, Jace discovered more hidden gems built into his house. He asked Yance if he knew much about its history, and why so much of the beautiful craftsmanship had been hidden away, but he said he had no idea.

His parents called to say they'd decided to stay in Monument through Christmas, given Jace was at the ranch and Yance had everything under control.

Billy called to check in, as did Tucker. Both wanted to know if he had changed his mind about coming south for Christmas.

"Have you heard from her?" Tucker asked.

"Not a word. Has Blythe?"

"Nope. She told me to ask you. I think her folks are gettin' worried."

"If she's in Idaho, she isn't alone."

"What's the story with this Red character?"

Jace told Tucker how Red had taken Bree under his wing. If Billy was right and something big had happened, at least she had Red to lean on.

Instead of dwelling on his relationship with Bree, Jace filled his day with more projects on the old house. He decided it would be better to paint the downstairs walls before refinishing the hard wood flooring. He also wanted to replace the linoleum in the kitchen. While he was at the hardware store in Helena, he picked out tile for both the kitchen and the downstairs bathroom.

"Back again?" asked the woman behind the counter. "You must have some big project goin'. Third time I've seen you this week. Don't think we've met otherwise."

Jace reached across the counter to shake her outstretched hand. "My name's Jace Rice, ma'am. My parents and I bought the Beiman Ranch."

"My, oh, my. Folks have been wonderin' when we'd catch sight of the cowboy who took over that place. Your parents have been to town. In fact, I invited your mama to join our bunko group."

"That was real nice of you," Jace smiled at the woman who had introduced herself as Vi.

"We haven't seen much of your parents lately. Everything okay with them?"

"They're traveling for the holidays," he explained.

"Thanks for your business, and I guess I'll see ya later this week," Vi smiled.

He was about to walk out the front door, but turned back. "I've been meaning to ask—do you know anything about the history of the main ranch house?"

Vi came around the counter. "I was wonderin' how long it would take you to ask."

She scooted Jace out to the sidewalk and turned the open sign in the front door to closed.

"Time for my break anyway. What do you say we have a cup of coffee over at the café?" She pulled him along with her, down the block, and across Main Street.

"My daughter owns this place. What can I get ya?"

"Uh, coffee would be fine, ma'am."

"Stop bein' so formal. Call me Vi, and make yourself comfortable. I got quite a story to tell you, cowboy."

Vi came back to the table with two coffees and two pieces of cherry pie. He hadn't realized how hungry he was until she set it in front of him.

"His wife designed the stained glass window. I'll bet that's the first thing you're curious about."

"I didn't know about it until a few days ago. It was hidden behind a wall of shiplap."

"Yep, Walt couldn't stand to look at it after she left."

"Was that when he had the carpeting put in too?"

Vi nodded. "Found the pocket doors yet?"

"Why'd he cover it all up?"

"Old man Bieman's wife was from Boston. Her family was loaded, if you know what I mean. She never did fit in too well around here. My mama told me she was mighty uppity for the wife of a rancher."

She went on. "Back in those days, it was as true as it was today—you never asked how much land a rancher owned, or how many head of cattle. It just wasn't done."

Jace nodded; Vi was right. Unless you were plannin' to buy a place, it wasn't polite to ask those kinds of questions.

"That was her first mistake. Comin' into town, braggin' about her husband's 'holdings,' as she called 'em. Wanted a big, fancy, East Coast-style house, too. Walt was close to thirty when they married, and all he had at the time was the land. It was her money that got that house built."

"I've been workin' on the main floor. Anything on the second floor for me to unearth?"

"Not on the second floor so much as the attic."

"Attic? I don't remember seein' access to it."

"There's an access door, probably painted over years ago, at the top of the back staircase. Used to be a set of pull-down stairs, unless Beiman took 'em out. If he did, get yourself a ladder."

"What's up there?" he asked.

"Can't say for sure. Some of what I heard might be true, but most is probably just rumor."

"I'm not gonna find any dead bodies, am I?"

Vi laughed. "Goodness, no, but I heard there are some treasures boarded up in there."

By the time he finished the second piece of pie Vi fetched for him, she'd told him all she knew about Walt's wife, Beatrice.

She'd hired an architect from Boston to design the house, but hadn't been able to convince the man to travel west to oversee it being built. Consequently, she wasn't happy with its quality of construction, so instead, Beatrice focused her efforts on the interior.

The stained glass window was only the beginning. There were lead glass windows and chandeliers, fancy bathroom fixtures, and a kitchen that was big enough for a full-time cook, even though they never had one.

"All that and she didn't live in the house more than five years."

"Where'd she go?"

"You heard why the Beimans were forced to sell?"

He had. They were caught driving cattle across the US-Canadian border. If what Lyric heard was true, Beiman's sons got into a lot of trouble for it.

"That ranch in Canada belonged to Beatrice's second husband. She met him at the Calgary Stampede. His family was from Vancouver, and appealed to her more 'gentrified' side. Did I mention she and Walt went to the stampede together?" Vi laughed.

"Walt wasn't the most observant guy," she continued. "He hadn't picked up on her affair until she told him she was pregnant. The story around town is that he picked her up, walked through the front door, down the porch steps, and told her to get the hell off his land."

"How did he know he wasn't the father?"

"He knew." Vi grinned.

"They had a kid before all this happened, a boy. When he forced Beatrice out, Walt raised him on his own. When that boy, Walt Junior, was in his early twenties, they got word Beatrice had passed away. Junior traveled to Vancouver alone for her funeral, even though he didn't remember much about her. While he was there, he met his half-brother, and the two became close."

Beiman never remarried, although Vi said she'd heard there was a widow from Butte he passed time with.

"You know much about Junior?" she asked him.

"Not really. I mean, I met both of Walt's sons when we made the offer on the ranch." Jace hadn't realized at the time the younger man wasn't Walt's biological son.

"Let's just say the apple didn't fall far from the tree. Junior was just like his mama, even though his daddy raised him. Soon as he could, he got off that ranch."

"I thought Junior lived in the second house."

"Nah, that was Walt's nephew."

Jace was confused. Maybe it was the nephew he'd met that day when they negotiated the sale.

"Not everyone is cut out for life on a ranch. They read books, thinkin' it's all romantic. When they get here, they realize it's isolated, cold, and lonely. Most of your time revolves around the livestock, which can be damn dirty work. I don't need to tell you that, though. You know all about ranching. You come from the land, Jace Rice. It's obvious."

"My great-grandfather was a rancher in Colorado, but he sold most of his ranch land to the Aspen Company, who used it to develop a ski area. I worked ranches growin' up, but my family didn't own one."

"You aren't married, are ya?"

"No, ma'am."

That was his cue to leave. Jace thanked her for the coffee, pie, and stories, and walked out the front door of the café.

"See ya later this week," Vi hollered after him.

Red and Bree spent an afternoon exploring Sun Valley. They had lunch, and then wandered through the shops. She found several things she thought would be perfect Christmas gifts for Cochran, but she wasn't in the right frame of mind to shop. Seeing all the families out, enjoying holiday activities, made her miss her own.

"Still with me?" Red asked. "I have one more stop I want to make."

Bree nodded and followed him back to where they'd parked.

She couldn't get her mind off the last few entries in Zack's journal. Had they really been that unhappy? So unsuited? Wasn't Zack her soulmate? Hadn't she believed she'd grow old with him? She wondered now. If he had lived, would they still be married?

Red put his hand on her arm. "You'll be bleeding soon if you don't quit chewing those nails."

She dropped her hand and looked out the window.

"Why don't you tell me what's got you in this state?"

"I wish I knew who sent the journals."

"You have no idea who did?"

"Maybe I should call his sister."

Bree hadn't kept in touch with Zack's family after the funeral. The conversation would be awkward, but maybe she'd get some closure.

Red pulled up to the town park.

"Where are we going?"

"You'll see. Follow me." They walked down a path that wandered into a heavily treed area.

Bree could hear voices and children's laughter. Both grew louder the further they walked. The sidewalk made a turn, and the canopy of trees opened into an area crowded with children skating on an ice rink. Red walked over to the concession stand and ordered two hot chocolates and two pairs of skates.

"What size shoe do you wear?" he asked.

"Oh no, I'm not getting out there. I'll wait right here for you."

"Give me a size seven," she heard him say to the teenager manning the counter. How had he known that was the size she wore?

Red sat down on the closest bench. "Come on. You know you want to."

She didn't want to, but Red was so good to her, how could she refuse to ice skate with him if that's what he wanted to do?

For the next hour, they skated around and around the rink. Christmas music played from speakers on top of the concession stand, and the skaters sang along.

"Look who's here," he said, pointing to the skater coming on the ice, dressed as Santa Claus.

The children out on the rink skated over and crowded around him.

"I brought my daughter here every Christmas from the time she could walk."

"I'm sorry, Red."

He looked at her, brow furrowed. "What for?"

"Being a spoilsport."

He smiled at her in the way her father probably would've, took her hand, and led her around the rink.

"That's enough for me," he said on their third lap.

"Me too. Thank you for bringing me here, Red."

"My pleasure, Bree."

"All that skating made me hungry," he said once they were back in the truck and warm.

"I could eat."

"What are you hungry for?"

"Anything, really. Whatever you feel like is fine with me."

"Okay, then." Red started the truck and drove out to the highway. "It isn't too far from here."

Bree's phone pinged, and she pulled it out of her pocket. "Oh, sweet boy," she sighed. "Look." She held the phone up so Red could see the photo her sister had texted. "This is Cochran," she said proudly. In the photo, he was asleep next to the Christmas tree. His cheeks were pink, like so many of the skaters they saw this afternoon.

Was she making a mistake, being away for Christmas? Maybe being around her family would lighten her spirits. If anyone could help her forget what was bothering her, it was Cochran.

Red pulled into the parking lot of the restaurant she and Jace had gone to the only other time she was in Sun Valley.

"I don't get down here often, but it's one of my favorite spots," he said, noticing the expression on her face. "Asian okay, or would you prefer something else?"

"No, this is great." Maybe Jace's friends wouldn't recognize her.

Red raised an eyebrow.

"No, really. I love Asian food."

"Uh huh," he answered, grinning back at her. "You're full of mystery today, aren't you?"

"I've been here before. That's all. And you're right, the food is great."

They were seated quickly, at a high top table in the bar area. Bree hadn't seen either of Jace's friends.

"I'd ask if this is someplace you came with Zack, but it hasn't been open that long."

"No, not Zack."

"Who, then?"

"Jace brought me here last summer. The husband and wife who own it are friends of his from Aspen."

"I see." He studied the menu. "Sake okay with you?"

"Uh, sure."

"Hot or cold."

"Hot, please."

"Good girl," he answered.

After the waiter took their drink order, Red sat with his hands folded on the table.

"Who should we talk about first?"

"What do you mean?"

"Jace or Zack. We're going to talk about them both tonight, so you decide which you'd like to talk about first."

"Red, I really don't—"

"Nope, I insist. If you can't decide, I will. Let's start with Zack."

She glared at him and folded her arms.

"You don't want to talk? I will. How long were you married?"

"Five years."

"How old were you when you met?"

"I was fifteen, Zack was seventeen."

"You knew him, what, ten years before he died? How many of those years were you together?"

"What's with the interrogation?"

"You've been frustrated with me in the past about… what was it you accused me of? Talking in riddles?"

"That's right. And telling me I need to figure things out for myself. What's with the sudden shift?"

"Maybe I'm feeling generous, given it's Christmas."

"You're giving me the gift of your wisdom, is that it?"

"Somethin' like that."

She leaned back in her chair.

"How old were you when you got married? Twenty-two?"

"Close. I was twenty-one."

"You aren't going to give an inch, are you?"

Bree shook her head.

Red continued asking her questions about her life with Zack. Most of her answers were no more than one or two words.

"What are you getting at, Red? Can you just cut to the chase?"

"I've been more than patient with you. Your turn."

"Oh, for Christ's sake," she groaned.

"Come on now, I think you're enough of an adult to have one frank and honest conversation about the mess you're making of your life. Don't you?"

20

"What did you say?"

"You heard me. Zack is dead, Bree."

"I'm very well aware of that, Red."

"No matter how many places you revisit that the two of you went, or how many letters you read, or pages in a journal, he isn't coming back."

Bree's eyes filled with tears. "I know that."

"I've spent a lot of time listening to you over the course of the last few months, and it wasn't until last night that I realized who you remind me of."

"I thought I reminded you of your daughter."

"You do. But you also remind me of my wife."

She tried to wipe the tears from her eyes. How dare Red do this to her in the middle of a crowded restaurant. Bree looked up just as Jace's friend approached the table.

"Merry Christmas. It's so nice to see you again, Bree."

"Hi, Jill. This is my friend, Red Dugan. Red this is a friend of Jace's, Jill Woodward."

"You look familiar," Jill said to Red.

Red told her about the ranch and that he'd eaten at the restaurant several times since they opened.

"Thanks for coming back," Jill smiled, looking back and forth between the two. "How's our buddy Jace? Since you're at a table for two, I assume he isn't with you."

"He's well," Bree answered.

"We were just talking about him," Red smirked.

"Sorry to interrupt. It was nice seeing you again, Bree."

"You, too."

Bree glared at Red and was about to tell him how little she appreciated the position he was putting her in, when a waiter approached the table, asking if they were ready to order.

"Not yet," answered Red. "But we're in no hurry."

"Speak for yourself," said Bree once the waiter walked away.

"Now where were we?"

"Your wife."

"That's right. Let's circle back to your husband first."

"What about him?"

"There is an edge in your voice when you talk about him. Did you realize that?"

"There is today, because I'm mad at him."

"Something in the journal made you mad. From what you said, it made you wonder if you'd made a mistake."

"Not that exactly. It just made me wonder. I'm not sure I ever really knew him."

Red sat back in his chair. "Tell me what's in the journals, Bree. Get it out."

"A few of the journals were written before he met me."

"What about the one you were reading earlier today?"

"After he graduated from the Air Force Academy, Zack, like all the other new lieutenants, had sixty days before they had to report to their first assignment." Bree told him that, in Zack's case, he had to report to pilot training in Texas. He proposed the day he graduated, they were married less than a month later, and the trip they took to Wyoming, Montana, and Idaho was their honeymoon.

* * *

Free from the anxiety of being in school, Zack was light-hearted and fun. Some days they knew what they would do, and some days they let the day lead them to their next adventure. It was the most uninterrupted time they'd ever spent together.

They fly-fished, and got to know Annie and Dave, who were the outfitters in Salmon. At the ranch, they rode, and fished, went for long walks, and sat on the porch of the main lodge, and talked.

Two days after they got back from Idaho, Zack left for Texas. Between then and the time he died, they were apart more than they were together. When he completed pilot training, he was stationed in Colorado Springs. Bree completed her bachelor's degree during that time and was thinking about graduate school.

Zack encouraged her to do it. She remembered thinking how good it felt to know he believed in her. "Do it now," he'd told her. Had he said "before we start a family," or was that just the way she remembered it?

With both of them focused on their individual pursuits, Bree didn't feel as though they saw each other much more than they did when he was in Texas. The only difference was, they slept together every night.

She brought it up to him one day, and he told her it would soon be worse. He was being deployed to Afghanistan.

The day before he left, one of Zack's buddies stopped by to see him.

"I can't believe he volunteered to go," the friend had said to Bree.

When Zack walked in the house, a few minutes later, Bree left. She told him she had errands to run, but the truth was, she was so angry, she didn't want to be around him.

She drove and drove, that afternoon, with no particular destination. When hours later she was still just as angry as she'd been when she left, she considered not going back to the house at all. In the end, she changed her mind, knowing she'd ultimately regret it if she didn't see him before he left.

When she came home, Zack was as angry as she was. They fought about the deployment.

"How can you not understand?" he shouted at her that night. He accused her of being selfish, and then he walked out.

Sometime in the middle of the night, she heard him come back in, but he didn't come into the bedroom; he slept on the couch. When she got up the next morning, his bags were packed and he was standing by the front door. Bree walked into the kitchen to get a cup of coffee, and when she came back, he was gone.

* * *

"That was the last time I saw him."

"Get rid of them."

"What?"

"The letters and the journals. Especially the journals. Don't read another word."

"Why?"

"As I said at the start of this conversation, there isn't anything that will bring him back. In fact, reading words that weren't meant for you, is doing the opposite. It's pushing him farther away. Let your memories be, Bree. Let the rest of it go. No good will come of you knowing what else there is in those journals."

"What do you think I'm going to find?"

"Who sent you the box?"

"I already told you, I don't know."

"There must have been a reason whoever it was didn't want you to know."

The waiter came back to the table and asked if they were ready to order. "Go ahead," she told Red.

He ordered for them both before he excused himself from the table.

Was he right? Should she just let it all go? Reading as much as she had certainly hadn't helped her either mourn him, or let go of him. It only reminded her that things between them were far more strained than she remembered.

Red sat back down at the table. "Ready?" he asked.

"For what?"

"Let's talk about Jace."

"Must we?" How much more of an emotional wringer did Red intend to put her through?

"Oh, absolutely. That's what I really want to talk about."

"Why?"

"You need to see what everyone else does."

"And that is?"

"Jace Rice loves you, heart and soul," he paused when Bree started shaking her head. "And what's more, you feel the same way about him."

"I don't know what you're talking about."

"Hear me out."

Bree sat back in her chair, her arms folded in front of her again.

"Didn't your mother ever tell you how rude that is?"

"What?"

"Folding your arms when someone is talking to you?"

Bree released her arms and rested her hands in her lap. "Better?"

"Much better. Now, as I was saying…"

December 23. He still had time to drive to Monument and spend Christmas with his family, but he would have to leave now. Jace went upstairs to pack a bag.

After he'd painted all the rooms on the main floor, he finished repairing the wood floor, and installed the tile in the kitchen and in the downstairs bathroom. He hadn't started the work on the upstairs of the house yet, but there would be plenty of time when he got back from Colorado.

Whenever he went up the back staircase, he thought about what Vi had said about the attic. There'd be time, later, to explore up there too.

Vi's words that day, not only about the house, stuck with him. "Not everyone is cut out for life on a ranch," she'd said.

The more time he spent at home, the more those words rang true. Even if a relationship with Bree was possible, how could he ask her to move to his isolated ranch?

The last time they spoke, he was in Vegas for NFR and she was on her way to Idaho. Was she back in Monument with her family? Only one way to find out.

"Hey, Mama," he said when she picked up the phone. "I'm fixing to leave now, so I'll see you sometime late tomorrow night, as long as the weather's good."

"Jace, you might not want to leave yet."

Before he could ask why not, he heard a rap at the door. "Give me a minute, Mama, someone's at the door. It's probably Yance. I asked him to swing by the house when he had a few minutes. I'll call you right back."

"Come on in, Yance," he yelled from the kitchen after he hung up. When the ranch manager didn't open the door and come in, Jace thought maybe he hadn't heard him.

"Got cotton balls stuffed in your ears?" He pulled the door open, and instead of Yance, Bree stood on the other side of it.

"Hi, Jace."

"Hi." Jace stood back from the door, where the wind blew snow across the threshold. "You must be freezing. Come on in."

He stood behind her and put his hands on her shoulders. "Uh, can I take your coat, or, uh, are you cold? Do you want to leave it on?"

"No, it's fine." She shrugged her arms out of it, and Jace hung it across the back of a chair in the dining room.

"Come in," he said again, motioning to the living room.

Bree stopped in front of the suitcase that sat at the bottom of the stairs. "Were you going somewhere?"

"I was, but that isn't important now that you're here." He put his arms around her and pulled her close to him. He leaned down and brushed her lips with his. "Why are you here, Bree?" he whispered.

"I needed to see you."

Jace walked to the couch, holding her hand. "Come sit down. Your hands are so cold. I'll light a fire."

He did, and then sat next to her.

"I missed you, Jace," she shifted back on the couch, farther away from him. "I'm sorry."

He moved forward, closing the gap between them again. He reached out and cupped the side of her face. "For missin' me? That's not somethin' to be sorry for, darlin'."

"I should've called first," she looked around, as though she expected to find someone else there. "You were leaving."

"It's okay, I already told you. That's not important now."

"Where were you going?"

"Colorado. Spur of the moment. I didn't want to be here alone."

"That's why I'm here. We need to talk."

"Okay."

"Jace...I...I've been wrong about so many things. About Zack, about you, about us."

"Bree, sweetheart—"

"Um, it was kind of a long drive. Sorry, but do you have a restroom I could use?"

Jace stood. "Of course, right here," he led her around the corner. "Can I get you anything? Something to drink?"

"That would be nice." She stepped into the bathroom, the one he'd just finished re-tiling, and closed the door.

Jace went into the kitchen. He didn't have much. There was a bottle of brandy in the cupboard, behind the bourbon. Maybe she'd like that.

He poured two glasses and went back to the living room. Bree had pulled a blanket off the back of one of the chairs, and was draping it over herself.

"I thought this might warm you," he handed her the glass.

"Thank you, Jace," she smiled up at him.

"You drove? Where from?"

"Stanley. I was at the ranch. Well, not the ranch, it was closed for the season. I was at Red's. He has a cabin on Pettit Lake. Did you know that? It's beautiful, really beautiful. And it was so gracious of him to let me come and stay."

His fingers caressed the side of her face. He leaned forward and kissed her. There were so many things he wanted to say, but instead, he'd listen. She came to him, and he needed to let her tell him why.

"Bree," he whispered. "Why are you here?"

"It's simple," she rested her head on his shoulder and wrapped her arm around his waist. "Because I realized there wasn't anywhere I'd rather be than with you."

Jace closed his eyes, took a deep breath, and tightened his arms around her. Before he could speak, Bree put her fingers on his lips.

"I care about you, Jace, but it's more than that. I want to be with you."

He wrapped his hand around hers and kissed her fingertips. "I want that too."

"I hoped you did. Red told me you did."

"Red had to tell you? You didn't know?"

She shifted so her back rested against his chest. "There's so much I've been wrong about. I didn't want to be wrong about you."

"What happened, sweetheart? Why did you go to Idaho?"

"When I got back from Thanksgiving break, I received a box. Someone, I still don't know who, sent it to me at the Air Force Academy."

"What was in it?"

"Zack's journals. There were letters in the box too. At first I couldn't read them. I started to, but it was too much. I called Red and asked him if I could come and stay, and then sent the box to him."

"Go on."

"I didn't read them all. I didn't have to. I learned more than I wanted to in the ones I did read. It wasn't what I thought."

"What wasn't?"

"Our marriage. Our life. My life with Zack. We weren't what I thought we were. Or he wasn't. Or I wasn't. I'm not making any sense, am I?"

"I'm listening."

"After he died, all I could think was that we would've been okay. When he came back from Afghanistan, we would've been okay. We would've started a family. Now I realize, we wouldn't have. We fought before he left. I told you that we didn't say goodbye."

"I'm sorry, darlin'."

"But, Jace, I don't want to talk about Zack. I want to talk about you." She shifted again, so she could look into his eyes. "No one else showed me the kindness you did. But more, no one has ever made me feel the way you do." She put her hands on his chest and clenched his shirt. "No one. Not even Zack. Especially not Zack."

When she put her lips on his, Jace couldn't hold back. His mouth took hers harder than he should've. He ran his hands down her sides and grasped her hips, pulling her closer to him. "I missed you so much," he said into her mouth, before his tongue tangled with hers. He stood, offered his hand. When she stood as well, Jace picked her up and carried her upstairs.

Bree filled her lungs with the scent of him. He must've taken a shower just before she got there. She kissed his neck while he carried her, and ran her tongue over his skin. She nuzzled his ear as he rested his knees against the edge of the bed and slowly lowered her onto it.

His breath was ragged as he pulled her sweater up over her head, and tossed it aside. His gaze idly drifted over her, down to her jeans. He unfastened the button, eased the zipper down, and slid them over her hips. He threw those in the same direction as her sweater.

His lips ran from her ankle, up, trailing soft kisses from her knee to her thigh. His hands stroked over her belly, and when he reached her bra, he pulled at it, exposing her breasts. Jace ran his lips where his hands had been just before. He sunk his teeth into the cup of her bra, reached around, unfastened it, and pulled it away from her skin with his teeth.

His lips returned, nipping, then licking to soothe the sting. Her muscles rippled beneath the heat of his mouth. She gasped, she sighed, she groaned. She may have even screamed. She couldn't hear anything above the roar of blood, pounding in her ears, her body, throbbing.

Bree watched Jace's fiery gaze sweep over her body as he stripped his clothes away. She closed her eyes, waiting to feel him rest on top of her.

"Open your eyes and look at me," he demanded. When she did, his eyes were trained on hers. "I want to know it's me you see. Me making love to you. No one else."

"I see you, Jace" she said, and gasped as he entered her. She dragged her nails down his back and felt him shudder. His slow, gentle movement changed. He quickened, bucking against her, slamming into her. He turned her brain to mush with his frantic, savage kisses. Soon, he threw his head back and groaned. She felt him shudder again, as she tightened her interior muscles around him, coming with him.

Jace didn't move away from her but rested his body gently against hers. She ran her hands down his back, stroking his flawlessly hard body, and rested them on his bottom.

"Did you feel it?" he asked her.

"I think so, but did I feel what?"

"Best. Sex. Ever. Wanna know why?"

She giggled. "Why?"

He shifted suddenly, startling her, getting right in her face. "Because I love you." His mouth descended on hers again. Forcefully, his lips claimed hers, as his body had staked its claim on her, in her, just moments before.

21

Jace kissed her. "Happy Christmas Eve."

"Mmm. Same to you too."

"How do you feel this morning?"

"Tired, a little sore, and very well sated."

"I have a little surprise for you, but it requires getting out of bed."

"Do I have to? Can't we just have breakfast in bed?" she smiled up at him.

"We could, but it'll be cold by the time I get back here with it."

"Huh?"

"We're having breakfast in Monument, darlin'."

"Oh, Jace," she sat up suddenly. "I'm so sorry. You were leaving last night, and I stopped you. Do you want to go now? I mean, I can—"

Jace kissed her, running his tongue along her bottom lip until she opened her mouth under his.

"Get up and get dressed, woman. We need to get to Helena before Ben's plane lands."

"Ben's plane?"

"You know Ben has a plane, right?"

"Of course I do."

"He's flying up as we speak, to ferry us down to Monument for Christmas."

"Really?" Bree squealed.

Jace smiled and pulled her out of bed. "Get dressed, or we'll be spending Christmas Eve and Christmas Day in Montana, in bed. I know you'd rather spend it with Cochran."

She smiled at him from the passenger seat of his truck. "I can't believe I'm going to be home for Christmas. Thank you, Jace, for making this happen."

He reached over and brought her hand to his lips. "My pleasure, ma'am."

When he told her he loved her, last night, it wasn't about the sex. He really did love her. There wasn't any doubt in his mind. They'd made love again, and then fell fast asleep. Jace still didn't know if she felt the same.

"It's so beautiful here. I had no idea." The ground was covered in snow, and the big Montana sky stretched on forever. Every so often the sun would peek out of the ominous clouds forming, making the snow glisten. "You must love it."

He did love it, but would she? Could she? For how long? "It's isolated," he muttered. "And cold."

"Jace," she laughed, "it sounds as though you don't like it at all."

"That isn't it."

"What is it, then?"

"It isn't an easy life up here, Bree. Not everyone is cut out for it." His tone was angrier than he intended it to be.

"You sound as though you're mad at me."

His face softened when he turned and looked at her. "No, darlin', I'm not angry with you."

His voice was soft and sweet, but Bree could feel an underlying tension emanating from him.

"We're here," he said. He hit the call button at the gate of the private air strip.

"Can I help you?" the voice on the other side bellowed.

"Jace Rice here. Has Ben Rice arrived? He was going to let you know—"

The box squawked, and the gate creaked open.

"I guess he's here," Jace muttered and drove through the gate. "Would be nice if I knew where I was going."

Jace's phone rang and he snapped it up. "Yeah?" Pause. "Okay, great. Thanks."

"Ben?"

"Yep. Guess he got the same warm welcome from the tower."

Jace pulled the truck close to the hangar, where there was a sign for parking. "It's a hike," he said. "And it's damn cold. I wish I could get you closer, but this is it."

He said he wasn't angry with her, but something was bothering him. His voice hadn't lost its edge.

"I'll be fine, Jace."

"I'll get our bags, you go ahead. The plane is on the other side of this hangar. Ben will be waiting for you."

"I can help. I'm not—"

He was out of the truck, the door slamming behind him, before she could finish her sentence. She opened her door and understood why he'd slammed his shut. The wind caught it, and she thought it would rip off the hinges. She managed to grab it with both hands and slam it closed.

"Go," he motioned. "That way."

Bree went in the direction he pointed. The snow was coming down hard, and it was difficult to walk into the wind. As she got closer to the hanger, she saw an open door.

"Come on in," a voice shouted to her.

Jace was right behind her when she got inside.

"Hey, Ben. Sorry to bring you into this weather," Jace said, shaking his hand.

"It's okay. Hey, Bree." Ben hugged her.

"Can we fly?"

"Waiting for word. The guy in the control tower said the weather is supposed to pass, but he didn't offer much more information about when."

"He was abrupt," added Jace.

"Yeah, you could say that," Ben laughed.

"I'm real sorry about this," Jace said again.

"No worse weather than we get in Crested Butte," Ben answered, looking at his phone. "Looks like it might be quick. It isn't much of a storm, and it's moving east. Come on over here; there's a heater."

Ben led them to a sitting area, furnished with a sofa that looked as old as Bree, and two ratty chairs.

"It isn't much," Ben said, noting the look on her face. "But it's warm over here."

Bree sat on the arm of the sofa. "I don't mind."

Jace took off his hat and ran his hand through his hair. "God, this is a clusterfuck. I'm sorry, Bree."

"For what?"

"For livin' out here, in the middle of nowhere. For gettin' you into this. You should be home, sitting by a fire, playin' with Cochran. Not up here, in a shit hole hangar, not knowin' when we can even leave."

"Wait just a minute," she snapped, and then looked at Ben.

"I'll just, uh, see if I can find a men's room." Ben walked away.

"Where is this coming from? You said you weren't angry with me, but you're sure acting as though you are. As far as what I should be doing, I came here, remember? I surprised you. If anyone should be sorry, it's me."

Jace looked at her but didn't answer. She stood and put her arms around his waist. "What's wrong? Please, just tell me. Is it because I didn't—"

Jace pulled her arms from around his waist and took a step away from her. "I'm tied here, Bree. I can't just walk away from it. It wouldn't be fair to my parents. They aren't cut out for doing this on their own. I can't just abandoned them if you aren't cut out for it either."

"If I'm not cut out for what?"

"Yeah, I guess I'm getting pretty far ahead of myself, aren't I? I mean, we haven't even talked about why you're here in the first place. Not really. I guess, I shouldn't go assuming anything about next week, let alone the future."

Bree sat back down on the arm of the sofa. "I'm not following you. I feel as though I'm supposed to read between the lines and figure out what you're trying to say, but I'm lost."

"You. Me. This place." Jace paced in front of her. "I live on a ranch, darlin', and when I'm not here, I'm in a rig, pulling a slew of bulls and broncs from one town to the next. It isn't romantic. It's damn hard work."

"There's only one thing I heard that you're right about," she stood and came toe to toe with him. "You're doing a lot of assuming you shouldn't be."

"Yeah, right. I got it." He turned his back to her and began to walk away.

"Wait a minute, *dammit.*" She grabbed his arm. "Jace? What is wrong with you? Why are you acting like this?"

Maybe she *had* been wrong about him. But last night, he told her he loved her. Did he regret saying it? Was that why he was behaving this way? Her eyes filled with tears, and she spun around, so he wouldn't see. Why did she have to start crying? Now he would feel sorry for her, and they'd never get to the bottom of why he was acting the way he was.

"I understand if you don't want me here. I should've called. I should've…well, there's so much I should've done. I'm sorry, Jace."

"I do want you here, Bree, but this is a damn hard life."

"I can't tell whether you're saying this for my benefit or yours. Quit talking in circles."

"I have responsibilities I can't just walk away from."

"Have I asked you to?" What was it about her that made Jace believe she was asking him to change his life? Why had Zack thought the same thing?

"I'm me, and you're you. Right, Bree? I'm a rancher, and a rough stock contractor. I get dirty, and I shovel a lot of shit in the course of a day. I made a commitment to my parents, and to my partners. I'm not in a position to renege."

She felt as though she was talking to a brick wall. "Why do you keep saying that, as though I'm asking you to?"

"Why did you come here? What is it that you want from me? If it's casual sex, I gotta tell you, I can't do it. Not anymore. I'm done bein' the detour. I'm done bein' the guy that offers comfort until you figure out what you want to do with the rest of your life, or who you want to spend the rest of your life with." He spun her around so she faced him. "I love you, Bree. I know that might not mean much to you. You may think I was in love with Renie, and Blythe. I did too. But I wasn't. Not like this. Nothing has ever felt like this."

She couldn't stop the flow of tears from her eyes. "Why are you pushing me away?"

"I ache for you, do you understand? Ache. I physically hurt, knowing you don't feel the same way about me. I want you every minute of every day, and when we're together, I get lost in you. Each time, I tell myself it'll be different. I let go of the fear, and then you stick me with the same knife you have every other time. Do you know how I felt when you called to say you were going to Idaho for Christmas? Do you?"

She was crying too hard to answer.

"Do you?"

"I-I'm so sorry," she hiccuped.

"Every time you pull away from me, you take another chunk of my heart."

"I don't want to pull away, Jace. I want this."

"For how long? This isn't you, living on a ranch. When you decide to leave, I'll be left here, with no choice but to board up that damn stained glass window all over again."

"Stained glass window? What are you talking about?"

"The one in the stairwell. When Beiman's wife left him, he couldn't stand to look at it, so he boarded it up. I know, now, why he did."

Bree stood in front of him, unable to speak, unable to do anything but cry. He said he wanted her, that he loved her, but he was convinced she either didn't love him enough, or wasn't strong enough to be what he needed. He'd already decided she couldn't do it. He was so sure of it, he wouldn't consider even trying.

"We're good to go," shouted Ben from the other side of the hangar. "Let's get on our way before the weather turns bad again."

Jace grabbed her bag and his. "Come on, let's do this."

The flight was short. It took them less than two hours to fly into the Centennial airport, south of Denver, but it felt as though it took them forever to get there. There was so much she wanted to say, but not in front of Ben. She needed to wait until they were alone.

She wished, now, that she'd read more of Zack's journals. Maybe if she had, they would've offered some clue as to what Zack was thinking about their marriage during his deployment. Had he decided, in the same way Jace had, that she wasn't cut out for their life together? Had he assumed she'd be unwilling to compromise so they could be together? Did he see her as being so selfish, she'd be unwilling, like Jace did?

They pulled into her parents' driveway less than an hour after Ben landed the plane. Jace brought her bags to the front door.

"Aren't you coming in?"

"Nah, I'm goin' straight to Tuck's. My family is stayin' there."

"Jace, we need to talk."

"Actually, we don't. I've heard those words often enough before to know what they mean."

He walked away and got in Ben's car.

"Well, hello," her father greeted her at the door. "I wasn't sure whether we'd see you for Christmas this year."

"Hi, Daddy. I wasn't sure either, but here I am, delivered safe and sound."

He looked behind her.

"They're gone already. Jace and Ben dropped me off."

"Nice of Ben to fly up to get you."

"I know. Very nice." She snuggled into her father's arms. "I missed you. I'm so glad to be home."

Bree's mom came around the corner. "There she is!" she shouted. "I've been so worried about you. When you didn't answer your cell, I didn't know what to think."

Bree hugged her mom, and then slipped off her coat, taking her cell phone out of her pocket. There were several missed calls from her mom, Blythe, and even Red.

"I'll take your bag up to your old room," her dad offered.

"I'll follow. I'd like to change," she said to her mom.

"Go ahead. I'll heat up some soup. Come back down when you're ready, and we'll catch up, baby."

Bree hugged her mother again before following her dad upstairs.

"I need to make a phone call, and then I'll be down."

"Take your time," he answered, closing her bedroom door behind him.

She hit the call-back button and listened while the phone rang. The call went to voicemail.

"Hi, Red, it's Bree. I'm sorry to bother you, but something's happened with Jace, and I need to talk to you. Can you, please, call me back?"

As soon as she hung up, she regretted leaving a message. Red had his own life to live, she shouldn't keep going to him for answers to her problems. She didn't need to wait to hear back from Red. She knew what she had to do.

"Hey, Tuck. Hi, Blythe," Jace said when they greeted him at the back door.

"We sure are happy to see you," said his mama, from behind them.

"I'm happy to see you too." He hugged her, and then his father. "Merry Christmas."

"I expected Bree to be with you," said Blythe.

"I dropped her at your parents' place."

"Okay. Well, I'm sure she'll be here later, with them."

"Uh, yeah. Not sure."

Blythe looked at him with a puzzled expression. He wasn't sure, because he hadn't asked. She probably would be, but that didn't have anything to do with him. She'd be here because that's where her family would be.

Tucker rubbed his chest and grimaced.

"What's wrong? Got indigestion from my cooking?" she teased.

"Not this time," he answered right before she slugged him.

"Got a minute?" he said to Jace.

"Got nothin' but," Jace answered.

"Good. Follow me, I need your help with something. Don't take your jacket off."

Jace followed Tucker out the back door, to the barn he'd heard Tuck had built, but hadn't seen yet.

"That was quick."

"Doesn't take long to raise a barn," Tucker answered. "Especially when Billy Patterson is involved." They walked inside where almost every stall was full. "Gotta get some of these buckers to Crested Butte after the holidays."

They were still working out the best way to organize how many bulls and broncs they would keep at each ranch.

"Bullet's got a spreadsheet, organized by rank. I don't know how he ranks 'em, or what it all means."

Once again, Bullet's organizational skills and what appeared to be inherent insight into rough stock amazed Jace. Same with Billy. He had a knack for reading animals like Jace had never seen in another human being.

"So tell me, brother, what's with the heartache?"

"Nothin'. It'll pass."

Tucker put his hand on Jace's arm. "No, it won't. Tell me what's going on."

"Hi," Blythe said when Bree walked in the kitchen. "I didn't expect you so soon, but I'm so happy you're here."

"Hi," Bree answered, returning Blythe's hug. "Have you seen Jace?"

"I'm fine, thanks. How are you?"

"I'm sorry. I'll catch up with you later. I really need to talk to Jace. He's here, isn't he?"

"He and Tucker walked out to the new barn—"

Bree was out the back door before Blythe finished her sentence.

"I'm sorry to interrupt," she said when she walked in the side door of the barn. "Actually, that isn't true. I'm not sorry at all. Jace, can I talk to you?"

Tucker stopped and hugged her on his way out. "He's all yours," he smirked.

"I don't know what the hell all that was about, earlier, but I have a few things to say to you, Jace Rice."

He sat down on a bale of hay, pulling out a piece to chew on. She hated the smug look on his face, as though he knew what she was about to say and was simply tolerating her saying it.

"You're such an asshole," she began.

"I am that," he smirked.

"Stop it. Do you understand me? You don't get to trample over me and talk to me as if you know what I'm thinking, or how I'm feeling, or what I want in life."

"Okay."

"In fact, I think it would be best if you just didn't say anything for a few minutes."

He nodded his head when she glared at him.

"I love you, Jace Rice. Do you hear me? I love you. And I don't care if you live in Montana, or Crested Butte, or Monument, or if you don't live in any of those places. I don't care if you're on the road all the time. I don't care as long as I'm with you.

"If you're in Montana, I will be too. If you're shoveling shit, so will I. If you're unloading bulls from the back of a trailer at two in the morning, I will be too. You aren't shutting me out. You aren't leaving me behind, or making decisions for me, or telling me what I can and can't do. Or what I want or don't want. You don't get to decide for me, Jace."

He nodded his head again. Bree could swear he was fighting the urge to smile.

"If you want to know how I feel, or what I think, ask me. Don't decide for me. Okay?"

He nodded his head again.

"You can talk now." She folded her arms in front of her and waited for him to say something.

"Well? I said you can talk now. Aren't you going to say anything?"

He stood instead, walked over, and grabbed her folded arms. He pulled them apart and brought her close to him. He leaned down and covered her mouth with his, snaking his tongue inside. The kiss felt like a continuation of their conversation. Instead of answering her with words, his tongue battled with hers. She kissed him back harder than he kissed her.

He ran his hands down her sides and lifted her so her legs went around his waist. He walked, with her that way, over to the side of the barn, and held her up against it.

"You love me?"

"Yes, I do."

"Say it again."

"I love you, Jace."

"What about the rest of it? You shoveling horse droppings. You sure about that?"

"I've never been more sure."

"It isn't easy."

"What is?"

"There are times you won't know what day it is, or one town from the next. You'll get damn tired of riding in the cab of a big rig."

"I don't care."

"You say that now—"

She kissed him again, to shut him up. Her cell phone rang, but she ignored it. The only person she needed to talk to now was right in front of her.

Epilogue

"What do you think is up there?"

"I don't know, but Vi assured me I wouldn't find any dead bodies."

Jace broke through the drywall in the ceiling and saw that it opened into the attic. "Old Man Beiman sure didn't make this easy."

"Do you see anything?"

Jace shined the flashlight around the dark room. "Not so far. Wait." He saw something over on the right. He focused the flashlight in that direction. "Looks like an old steamer trunk."

"Big enough for a body?"

Jace laughed. "Uh, yep."

"Then you're on your own, cowboy. I'll be waiting down here."

Jace pulled himself up into the attic. Once he stood, he shone the flashlight around the big, open space. He drew back the heavy tarps that blocked the light from coming in the windows. There were three windows in the attic, and once uncovered, it was light enough to see. The only thing up there was that big steamer trunk.

"Here goes," he shouted in Bree's direction.

"Good luck."

He unfastened the latches and pried the top open.

"No bodies."

"Glad to hear it. What's in it?"

"I'm not sure. It looks like a bunch of old books. And some clothes."

"I'm coming up."

"Wait for me—"

She pulled herself up into the attic before he could walk back over to the opening. "I'm fine, Jace," she said when he put his arms around her.

"Not just you I'm worried about, stubborn woman."

"You don't have to coddle me."

"Ha! As if that would ever happen," he rubbed her belly. "Precious cargo in here, darlin'. How 'bout if I just coddle her."

Bree smiled and rested her hand on top of his. "Or him."

She walked over to the trunk and pulled out a book. She blew the dust off the cover and opened it.

"It's someone's journal," she said and closed it.

"Whose?"

"I don't know and I don't care." Bree set the book back in the trunk where it had been before and closed the lid.

"Not even curious?"

"Not in the least."

"What should we do with it?"

"Leave it where it is."

Bree hadn't asked Red what he did with Zack's journals. She flew into Idaho the day before she and Jace were getting married, but the ranch staff already had everything set up, so she and Red went fishing. Just like the first time, they didn't talk about Zack, and they never would again.

About the Author

USA Today and Amazon Top 15 Bestselling Author Heather Slade writes shamelessly sexy, edge-of-your seat romantic suspense.

She gave herself the gift of writing a book for her own birthday one year. Forty-plus books later (and counting), she's having the time of her life.

The women Slade writes are self-confident, strong, with wills of their own, and hearts as big as the Colorado sky. The men are sublimely sexy, seductive alphas who rise to the challenge of capturing the sweet soul of a woman whose heart they'll hold in the palm of their hand forever. Add in a couple of neck-snapping twists and turns, a page-turning mystery, and a swoon-worthy HEA, and you'll be holding one of her books in your hands.

She loves to hear from my readers. You can contact her at heather@heatherslade.com

To keep up with her latest news and releases, please visit her website at www.heatherslade.com to sign up for her newsletter.

MORE FROM AUTHOR HEATHER SLADE

BUTLER RANCH

Kade's Worth
Brodie's Promise
Maddox's Truce
Naughton's Secret
Mercer's Vow
Kade's Return
Butler Ranch Christmas

WICKED WINEMAKERS
FIRST LABEL

Brix's Bid
Ridge's Release
Press' Passion
Zin's Sins
Tryst's Temptation

WICKED WINEMAKERS
SECOND LABEL

Beau's Beloved
Coming Soon:
Cru's Crush
Bones' Bliss
Snapper's Seduction
Kick's Kiss

ROARING FORK RANCH

Coming Soon:
Roaring Fork Wrangler
Roaring Fork Roughstock
Roaring Fork Rockstar
Roaring Fork Rooker
Roaring Fork Bridger

THE ROYAL AGENTS
OF MI6

Make Me Shiver
Drive Me Wilder
Feel My Pinch
Chase My Shadow
Find My Angel

K19 SECURITY
SOLUTIONS TEAM ONE

Razor's Edge
Gunner's Redemption
Mistletoe's Magic
Mantis' Desire
Dutch's Salvation

K19 SECURITY
SOLUTIONS TEAM TWO

Striker's Choice
Monk's Fire
Halo's Oath
Tackle's Honor
Onyx's Awakening

K19 SHADOW OPERATIONS
TEAM ONE

Code Name: Ranger
Code Name: Diesel
Code Name: Wasp
Code Name: Cowboy
Code Name: Mayhem

K19 ALLIED INTELLIGENCE
TEAM ONE

Code Name: Ares
Code Name: Cayman
Code Name: Poseidon
Code Name: Zeppelin
Code Name: Magnet

K19 ALLIED INTELLIGENCE
TEAM TWO

Coming Soon:
Code Name: Puck
Code Name: Michelangelo
Code Name: Typhon
Code Name: Hornet
Code Name: Reaper

PROTECTORS
UNDERCOVER

Undercover Agent
Undercover Emissary
Coming Soon:
Undercover Savior
Undercover Infidel
Undercover Assassin

THE INVINCIBLES
TEAM ONE

Decked
Edged
Grinded
Riled
Smoked

THE INVINCIBLES
TEAM TWO

Bucked
Irished
Sainted
Hammered
Ripped

THE UNSTOPPABLES
TEAM ONE

Furied
Married

COWBOYS OF
CRESTED BUTTE

A Cowboy Falls
A Cowboy's Dance
A Cowboy's Kiss
A Cowboy Stays
A Cowboy Wins